CHOSEN

an autobiograpical novel

by

Helen Reed Trobian

To Irene and David
with love,

Helen

Copyright © 1999 by Helen Reed Trobian

ISBN 0-7414-0181-9

Published by:

Buy Books on the web.com
862 West Lancaster Avenue
Bryn Mawr, PA 19010-3222
Info@buybooksontheweb.com
www.buybooksontheweb.com
Toll-free (877) BUY BOOK

Printed in the United States of America
Printed on Recycled Paper
Published June-1999

To honor the memory of Albert Lori Trobian who understood and shared the synergetic power of Universal Love through his conception of a life principle which he called the Lori Family Concept.

PREFACE

Writing an autobiographical novel is a challenge. Life thrives on challenges and I wanted to prove to myself I could accept this one. Friends and relatives said it should be written. It is my hope that it makes a small contribution to racial understanding, serves as a reminder of civil rights history, and shows that "outsiders" can contribute to an "insider" community. At the same time it shows how spouses from radically different backgrounds can find true love regardless of difficulties encountered. For both spouses, true soulmates, this life story shows that love is a potent influence in surviving childhood problems and becoming responsible members of society.

ACKNOWLEDGMENTS

Audrey Carol Miller, an army friend, inspired me with her *How I Climbed the Learning Tree,* (Pearl Street Press, Rossville, Kansas, 1991.) She said writing would be therapeutic and she was right. I am grateful for her friendship and for my sister Grace's encouragement and her contributions to knowledge of my early life.

I am especially thankful for the faith and love of Albert's sisters, Irene Ross and Lucille Ciccarelli, and to Barbara Walker for her insights leading to the title *CHOSEN.* I thank Joyce Calloway for frequently suggesting that I write this book.

Barbara Cockrell, my Mentor and friend, has been of inestimable help.

My thanks to Barbara Allen for thoughtful and professional preparaton of the manuscript and to "Buy Books on the Web.com" for creating a "new publishing idea."

TABLE OF CONTENTS

PROLOGUE

Parsons, Kansas - 1920

PAPER CLIP REMOVED —CHILD RECOVERING

Galesburg 2 Year Old Girl Again
Able to Speak after Remarkable Operation Here.

Little Helen Reed, two year old
daughter of Rev. and Mrs. C. M.
Reed of Galesburg Kansas, has been
taken to her home after a ten days'
stay at Mercy Hospital where she had
undergone a tracheatomy operation.

The little girl lost her voice some
five months ago, following what
seemed to be an ordinary attack
of tonsilitis. Along with the loss
of voice she became very thin and
pale, was breathing with difficulty
and would have frequent spells in
which she would struggle for breath
and get cyanoticor blue. These at-
tacks got so bad that the parents
thought the child would surely die in
each one. She was taken to several
physicians but the case presented
some unusual aspects and appeared
to be a tubercular laynogitis. Little
hope was entertained for her recovery and the parents were advised
to take her to Arizona.

A Parsons specialist was called in
to make an examination of her throat
and he diagnosed the case as a foreign body located in the trachea, and
suggested taking an X-ray. The
little girl was brought to Parsons
and the X-ray picture revealed a
wire paper clip located in the trachea. or wind pipe, just below the
vocal cords.

She was taken to Mercy Hospital
and an opening was made in the
trachea in order to insert a silver
tube through which the baby could
breathe. The paper clip was removed
and the tube was left in a few days.
after which it was removed and the
little patient again breathed the natural way. She made a splendid
recovery and the parents returned
home with her unable to express
their gatitude.

CHAPTER 1

Early Years

My parents had been sent to the waiting room while the x-ray was being taken. The young doctor was standing up with the x-ray picture in his hand.

"Reverend Reed," he began, in a low, sympathetic voice, "this is a rare case. Your child is not likely to survive. I believe, however, there **is** a possibility of an experimental tracheotomy."

He then quickly described the operation and asked, "Would you be willing to authorize me to attempt it in the interest of science?" My father told me he responded urgently, "What are you waiting for?"

As the newspaper item relates, my life was miraculously saved at the age of two years. Being an inquisitive child, I had taken a paper clip, really just a piece of wire bent like an X with a top, from my father's desk and for about six months it was gradually encapsulated in my windpipe as my tissues grew around it.

Dr. Landis wired Kansas City, Missouri for special surgical instruments which were sent on the next train south. The Sisters at Mercy Hospital in Parsons, Kansas prayed for the child of the Methodist minister from Galesburg, Kansas.

I attribute the saving of my life to Dr. Landis' skill, the

Sisters' prayers, and Divine Providence. At the hospital Mama slept in a bed beside mine. "I knew that Helen was getting better when she stood up in bed and threw a wet towel on my face." Mama retold that episode from time to time.

She also related that many of the church members gave advice during the "illness." "She has consumption. Tickle the back of her throat with a feather dipped in kerosene." The final advice was to go to Parsons, Kansas to an eye-ear-nose and throat specialist who had access to a new machine called an x-ray, the only one in southeast Kansas.

As a college junior, I wrote to Dr. Landis who replied immediately. He said the operation was a highlight of his career and that my picture still hung in his office.

Because of the tracheotomy's effect on my vocal chords my voice throughout childhood was "husky." I made gradual improvement, but was never able to shout. My sister, Grace, five years older, helped me learn to speak. Reminiscing about this process, she wrote to me years later.

> I still remember seeing you in the hospital with a metal tube sticking out of your throat and two nuns bending over you. One of the nuns said, "Your little sister is very brave." I was speechless, and all I could do was stare.
>
> When you came home I was told that it was my job to get you to speak. Papa got us a little table and two chairs and I suddenly became a schoolteacher at the age of seven. Finally you **whispered**. It was a great day. Then later maybe one word of a sentence would come out loud. The whispering gradually ceased and your voice got back to complete sentences. But your voice was never normal because the injury had been

too great.

I had been born in August 1918, a few days before the World War I Armistice was signed. Grace remembers going at the age of five from Coffeen, Illinois to Hillsboro (county seat) Hospital to see me.

> I remember very definitely standing with Papa in front of a huge glass window. He was in an army uniform, and told me that he was going across a lot of water called an ocean to be Chaplain in the army. He said I must take good care of Mama and baby Helen while he was gone.
>
> However, the Armistice was signed a few days later and Papa never went. The day the war ended the town whistle blew for an hour from noon 'till one o'clock. *I can still hear it!* They made a Kaiser out of straw and hung him in the town square and burned him down. Papa taught me to sing, "It's Over, Over There." I raced up and down the front porch singing it at intervals all day long. I didn't really understand the whole thing, but I knew everybody was exceedingly happy, so I was happy too.

Papa and Mama had been Mennonite students at Goshen College, Goshen, Indiana, who eloped to be married in 1909, leaving the college and the Mennonite tradition. They became Methodists. We were never told why, but figured out later that their relatives felt their behavior was not consistent with Mennonite beliefs.

Soon after my arrival, the family moved from Coffeen to Bone Gap, Illinois, and the next year to Galesburg, Kansas.

By that time Papa, a teacher and preacher, had been ordained and was accepted into the Methodist Episcopal Conference.

In 1963 at age seventy-seven, Papa wrote an informal record entitled, "Reed-Weaver-Good-Ressler Family History." It included genealogical trees showing, after five generations, that the Reed heritage is "Swiss-German-Irish." Since there was no conversation at home about his past, it was interesting after his death to read his research. Never having met my Mennonite relatives, I grew up knowing very little about them.

In his "Family History" Papa described his first meeting with Mama.

Susanna Good came north from Tennessee and stayed at her uncle Levi Ressler's home, one-half mile east of the Union Township Center School. (I taught this district rural school 1912-13). Susie came to the Salem Mennonite church where I was the Superintendent of the Sunday School at age 18. I did not know she was there until we went to a Sunday School Convention at Emma, ten miles north of Topeka, Indiana, where I read a paper I had written on the history of the Sunday School. On the way home I made a date with Susie for Saturday evening at her uncle's home. She talked to me three hours while she sat on one side of the room, and I on the other side. It was all about the Good families. Then she walked across the room, handed me my hat, and I made a hasty retreat to the Reed farm. This is how I met the South.

The Early Years

Papa depicted his father, Noah W. Reed, as

> ...a strong muscular, lean man. He was a skilled machinist, a blacksmith, a wheelwright, a wagon maker, a sawmill and lumber man. Just as his father had, he enjoyed the workshop. As a young man he was a blacksmith, and continued to do some work for the neighbors after he located on the sixty acre homestead in Elkhart county. At age 34 Noah Reed married Catherine Peppel and operated two threshing crews for fourteen years in northern Indiana.

Papa described himself as "Artisan-Craftsman-Teacher." Several times he was teaching and preaching at the same time. He classified his professional experience as twenty years in the Methodist Ministry in southern Illinois, Kansas and Missouri; five years in southern Illinois high schools; seventeen years in Kansas high schools, and four years teaching in the Civilian Conservation Corp.

During the summer of 1904 he was an apprentice painter of farm buildings. He established an adult woodworking shop, "during the Great Depression" under the FERA (Federal Emergency Recovery Act) at Bolckow, Missouri where he taught boys to operate power tools and make furniture.

Papa's mother, Catherine Peppel, died in 1892 of "consumption (TB) and child-bed fever." In 1894 his father married Barbara Metzler. "She was a wonderful mother to our bereft family," he said. Mama's mother, Susan Ressler, married Henry Good in 1871. He was a Mennonite minister who had moved from Wayne County, Ohio to Concord, Tennessee, described as an excellent farm leader. Susanna, my mother, was their seventh child. There were several more.

After the death of Henry Good, David Hostettler became Mama's step-father in 1914.

Included in Papa's "Family History" were three "Stories of Youth": Threshing Day, Fishing, and Butcher Day, giving a personal account of Mennonite farm practices. There was also a poem written *In Memoriam* of his brother William A Reed, who was killed in the battle of the Argonne Forest, World War I. Another poem, "On this Circuit," was composed in 1935 while Papa walked his twenty-two mile circuit ministering to three churches in Andrew County, Missouri—Bolckow, Walnut Grove, and Wyeth.

The Early Years

A. Papa Reed
C. Helen

B. Mama Reed
D. Grace

Chosen

CHAPTER 2

Childhood Years

My childhood was spent in a series of Methodist parsonages in Kansas—Galesburg, Pleasanton, Gardner, Baldwin, Jamestown; and northwest Missouri—Pickering, Westboro, and Ridgeway. I have distinct memories of each place, including my efforts to be creative in the workshop and to learn how to do things by myself. I was conscious of some kind of tension between Papa and Mama, but didn't know the cause. As I recall my behavior and the consequences of moving each year, I am surprised at what a deceitful little person I was and how much I got away with.

Papa was an easy-going, kind-hearted, helpful father, artistic and literary, who taught me to read and to use woodworking tools. Mama was not motherly in the traditional sense of being affectionate. She never touched me except when I got a spanking. She would say to young mothers, "I never picked up my babies every time they cried. They soon learned to be quiet." She frightened me with her harsh commands. Her "iron hand" ruled.

I have some memory of having been a three-year old living in Galesburg, Kansas. There was a picture in an old family photo album. Dr. Scott, a Methodist Superintendent, was photographed standing between the church and the parsonage.

Chosen

When I saw the picture, so I was told, I said, "Is that God?" At the church there was much talk about God so I thought since Dr. Scott came to see about the church, he must be the one.

I was four, five, and six in Pleasanton, where the parsonage was on a corner and the main line of the Santa Fe Railroad ran behind the house just beyond the barn/garage. I would wait for the train so I could wave to the engineer who would wave back.

This was a convenient stopping-off place for hobos. They would stop at our back porch and ask for food. Mama's practice was to give a paper bag lunch which could be eaten on the back steps. Once a hungry man said, "If I ain't good enough to come in and eat at your table, you can just keep your old food." He left Mama standing with her mouth open.

The road beside the house crossed the railroad tracks. One day a Ford Touring car with two foreign-looking strangers stopped just past the tracks by the side of the house. One man in a black suit stood by the side of the car holding up a bright orange ball, trying to get me to come and get it. I ran in the house and looked out the window. The enticement activity continued. Mama took one look and called the police. We left the window and the car drove on.

Mama went to the hospital when I was four. It was a big mystery. Now we know she had a hysterectomy. Papa was holding evangelistic meetings nightly in the city park. I had the Whooping Cough. Mama told us that she insisted on leaving the hospital early because she felt that the nights in the park could ruin me. Then her operation wound opened up and she had to go back to the hospital to have it closed. During part of the time Mama was in the hospital, Grace and I were monitored by a large black woman known as Aunt

Hallie. "Helen, you take a piece of cheese with a fork, not with your fingers." There were two young black women who assisted us for a few weeks with housework.

Both Mama and Papa were Scout Captains. Once we went on a family picnic to enjoy outdoor cooking. Mama prepared sliced potatoes and onions with Crisco in her black cast-iron skillet. At the river a fire was built. Papa caught catfish, cleaned and cooked them. We had a delicious fish- fry. This is one of my memories of happy family life.

Our dining room had a large round pedestal type table. Mama made a large cake, put chocolate icing on it and placed it in the center of the table with strict instructions, "Do not touch it." When the icing ran down some on the plate I figured it wouldn't show if I just took a little finger. At first it didn't show, but the chocolate became addictive and the finger went all around the cake. By the time Mama came back it was obvious. I got a spanking and had to sit on a little chair in a dark closet for a long time. I was not afraid of the dark, but I hated being punished.

One summer Papa took the family to spend two weeks at a Boy Scout Camp in the Ozarks near Neosho, Missouri. The boys took me canoeing, which I enjoyed. I did not enjoy my dull brown, homemade, poorly fitting romper suit that served as my swimming suit. Grace and Mama had real suits, ridiculous looking garments.

The year I was five I broke first one arm then the other, each through the elbow. In August I fell out of a little wagon; in October I fell out of a swing we had in the barn.

Each evening, as I sat on Papa's lap, he would read me the Uncle Wiggly story from the newspaper. When he found I was reading the story, too, he supplied me with a Kansas Primer, First and Second Readers, and Indiana First and

Second Readers. In Kansas one had to be six years old to start school. With a birthday on August 28, I felt I was delayed a year. By the time I got to go to school, I had read five books.

In the First Grade when each pupil was to stand up front and read a sentence, which others did haltingly, placing one word slowly after another, I would breeze hastily through a paragraph. The teacher suggested that perhaps I should be promoted to Second Grade. Papa said, "No, she needs to stay with her own age group."

I had the misfortune to walk into our parents' bedroom while a fist fight was occurring. They were standing up in the middle of the room. Papa seemed to be trying to hug Mama. She was slapping him and he was fighting back. I had no idea what it was about except that I knew it was not right. I stopped the fight, but Mama made me sit in the dark closet for a long stretch. I wasn't sure why I was being punished, I just felt very bad.

Papa won a radio in a newspaper contest. It had two headphones and two huge batteries. He was given a purse of forty dollars at a Testimonial Dinner in his honor just before we left Pleasanton for Gardner.

After reading my notes on Pleasanton, Grace wrote me a long letter validating my remembrances and telling me some of hers.

At Pleasanton we had a nice big yard on the right side of the house. It was full of trees and birds. Sometimes we found dead birds on the ground and had bird funerals. A matchbox made a good casket and I would do a small funeral sermon and sing part of a song and then we would put the bird in a hole we had dug at the end of a flower garden. When Papa came here to Akron to live with me he told me he remembered my bird funerals. I was astounded. He said he was listening from his Study window.

Mama went wild one summer afternoon and gave both of us very brutal switchings on our bare legs. We went round and round the dining room table screaming and crying. I kept saying, "Not Helen, not Helen!" But she kept right on, and our legs hurt awful. She had warned me previously that she was going to **cut the blood out of me**. I didn't understand what she meant. But I understood it that day. She finally flung us into our bedroom and put her switch away. We screamed and cried for a long time.

Papa was at the church, but when he came home we went to the Study and told him we had not done anything wrong. When he saw our awful looking legs he told Mama to come to the Study and he told her he would have her put away if she ever did that again. It took a long time for our legs to heal.

About a week later the Women's Home Missionary Society met at the Parsonage and we were in the living room and one woman noticed our legs. She wanted to know what had happened to us. Mama said we had helped out in the garden, and accidentally gotten into the barbed wire fence. That day I learned that Mama was an expert liar. Sometimes it is necessary to lie.

I finished the Third Grade at Pleasanton. Three black boys sat in a back corner of the schoolroom. I had seen black people but was very curious of the fact that they were **down**. I was also **down**. Strange as it may seem I loved those boys, and they loved me. Every recess they would go off on the playground by themselves and I would go and get them and welcome them into our games. **Always** they went off by themselves at recess. I left Pleasanton when I was in the Sixth Grade and all that time it was the same story over and over. This is the truth. I knew nothing about slavery. I just knew that **something** was wrong.

Mama told me once when she was in college she took a trip back to her home, and one of her maids, May Lily, had gotten married. Her husband had built a house back in the woods. She took Mama to her house and gave her blackberry wine she had made. Mama said it tasted very good. Apparently they were glad to see each other, but this still didn't make slavery right.

The black twins who came to dust on Saturday morning were about ten years old, the same age as me. I was not allowed to speak to them because they were servants. Mama grew up with two black servant girls so she was pleased to have Eleanor and Elvira to come on Saturday mornings. Mama told me not to talk to them and to practice the piano while they were dusting in the dining room. But I wanted to talk with them because I was very curious about them. Mama told me that black people were to wait on white people. That was the way things were in the world. But Papa and I could not swallow this. We knew better.

One Saturday morning Mama had to go someplace and as soon as she was out the front door I went to the bedroom where Eleanor and Elvira were dusting.

Papa wanted to talk with them so I invited them into the Study. The four of us had a grand time talking. We found out how they lived. They said they knew about gardening and cooking and wanted to get married when they were older.

They were not allowed to go to school. Black boys went to school **but not girls**. Papa thought it was unfair and initiated getting the law changed. Papa was very kind to them. I had them touch the piano keys. Then they went back to the bedroom.

When Mama came back I was playing the piano, Papa was at his desk in the Study, and we were triumphant. Mama never knew what happened while she was gone.

Going to the Governor's Mansion on my bicycle with you on the saddle we upset in the park at a very bad place where we both got dirty. I was embarrassed to no end because the Governor's house was a special place, not an ordinary house. The governor's wife was very kind and she understood our predicament.

Listening to the radio at Pleasanton with the headphones on I heard somebody play the piano in New York City. I was thrilled. Papa told me that the best was yet to come. He said that someday there would be a picture box called television, and I would be able to **see** somebody in New York City. I didn't believe a word of it. I knew very well that was an impossibility. I still think so even when I'm looking right at it.

By 1923-24, Papa had decided to work toward completion of a college degree. The Methodist Episcopal Conference gave him a charge at Gardner, Kansas so he could commute to Baker University in Baldwin. It was expected that the family would live in Baldwin, but Mama decided for her and her children to occupy the parsonage in Gardner, with Papa coming home to preach on weekends.

The house had not been lived in for many years. One end of the dining room was several inches higher than the other. There was a cistern by the front porch. At the back of the lot there was an outhouse and a garage. Heating was done by a wood stove with a stove pipe that came up through a bedroom. When people were conversing downstairs after I had been sent to bed, I would lie on the floor with my head next to the opening around the pipe. I had to know what was going on.

It was in that old house that Mama made me lie on my back on the kitchen table on Saturday mornings, with my head hanging down into a pan of soapy water, while she scrubbed my head with a vegetable brush, courtesy of the Fuller Brush Man. I was in agony. Grace had beautiful long auburn curls, done up each night on long white strips of cotton cloth. My hair was afflicted with a large cowlick caused by an early effort to cut my own hair.

Just when my legs had grown long enough to ride Grace's bicycle, it was sold. Adrian Young, a bachelor who lived next door, took pity on me. He took me to his hardware store and gave me a scooter. It was a good one, solid, secure and very functional. I rode it for years even after I was too old for such a vehicle. I had no words to thank him. We had not been taught to say polite niceties. I just looked into his eyes and rode home.

Directly across from the parsonage lived Mr. Bray, an elderly man who would invite me to swing with him in his double lawn swing. His death was my introduction to what happens at the end of life. I saw the flowers covering his casket as it left the house. Papa administered the funeral. Mama made me stay home. I was too young, or too good a friend, or I just wouldn't understand. I was not to go, period. It was all very strange, and yes, Mama was right, I did not understand.

At Gardner, Grace was introduced to child labor. We are old enough to remember silent movies.

I played the piano for two weeks at the Theater because the regular lady had to go to the hospital. I played two nights a week and it was **work**. I got seventy-five cents a night, **CHILD LABOR.**

I was very sad and also very mad about my bicycle being sold. It was turned in on the grocery bill.

By our second year at Gardner, Mama had had her fill of primitive life in a dilapidated parsonage. Papa felt we should live in Baldwin in "light housekeeping rooms."

Mama regarded herself as a prominent member of the Methodist church in Baldwin. She was fond of recounting an episode with our new car, the Willys-Overland, one of the first closed-in cars. "I had learned to drive the new car quickly and was very proud of the car and my driving ability. While Charles was completing his degree at Baker University I was active in women's organizations at the Methodist Episcopal church. For an auspicious district convention I volunteered to assist with transportation for visiting dignitaries, platform guests and speakers. Very pleased with myself, I picked up the designated women at the train station.

They were happy to ride in the new car, and I was obviously pleased to drive it. When we started up a hill, the wonderful car began to chug-chug, sputter, groan and bounce. I didn't know what to do so I just kept going, my embarrassment increasing to the top of the hill. Then I discovered I had driven up the hill with the brake on. I didn't apologize, just kept going with a red face."

I never liked breakfast and was sometimes allowed to go without. One cold morning I was served **Cream of Wheat**. "You are not to leave the table until it is all eaten," Mama commanded. "I can't eat it." A battle of wits ensued. Much as I wanted to go to school I still could not eat it. When Mama saw she had an impossible situation, she let me go to school. Crossing the Baker University campus after school had started was a cold, cold, lonely trip. There seemed to be no one but me around. I felt like a fugitive from justice. When I got to my classroom the teacher wanted to know what had happened. "Nothing to worry about," I told her.

During vacation, Papa did construction, remodeling, plastering, and cement work on a house in Baldwin. I was permitted to sift sand and was shown all sorts of interesting things. It amazed me that Papa could do so much. His early Mennonite training had been extensive and practical.

Papa finished his BA in April with majors in English and History and was immediately transferred to Jamestown in northcentral Kansas not far from the Nebraska line. Jamestown had not had rain for a year although some towns in the county had. On the day we left Baldwin it rained steadily. The folks at Jamestown said we brought good luck since the rain came with us.

The church was well supported. The parsonage next door was one of the best houses in town. After our living quarters in Gardner and Baldwin, the house seemed luxurious with its indoor plumbing, two bedrooms and bath downstairs, large living, dining, and kitchen and three rooms and walk-in attic upstairs. I loved to go upstairs to Grace's bedroom window to watch the sun set on the wheat field across the road. There was a glorious, esthetic glow.

Behind the church was a splendid tennis court. For me, sitting in a tree, it was a spectator sport. The young people played lots of tennis. Grace and I both had tennis racquets. She played, I watched.

Jamestown was a comfortable place to live. On May first, the church people gave the minister's family a big May Basket. A decorated bushel-basket held all sorts of food and while that was at the front door two men delivered a one-hundred pound sack of sugar at the back door. Mama really appreciated that sugar supply and took full advantage of it. She made lots of candy, especially some to give away in Christmas boxes.

The church had a small Sunday School Orchestra that was of interest to me, especially the clarinet, but I had been observed making motions as if I were playing a violin. Papa went to Concordia, the county seat, and came back with a three-quarter-size violin. There was no violin teacher in town so a woman who played the cello came and "explained" the violin. She admitted she didn't know much about it. She couldn't teach me how to tune it or how to hold the violin and bow. It was a miserable experience. There was no music book, no directions, no guidelines, no pictures, no rudiments of music. Why was this happening to me? **I could not play the violin.**

Frequently I was sent to the grocery story about four blocks from home. At the store I had a system of adding to

Mama's order. All I did was point to the cookie bins and say how many. I was skilled at getting just enough cookies that could be eaten before getting home. There never was any money involved because a bill was run up and paid whenever Papa was paid. As far as I know, no one ever questioned the bill and my quilt was not very deep. It was a secret I kept from Mama.

Past the tennis court, where Grace valiantly won a Tournament, stood a tall pine tree. I was very much into climbing that summer and climbed everything I could. The pine tree presented a challenge. I got way up, then got frightened about getting down, but that fear was not as great as the fear of getting caught by Mama and the subsequent trouble that would ensue. It took a long time but I got down safely and it took hours to clean the resin off my hands. Two other events that summer when I was nine made a deep impression.

Mama's youngest sister, Aunt Mary, was a Mennonite missionary in a girl's school in Dhamtari, India. She was home on furlough for the year and she and Cousin Willy Jennings, Aunt Anna's son, spent a week with us. She wore the Mennonite prayer-head covering (little crinoline cap), signifying being in prayer at all times. She had to have her own tea brewed in a little metal ball. She taught us to sing *"Rajah ishue eye ah,"* *(King Jesus is Come).* I still remember the words and the tune. Aunt Mary was different from anyone I had ever known, but like Mama she showed her fierce independence.

The second event was that Papa took me to an Epworth League Summer Institute (teen-age summer camp) at Kansas Wesleyan College in Salina. We were there for two weeks. I was too young for Epworth League, but I acted like I didn't know the difference. I loved the Institute (this is a favorite memory) especially the Dining Hall. There were many tables with not more than ten at a table. While the food personnel were preparing to serve the tables there would be table to table songs such as "What did Idaho, boys, oh what did Idaho? I ask you now as a personal friend, what did Idaho?" Then some other table would answer, "She hoed a Maryland, boys, she hoed a Maryland. I tell you now as a personal friend, she hoed a Maryland." There were lots of states to sing about. It was good fun. We all felt good and had a great sense of belonging.

Just before the end of the school year Papa was transferred to a three-point charge in Missouri—the town of Pickering and two country churches: Myrtle Tree and Mozingo Valley. At the first Sunday Service, even before our furniture had arrived, I got acquainted with a kid and cut up in church. I was always easily amused, but it wasn't funny to Mama. She marched me over to the back porch of the parsonage, picked up an old overshoe left in a corner and spanked me real hard.

During a funeral at Myrtle Tree I had to stay in the car and the honk got unscrewed and a spring jumped out. There I was, completely innocent of course, having nothing to do with the fact that the car started honking on its own accord. Mama came running out of the church. She was angry, red in the face, and there was nothing I could do about it. I was in disgrace for weeks.

During the summer, Dean Wiley, a red-headed boy from across the street, and I played together. We were very good friends. We worked in our garage workshop many hours while constructing a "soap box derby car." It worked but it didn't last long. The steering and braking mechanisms were too weak in spite of my "inventions."

Chosen

Pickering was about twenty miles from Maryville, county seat of Nodaway and home of Northwest Missouri State Teachers College with a Conservatory of Music. Grace was enrolled for piano lessons with Mrs. Caldwell and distinguished herself in pursuing her piano career.

I was registered for violin lessons with Miss Helen Schwarzkopf. Just entering her studio scared me. She did not know that I had no background in music or violin. I didn't tell her anything, but it soon became obvious that I was totally devoid of knowledge and skill. "All right, Helen. Sing do-re-mi along with the piano," Miss Schwarzkopf ordered.

"I'm not supposed to sing because of my voice." I did not explain in detail. The conclusion was that I had no ear for music. She continued to work with me. (If only she had taught me a proper way to hold the violin and bow!) I was forced to play in a recital held in Social Hall at the college. My dinky, little piece was "The Happy Farmer." On the same program, precocious little Sarah Caldwell, only five years old, half my age, played a Mendelssohn Concerto. It was embarrassing. To add to my hurt, Mama insisted that my teacher go on a picnic with us after the recital. I think most children would have cried under the circumstances, but not me, it wouldn't have been allowed. Another insult was added to my tender, buried pain when soon after that Sarah played at our church in Pickering, with her mother at the piano. I had a severe case of inadequacy. I knew I would never be a violinist. Music was for other people.

NOTE: Sarah Caldwell became a famous opera conductor in Boston. I saw her picture on TIME magazine. I have been a successful band and orchestra director and have taught string classes for music education students and several adult beginners. Grace has taught piano for over fifty years in her own studio in Akron, Ohio. She has thirty students each week and gives recitals in Steinway Hall.

I completed the sixth grade and the first twelve weeks of the seventh grade junior high in Westboro, Missouri. Westboro schools were very progressive. This meant an art class and a cooking class in addition to other subjects. For cooking we learned to make muffins, cocoa, and applesauce with red hots. The rest of the time we sent letters to companies for free recipes and information. We sat around a table, were free to talk and be ourselves. It was like becoming an adult.

During the summer I had a playhouse in the box the piano was moved in. A board nailed up in a tree sufficed for a "tree house." Another wooden box close to the chicken yard provided a cover for my secret smoking activities, i.e., learning to smoke. From a piece of corncob and short stem of hollow catnip I created a pipe to smoke the tea and coffee I would steal from the kitchen while Mama was taking her afternoon nap. She had a regular sleep time we could usually count on.

Betty and Joe Utter, who lived caddie-cornered across from us, were also into smoking. They had a little doghouse we could crawl into. Simulated cigarettes were made by folding over a piece of toilet paper and rolling it tightly. Thank Goodness there was no idea at any time for anyone to inhale. Besides, it was secret.

Mama had a mysterious illness for a few weeks. She said her nerves were crawling, stayed in bed, acted hysterical, and was given a shot of morphine. I was mystified, scared, and kept out of sight as much as possible.

23

Chosen

Our exodus from Westboro is still a vivid memory. Papa
had traded the Willys-Overland for a Whippet. He had not
discussed it with Mama and she was furious. For the
departure there were two trucks, one for books and tools, one
for everything else. At the last moment the back seat of the
Whippet got so filled with luggage and other things that Grace
and I had to ride in the furniture truck with the driver, Edgar
Polley. A chair was sticking up too high when we had to go
under a railroad viaduct. He did some reloading while saying
he wanted to swear, but wouldn't because we were preacher's
kids. Even after all that the truck got to Ridgeway before the
Whippet. Grace and I were delivered to the home of some
church family. That evening they were hosting a skating party
for church youth. It was cold. We all huddled around a stove.
We had not had any training about how to introduce
ourselves. We exhibited no social graces. We were tired,
awkward, shy, introverted, and we hoped our parents would
soon show up. The one thing we had always been taught was,
"At the new place you never mention the old place. You
learn the names of the people and behave yourself." That was
Mama's "rules and regulations." Incidentally, the Whippet
either fell to pieces or was sold soon after we were settled in
Ridgeway.

We lived for the next two years in a parsonage next to the
church. It had indoor plumbing, four bedrooms upstairs, the
kitchen had a big range. There was a cave in the yard, just as
in Pickering, but this one was easier to get into. One side of
the basement housed Papa's workshop.

While we were just getting settled, the church people gave
us a food shower. Mama was upset that they came before she
got the curtains up. The group had not planned what to bring.
Almost everyone brought candy, especially divinity. It was all

24

over the dining room.

At Ridgeway Papa slept in my bedroom. Mama made me sleep with her. I hated that but there was no way out of the problem. It was not subject to discussion. Papa had a study upstairs. It was lots of fun to play with his colored inks, make colored parchment paper, browse in his old magazines, books and papers. During one of those explorations in Papa's file cabinets I found something I blew up as a balloon. Papa said, "Put that away. It's not a balloon." I didn't tell him I had also sampled the small chocolate bar found in another drawer. It was ex-lax. It took a day or two to get over it.

Reading catalogs, either Sears Roebuck or Montgomery Ward, was a time consuming sport. Other kids had play clothes, shirts and slacks. After much begging, a pair of blue slacks and a light tan shirt were ordered. These new clothes made me so happy that I ran around the neighborhood for hours after supper, in great glee that I now had appropriate clothing for playing active games.

Grace had the room on the left at the head of the stairs. Mama was in her room yelling at her. She was beating Grace's bare legs with a green switch. What had Grace done? She had hung all her clothes on one hook and her closet needed cleaning up.

When I started the Eighth Grade, Grace was starting her first year of college in Maryville. She had a Methodist student loan and lived at Residence Hall, the women's dormitory. Majoring in both music and art, after her First Quarter she became ill and came home. She was too fragile for dorm life. While she recuperated she taught art to several students and I was permitted to join the class. I acquired some useful knowledge.

Papa played the lead for a week of performance in *Ten*

Nights in the Bar Room, a play put on in Bill Leonard's Theater by a community group. It portrayed the evils of alcoholism. Mama condemned Papa for playing such a bad character, but his performance was a big hit. The public admired him. Leonard also had a summer traveling tent show featuring "Tess of the Storm Country." He came to the parsonage once for dinner. Mama served her mincemeat pie. She had a special way of grinding meat and spices, canning for future use, then making a pie. Did the meat ferment? I don't know. Bill Leonard loved the pie and announced from the stage of his theater that the Methodist minister's wife made special mincemeat pie with reference to the possibility it had been fermented. Mama claimed to be embarrassed, but I think she was really flattered. Incidentally, I have never had such delicious pie in any home or restaurant.

Because we had been accustomed to the Methodist Conference moving Papa to a new charge each year, when he went off to conference, Mama started packing. She would be prepared to move with alacrity when he returned. As soon as he got back we crowded around him, "Well, where are we going?" Papa nonchalantly said, "We are not moving. The Official Board contacted the Conference and asked to have me returned to Ridgeway."

One of the few times that Mama praised Papa was in Ridgeway after he had conducted a funeral for a baby. It was good to hear that kind of praise for him since we were so accustomed to hearing condemnations.

Mama had a series of tales she loved to tell. One was about how in the middle of the night she heard Papa downstairs praying aloud! "I thought he was getting 'born again religion' or having something special happening to him, and ran down the stairs to join him. There I was in my flimsy nightgown interrupting a solemn marriage ceremony. A couple had come down from Iowa and he had agreed to marry them since otherwise they would have to wait three days. I retreated back upstairs in haste."

Papa was invited to take a group of young people to tour the Abbey at Conception, Conception Junction, and Clyde, Missouri. A convent had a Chapel of Perpetual Adoration. We were told it had been in existence for more than forty years. No less than two nuns were at the altar, always with a quiet system of replacements. From the back we saw four nuns on their knees at the altar. Near the back of the chapel a small group of us were greeted by the Mother Superior. She seemed to float as she stepped forward toward us and **I saw about her head, an aura**. For some reason she chose to single me out to give a special greeting with her eyes. Her voice was smooth as silk. For me it was a new experience, like meeting purity. I was in a trance and felt as if she were purifying me. For the rest of the tour I was in a daze. Years later I read about the phenomenon of seeing an aura, an experience that does not happen to everyone.

In August, Mama announced she would take Grace and me to Maryville and we would rejoin Papa for the next summer. The exodus was heart-breaking. Mama said it would be better for Grace to go to college without living in a dorm, and for me to be in one high school for four years instead of moving every year. Someone drove a car up to the front of the house. Papa stood in the doorway saying to me, "I thought maybe you would stay with me!" I couldn't say anything. We both knew it was useless. It was extremely painful. It had not been discussed. There was no emotion of affection shown, no good-byes.

Chosen

CHAPTER 3

High School in Maryville

"Thump, thump, thump." All night long the freight cars were being loaded. The small cottage Mama rented in Maryville was close to a Railroad Freight Depot and the back entrance to the college campus. The place was a shack, but since we expected to join Papa for the summer, we regarded it as temporary.

The front door was reached by a half dozen steps up from the sidewalk. There were five rooms—a center room with a small coal-burning stove, living room, two tiny bedrooms, and a kitchen. To the right of the kitchen was a semi-enclosed back porch with a camp-type toilet. The kitchen sink had a hand pump. During the winter the coal was delivered in one big chunk that I chopped up with a Scout ax while coal dust got in my eyes and lungs.

Grace got the bedroom with a cot. There was no alternative to my sharing the only bed with Mama. There wasn't even any way to protest. Mama and I never talked about it. There was no affection between us. Grace lived in her own world. She and I didn't engage in any idle chatter. College and high school were very different. She was occupied with her music and art.

The school friends I acquired never talked about their

parents or about "feelings." Adolescence was a time to be frivolous, ignoring whatever was really developing within us. There was great need for secrecy about everything. To be a cool kid you had to learn to smoke. Even though I had tried experiments as a child, I never succeeded in really smoking. (I'm grateful for that.)

Now that I was fourteen, it was time to grow up. I had matured physically, but not socially. All the way across town to the high school was a long walk, but it gave me time to adjust my mind to all the new things that were so different from the small towns we had lived in and the reality of not being a "preachers kid" anymore.

The high school was a different world. There everyone had a locker. In addition to books and wraps it housed my small bean-sandwich I could eat in the study hall on the noon hour. That seemed weird. Not everyone was hit by the "Depression" as hard as my family was. Physical Education was scheduled on alternate days of the week. The activity itself was not hard to manage, but undressing and taking a shower with thirty or more kids was not easy for me. I was the only one wearing a dyed rose-colored homemade (flour sack) slip with wide straps, no bra. My underclothes were an embarrassment, so I always changed swiftly, doing my best to hide the incriminating evidence of poverty. Eventually I came to appreciate the showers. Taking a bath at home was to be avoided if at all possible. "I had a bath at school," was highly preferable.

I had no difficulty making my grades, but every so often I was called to the Principal's Office. I couldn't always behave. One day the Superintendent of Schools came to make a speech to our English class. My seat was in the front row. He admonished all students to behave themselves. He said things I regarded as funny so I laughed. After he left the teacher gave me a long lecture, a dressing down in front of the class about my "over developed sense of humor." I was hurt and embarrassed and wondered if there was some way I could run away. All the way on the long walk home after school I tried to think up some way to avoid going back to school the next day. I never came up with any plan.

After Christmas the canned fruit and vegetables we had brought with us from Ridgeway had all been consumed except green beans. Papa had been moved to Helena, Missouri, another poor church, and he had not sent any money. We started having nothing but green beans for supper and nobody worried about breakfast anymore.

Mama joined the Methodist Church and went around telling people about bringing her children to Maryville to go to high school and college. That was embarrassing. At church organizations she would meet people and make appointments to go to their homes to sell hosiery and lingerie. Since our meals at home were insignificant, the occasional Wednesday night potluck suppers at the church were enjoyed. I know that during the "Depression" lots of people went hungry. One can get accustomed to eating less. It is said that the stomach shrinks.

At the end of the school year Mama took Grace and me and our furniture to Helena to be with Papa. Even though I was still forced to sleep with Mama it was good to be a family and have a father again. There was no show of affection. Each member of the family took everything for granted. I don't remember being very hungry, just generally miserable, especially since Mama made me go to bed at 7:30 each evening.

We were able to eat from the garden. One morning I was

31

sent out in the hot sun to pick peas. The peas were prolific and picked easily. On the back porch I was put to shelling them. Soon something strange happened. I didn't know what was happening to me. Was I going blind? I started falling off the chair. Next I could feel Grace and Mama walking me to a cot in a bedroom. I had fainted. It took me quite awhile to recover. I stayed in bed for a couple of days until I felt stronger. No doctor was called. I wondered to myself if I might be more fragile than Mama realized.

Mama arranged for me to baby-sit at a home close to ours. There was no work to do, the child was in bed, I wasn't even introduced to him, but every time I had to baby-sit I was a nervous wreck worrying until the parents returned. If an emergency had occurred I would have been totally inadequate. The fact that I did not want the job did not phase Mama. She collected the pay.

When the summer was over we returned to Maryville to a second floor room Mama had arranged to rent at Mrs. J. Russell's house. Grace, Mama and I shared a room with a bed and a cot, and "kitchen privileges" in the basement. We still had the small walnut desk Papa had made for me. Grace's piano was stored in a practice room at the college conservatory. She did her art work on a card table, I studied at my desk, and Mama sat on a chair with a small bedside table on the far side of the bed, studying her efforts toward business enterprises.

There were several other renters. The minister of the Methodist Episcopal Church South had a room next to ours. Downstairs with Mrs. Russell, lived Roland Russell, a college student currently home recovering from a collapsed lung, and his divorced sister Mildred, an elementary teacher with a six-year-old son, Billy. The house was comfortably crowded with people. Roland's older brother, Donald, came for visits from time to time and Mr. Russell came in from his farm about once a month.

By my second year of high school I started wearing a "boy-bob." Mama didn't object since she provided no money for professional hair care. Although the "boy-bob" was not feminine, it was distinctive and saved time, energy, and money. I had a special way to have some cash available. I sold my textbooks from the previous year and converted the money into small change kept discretely on the top shelf of my locker. On the noon hour I could get a five-cent White Tower hamburger and when my friends, Margery Rose Sauceman and Marcia Tyson, invited me to go with them after school to "The Granada", the local soda shop, I had the resources for a fountain coke.

Seated in a booth at "The Granada" one day, comfortably relaxing while slowly sipping my coke, I looked up toward the long drugstore counter near the entrance. To my complete surprise there was Mama. It had never occurred to me that she would come in. My heart skipped a beat. She did not know I had a source of cash. I was supposed to be in the Public Library. What would I do if she came back to the booths? I didn't tell my friends what was happening to me, as I became quiet, imagining myself to be small and inconspicuous. Mama sat at the counter, had a drink, and left. I could see her, but she did not see me. I breathed easier when she was gone. I had a plan in mind by which I could justify not telling the source of my cash. Since Mama didn't tell us anything about her financial affairs, I didn't tell about mine. The incident made a deep impression on me. Why was I so scared of her? Some other kids had parents they never talked about so is this normal behavior? I wondered about

33

how other people lived. Certainly my life as it was being lived was not like the lives of people I was reading about in books.

After school the Public Library was a place to read, study, hang out, cut up, and get into trouble. For disrupting the peace of the library, three of us were reprimanded by the Mayor in his office in the basement of the library. We all promised to behave ourselves in the future.

Sophomore English was taught by a woman near retirement age. We had "Oral English." After I gave my speech she told me to see her after school and she would teach me how to talk. I was upset. Kids who knew me told me to forget it. At home I burst into tears. "What is wrong with you?" Mama barked at me. Crying was something I did not do at home.

I recounted my problem. The teacher lived next door to Russell's house. Mama went to that house that evening. She didn't tell me she was going nor give me a report on her visit. I didn't ask any questions. We were not accustomed to discussion. The teacher never mentioned Mama or my voice, but there were no more problems with "Oral English."

Without asking me if I wanted the job, Mama arranged for me to earn ten cents per evening. I was told that an elderly widow with arthritis needed to have a companion and someone to cook breakfast for. At first when I arrived I would sit in the "parlor" and engage in polite conversation. We had nothing in common and there was not much to talk about. Soon I would take my books and go upstairs to the bedroom. The woman's arthritis kept her from going up to the second floor. It was like an attic with a bed that had a "feather bed" to sleep under. It was good to sleep alone although I felt strange in the house and did not find it easy to be friendly. In the morning she made pancakes while I sat at the kitchen table. The place was not clean, nor was she. She would put her dirty looking hands into a box of pancake mix to take out a handful. That was revolting to me, especially since I was not accustomed to having breakfast. If Mama thought the food would be good for me she was mistaken. I like pancakes but couldn't possibly eat those dirty ones.

One night after going upstairs to bed, I opened a window and lighted one of my secret Sir Walter Raleigh cigarettes that my friend Winifred, had given me. I thought that with my head in the window it would be safe. I was mistaken. The woman smelled it right away and called up the stairs. I made some wild explanation, made a production of closing the window and that was the end of smoking. The job didn't last long. I begged to quit and when I did I imagine the poor old woman was glad to be rid of me. I was actually glad to get back to Russell's house.

One morning I failed to get up and go to school, just couldn't make it, complained of aches and pains. Was it rheumatic fever, or anemia? I stayed home a few days and was told to take aspirin. Was I fatigued from the tension of sleeping with Mama? Why was I so scared of her? She would not let me turn over or move in the bed. The slightest movement would cause a sharp, angry command: "Lie still!" If my illness bothered her, she did not show it.

It would be nice to say that Mama dressed up each day to go out to sales appointments, but to be truthful she wore the old clothes she had. As a minister's wife she had dressed discretely, mostly in a black or navy suit. She never divulged details of her profits. I remember she occasionally would say she had been invited to stay for lunch in someone's home after making a sale, and she was a regular customer of a taxicab company.

At school two of my friends, Winifred and Marguerite, decided to try smoking in the Restroom on the second floor. I agreed to watch the hall and give warning if anyone was coming. They smoked. We each returned to wherever we belonged. Not long after, Principal Thomas called me to his office. "Did you smoke?"

"No, I only watched the hall." When he told me that Winifred and Marguerite were being expelled for a week until their parents reinstated them, and that I could be expelled too, my eyes nearly popped out of my head as I visualized what Mama would do to me if I got expelled. I was so frightened I could not speak. I felt paralyzed. As far as I know Mr. Thomas never contacted Mama. State Law prohibited smoking in the building. I was glad I had not smoked.

The most important feature of my sophomore year was becoming a member of the newly created band and orchestra. Mr. William Gaugh, taught Winifred and Alice and me to play string basses for the orchestra. The parts were simple. We didn't need to know very much. I didn't talk about this at home until one night I had to because the orchestra was scheduled to play at a church. Having been a failure on the violin I was hesitant, thinking it best to keep it a secret in case it was temporary. Then the band needed tuba players, so very quickly I learned enough to play in the band. Little did I realize at the time what a difference being a member of the band and orchestra made, or the positive influence that Mr. Gaugh, a quiet, unassuming, married man with children, had on me.

For the next two summers, we lived with Papa in Bolckow, Missouri.

In September, back in Maryville, the Russell's decided to

move next door to a larger house. The renters moved too. Grace got a small room of her own. I had to sleep with Mama. "No alternative."

For the 1935 All-State High School Orchestra, Mr. Gaugh took three string bass players and one violinist to Kansas City where the orchestra played for a State Teachers Meeting. A local school supplied the basses. After the rehearsal we were free until 4:00 p.m. when we were due on stage to perform. Our group decided to see the changing light tower on top of the Kansas City Light and Power Building. We took the elevator to the top. When we were ready to descend, the elevator did not come. Not having any idea how long it would take, we were all in a panic. Kenny Tebow (violinist) said we should walk down. So we ran, and ran, and ran, down seventy-six flights. We were too scared to realize what we were doing. We arrived back at the stage at the last minute. Poor Mr. Gaugh was getting worried about us. We played. My legs felt like rubber. After the performance Mr. Gaugh took us to a cafeteria, a new experience for me. Not knowing what to take I kept going in line until near the end I saw a steak covering a plate. "Do you really want that?" asked Mr. Gaugh.

"Yes, that's all." It probably blew his budget. I ate it all.

That evening we were guests of the Kansas City Philharmonic. Brahms Fourth was thrilling, but before the end of the concert I fell asleep. We were all riding in Mr. Gaugh's car. We got home about four o'clock in the morning to find that a tornado had struck Maryville. There would be no school for a few days because the roof of the high school building was twisted and partially destroyed. For a few weeks we had classes in nearby churches.

The Presbyterian Church had a Sunday School Orchestra

---

directed by Mr. Gaugh. He let me play the old cornet I had bought for five dollars in a junk shop. I went to Christian Endeavor on Sunday nights. Before long, I was appointed Secretary of the Sunday School, kept the attendance records, and counted the class collection money. On the Sunday I joined the Presbyterian Church Mama showed up uninvited. We did not talk about it. Having been born a Methodist, this was a rare assertion of independence.

Toward spring I had another period of extreme fatigue and simply could not get up and go to school. During the time I was bedridden, Hope Miller and Marguerite Curfman and a couple of other girls came to my bedroom and planned a picnic. That surprised and embarrassed me. I was not diagnosed as having any recognizable ailment, and Mama didn't seem disturbed by my illness.

The Russell's decided to go back to their farm. Roland's lungs had healed and he graduated from college. He was a Captain in the National Guard. His room was off the living room through which one had to go to the front door. In the living room he had two large shells that looked like huge bullets. I was very curious, and Roland, who didn't usually talk with me, was pleased to tell me all about them. He and I communicated. I was thrilled that this "college man" I admired so much, talked to me like a friend. (During WW-II he was a Brigadier General on duty in London.)

From the Russell's house we moved to Mrs. Wilson's rooming house. There I spent my senior year. On the second floor we had a kitchen, Grace had a bedroom and Mama and I had a bedroom. Once again for me there was "no alternative" to sleeping with Mama. Down the hall was a bathroom and another room inhabited by an old woman whose enemas taken with a bucket in her room were a disturbing noise while I studied at the kitchen table. Downstairs lived a group of teachers, one of whom was my typing teacher.

Being a senior in 1935-36 meant that I was eligible to apply for a "job" at the high school under the NYA (National Youth Administration).[1]

I succeeded in being employed at the high school and worked for a math teacher, a history teacher and Mr. Gaugh. For sixty hours a month I drew a check for six dollars. I graded papers, duplicated tests, and copied music. It was my money, but Mama saw to it that enough was saved so she could make me a spring outfit: a light green skirt and three-quarter coat. Most of my high school days were spent in a brown skirt and sweater with plaid zipper jacket for a coat. I wasn't very happy about the spring outfit, but it made Mama very happy!

Maryville High School offered for the first time a *Fundamentals of Music* course. Mr. Gaugh made it a college prep course with an introduction to harmony, composition, orchestration and conducting. The class was small, not more than twelve. While I had no intention of taking music in college, I took the course seriously. I loved it when we each got to conduct the band, playing our original compositions of

---

[1] President Franklin D. Roosevelt's New Deal was said to be "an amalgam of 'alphabet' agencies (AAA, NRA, WPA, SEC, DIC, NLRB. Unemployment and homelessness was widespread. There were many "work-relief" projects that set the jobless to work building dams, bridges, highways and airports. Congress enacted reforms such as Social Security, unemployment compensation and federal insurance of bank deposits." (See George J. Church writing on the 1929-39 years in the 75th Anniversary issue of *TIME.)*

sixteen measures. It was obvious that I had a flair for conducting. My composition sounded good too. I had worked it out very carefully. Later, when grades were posted, Kenny Tebow, who came from a musical family, asked in class, "How come Reed got an A, if I didn't?" Mr. Gaugh, ever the calm, cool, collected more than adequate teacher, explained, "Reed deserved an A. She worked for it." It was the only A in the class. I was slightly embarrassed, but pleased. I started staying after school and playing various instruments in Beginners Band. Once Mr. Gaugh even let me play his own cornet.

I had been playing an E-flat Sousaphone in the band. A fine BB-flat York Tuba with recording bell was donated to the school. It was a splendid instrument, fun to play, and heavy as lead. Marching with it was a problem, even with a belt around it and me. I always coped, even when we were parading in downtown Maryville and my homemade garter fell off and my stocking started falling down to my ankle inside the white duck pants. The uniforms were dark blue jackets and hats. We furnished the pants. Mine fitted well; I had a good figure.

In retrospect I am amazed at how much I owe to Mr. Gaugh for giving me a large measure of personal respect. Even when three of us were practicing in the "Men's Room" next door, with our music placed on the top of the urinal (the room was available to girls while the roof was being repaired after the tornado), he came and got us to take us through our parts on a new piece that had a short passage that was difficult for us and I being in a mischievous mood, took my sousaphone into the band room with water in it and squirted it out, a totally unnecessary prank. Even then he didn't get angry with me. In my senior year he gave me a tuba piece to play at the district contests at the college. I think that must have taken considerable faith. I played the piece and won a quarter of private piano lessons at the college during the summer. At the time I wasn't appreciative, but years later realized it had been beneficial.

I planned to enter college for the summer quarter of 1936 at Northwest Missouri State Teachers College. By staying in college each summer, I could get my degree in three years. The sooner I could become self-supporting the better. The necessary eighteen dollars for tuition for the summer was not forthcoming. I was very disappointed.

Two weeks of the summer were spent at Missouri Valley College in Marshall attending a Christian Endeavor Conference. The Presbyterian Church paid all of my expenses. I was grateful for the "vacation" and in a zealous moment I almost answered a call to the Christian ministry. (I thought it would give me a scholarship at some Presbyterian College.) I decided I was meant to do something of value, but that teaching was also a "calling."

Papa had left the Methodist Conference (or it left him) and he was teaching nights in a CCC camp (Civilian Conservation Corp) near Savannah, Missouri. He had rented an old house, furnished the kitchen with a cot, put his books and papers on the second floor and turned the first floor into a woodworking shop with power tools. I spent a week with him making bracelets and other salable items on the lathe. For me to have this privilege, Mama's arrangements included my earning board and room at a local parsonage. That minister's wife was cruel and abusive. The dish washing was an enormous chore. I also had to let the dirty water out of the bathtub for the minister and his teenage son. Why they couldn't do that was beyond my comprehension.

Papa was teaching mathematics and Spanish for the CCC. When I asked him how he knew Spanish, he said he was learning while teaching it from a good textbook. He would teach anything the CCC asked for.

The rest of the summer I coped with hayfever while delivering packages to Mama's customers. For a few days I went to the college typing room which was open to anyone and practiced typing, since I knew I needed to get ready for writing college papers.

Looking back on my four years of high school I have ambivalent feelings toward Mama and myself. She was tenaciously independent—determined to make a living as an entrepreneur. Did I inherit independence or learn it from her and Papa? When I was so dependent on her why was I so afraid of her?

I was aware that not having "a room of my own" was not normal. Under the circumstances I was grateful for what little we had, but how I hated sleeping with Mama! Deep within me I felt as though the fact that she wasn't sleeping with Papa was somehow my fault because she was using me instead. Not all abuse is physical—there were many ways Mama's frustrations were subtly planted on me. She treated me like I was made of steel instead of flesh and bone. I think we both acted as if we were indestructible.

At the high school it was easy for me to make good grades and easy to get into trouble. Several times teachers reprimanded me for "cutting up." I was called to the Principal's office several times.

The one teacher to whom I will be forever grateful was Mr. William Gaugh, for giving me band and orchestra membership. This type of experience is probably why I turned out as well as I did, and why, much later, I became a band director. (No, I did not have a crush on him.) In my opinion any student who has not been a band member has missed the best possible education of their youth. In my case there was also the healing of the pain of my childhood failure to become a violinist. His personal faith in me as a student and as a person served to mitigate the unhappy experiences of home and family.

During these high school years there were opportunities for me to "crack up." In each instance I resisted sufficiently. Were those undiagnosed illnesses indicative of what much later became "congestive heart failure," or was I simply undernourished, anemic, and tense? Was I just sick of life as it was being lived? Joining the Presbyterian Church was a significant step forward for me in my junior year as an assertion of my independence. The Lippman family at the church, was kind to me. They helped me feel a sense of belonging to a group and being a worthy member of society. They had four daughters playing in the Sunday School Orchestra.

The NYA was my introduction to federal aid, politics and low wages. After graduation it would have been ideal for me to go through college in three years. I was all psyched up to do it and couldn't get hold of the tuition. For all I know, now that I can judge in retrospect, my deep disappointment may have been a blessing in disguise.

Chosen

Helen Reed - High School, Maryville, Missouri

CHAPTER 4

College Years at NW Missouri STC

As my freshman year of college commenced, we were still living at Mrs. Wilson's rooming house. Each night I studied at the kitchen table. There was plenty to study since the "studying" done in the college library was not productive. Some of us would congregate in a small back room. We tried to study, but told jokes, made fun of professors, and were laughing most of the time. We were a giddy, nervous bunch. After we came to the attention of the library staff, the privilege of the back room was revoked.

Freshman English, that bugbear of many students, proved to be just that for me. Dr. Lowery was an imposing, authoritarian professor. She wore a large black wig and a black silk dress, always the same each day. When she stood in front of the class, I felt claustrophobic just from her presence. I said to myself, "If I am going to feel like a scared rabbit, how am I going to learn what I need to know? If this woman is an example of a scholarly college professor I must be in the wrong class."

I soon learned that Dr. Lowery had an aversion to any student from Maryville High School. She made her opinion clear to the class.

"You students from Maryville High School are not

prepared for this course. Students from that school have not been properly taught. You are not prepared for college. Those Maryville teachers are antiquated."

She raised her voice and repeated her denigration of our former teachers. I looked around and recognized almost half the group as former classmates. It didn't seem right to put up silently with personal condemnation at the beginning of the course. I was in college now and I expected to be treated with respect, even if I was ignorant and underprepared, so I caused an "incident."

"Dr. Lowery, you are being unprofessional," I said in a nervous tone of voice. (I didn't know the word "unethical.") I didn't argue that her opinion was wrong because I knew that by college standards I was not ready for Freshman English, probably never would be, but nevertheless it was her job to get me through the course. She didn't argue with me, looked shocked and stared at me for a moment, (I felt a chill), then proceeded as if nothing had happened as she made the assignment for the next day. I made a solemn vow to myself to keep a positive attitude. After class some kids thanked me, some told me I was brave, one said, "You'll flunk this class."

Little did I know that in two years I would have a column of my own as a feature writer on the college weekly and would watch students picking up their paper, turning the first page over to read my column first!

After a few weeks, I got called to Dr. Lowery's office.

"Miss Reed, this paper is not presentable. Why was it written this way?"

"I used a carpenter's pencil. It was all I had available," I muttered.

"Your sister's papers were done in India ink with a Spencerian pen."

"She's an art major. Next time I'll use a fountain pen."

From my present perspective I imagine that since Dr. Lowery considered herself a "Blake Scholar," she probably resented having to teach Freshman English.

In later years I developed great respect for the learnings of that Freshman Year. The college had newly adopted a University of Chicago plan for the first two years of college. The professors who lectured for the Humanities course were superbly competent. It was impressive to hear the professors coordinate the knowledge. Only years later did I realize how scholarly they were. The examinations were also special. They were given in the auditorium. Each student had two rows vacant in front and back and two seats on each side vacant, during the exam. It was said that the college lost half the freshman class after the first Humanities exam. It was easy to "flunk out."

Before the end of the freshman year we moved to Bill Burr's house, built in 1875, that had not been inhabited for years. It was like living in a museum. Back in high school, one night when Marguerite Curfman and several friends were riding around in her car, she said, "Let's go look for ghosts in the old 'Castle'." Some people called it the haunted house. Her father had a machine shop in the Carriage House on the lot next to the "Castle." She said people had reported blue lights seen flickering in the attic windows. We looked and didn't see any lights. The ancient, large, uninhabited brick house was scary enough. It felt ghostly just to look at it at night. Then Marguerite said, "Let me tell you another story. The man who built the house had a wax figure of his wife made, after her death, and propped it up at the dining table to have meals with him."

At that time I had no idea I would some day live where the

blue lights were supposed to flicker. When we moved into the house, right after Bill Burr, County Superintendent of Schools, bought it, I kept remembering the tales I had heard and wondered what truth there might be in those stories.

A magnificent American Walnut staircase wound its way to the third floor. A servant's stairway could be entered from the back. We had a second floor kitchen and a bedroom with an unusable bloodstained fireplace. The house had been used as a hospital at some time in its history. Mama continued her sewing, and her selling of hose, lingerie, and housedresses.

The college authorities did not discourage me from taking Industrial Arts my freshman year. As the only girl I was careful not to bother the boys or the instructors. After making it successfully through several courses I eventually had to get boys to help me with the heavy clamps used on hot glue jobs for my furniture. Being the only girl was not fun and I became skeptical of Industrial Arts as my major. It didn't seem right anymore, nor did my haircut.

In a few months, Mama decided we couldn't afford the kitchen, and we moved to a third floor room. In the hall outside our room was a kerosene stove. Food, if there was any, was kept in a box outside the window.

One morning, Mama got up early, went out to her work, and returned to find me still in bed when I should have been at school. She had just received a "pink slip" showing that at Mid-term I was failing in French 101.

"This is inexcusable. I'm working my fingers to the bone every day and pounding the sidewalks to keep a roof over your head and you are too lazy to get up and go to school. You don't have sense enough to appreciate what is being done for you. You ungrateful child, you don't deserve all my hard work. Get out of that bed now!" She went on and on with her tirade as I went more and more into the fetal position in the bed and responded quietly.

"It's not my fault. I didn't ask to be born."

"Oh, yes you did. For nine long months you did."

After that, no matter what, I went to school even if I had to take a nap on one of the cots provided in the Women's Restroom on the third floor of the "Old Main" college building.

It was no surprise to me that I was failing in French. In each class Dr. Dow would have each student translate a sentence. I never prepared my lessons and could not translate. When I could see my sentence coming up I would panic and bolt for the rear door. Why couldn't I cope with French? Could it have been partly that I could never comprehend the mechanics of English, let alone any other language, or because I never learned to diagram a sentence, or was I simply stupid, or just lazy? There must have been an emotional block and Mama's outburst didn't help.

I kept expecting Dr. Dow to question me about my exits via the rear door, but she never did. The class was just before the lunch hour and after class she would see me sprawled on a bench outside the Bookstore having a candy bar for my lunch.

When I had to take the end of the term exam my emotional and verbal numbness turned into acute pain. For our final exam Dr. Dow told us to write a letter in French to a student in France, describing our family. My first reaction was completely negative. Had someone put a knife in my throat? No, I will not cry! I shot a vicious abusive glance at Dr. Dow. How could she do this to me? Then I settled down and proceeded to write the story of my family pain—pain I could not describe—in a language I did not know. Any word I didn't know I just gave a French ending. Perhaps there was a certain type of therapy built into that exam. I passed the course. The next year, while working in the Registrar's Office I looked up Dr. Dow's comments on my grade slips. "Genuine intellectual curiosity, but apparently no time to study French." When I was overseas during World War II, I sent her a card from Paris. She surprised me by responding, which made me very happy. By that time she was President of Cottey College in Missouri. (I was surprised that using my poorly learned French I could ask questions on the streets of Paris and understand the answers.)

Before I had fully recuperated from the "pink slip" episode I was in for another frightening event with Mama. Papa divorced Mama on the grounds of desertion. We were in the third floor bedroom at Burr's "Castle" when she received the papers. It seemed to be a bigger surprise to her than to Grace and me. *After all, she had left Papa.* We were accustomed to coping with her sudden violence, but this seemed different. We were frightened into silence by her extreme physical and mental need to act out her negative feelings. To vent her anger she kept saying over and over, as she stood rigidly in the middle of the room, "I should have married A. K. Rupp. He became a banker. I had to choose between the two of them. I chose the wrong one." Then she took our family photo album, started ripping pages out and ran down all the stairs to the back alley where garbage was burned, yelling that all pictures of "that man" (our father) were going to be burned. We did not accompany her. We were not sure it was safe to be near her. I did not feel like talking. What was there to say? I was emotionally numb. It was best to try to ignore the situation. Once the episode was over, there was never anymore talk about Papa. His name simply did not come up.

If any tears were shed, we did not see them.

For my junior year I was hired as a Student Assistant by Dr. O. Myking Mehus, head of the Sociology Department, who was very busy campaigning to become President of Winona College in Minnesota. He trusted me with many types of work. I made exams for all his courses: objective tests with completion, true-false, multiple choice, and matching questions. I could grade them, post the grades, and occasionally monitor a class. I also wrote publicity releases for the Missouri Society for Social Welfare, which he headed.

I was invited to write a feature column in *The Northwest Missourian*, the college weekly. I was attracted to Virgil Elliott, the student editor. Each week I filled a space with light satire, usually on current college happenings, such as the time the Greeks stuffed the ballot boxes for the Student Senate election.

Virgil Elliott had a sister whom I did not know. She lived in an approved college rooming house where she and Virgil shared a kitchen in the basement. It was near the back entrance to the campus. One day when she was out of town Virgil took me to their kitchen for lunch, a very rare happening. He sent me to a small store, a couple of blocks up from the house, to buy a loaf of bread. "Just tell the man to put it on my bill," he said. The bread would be ten cents. How I wished I had a dime so I could just buy the bread. I wondered what the man would think. It didn't bother Virgil, he was tall, self-composed, secure. I came back with the bread, but was so nervous, so pleased to be alone with Virgil, I could hardly eat the fried potatoes he cooked.

During the summer vacation I was hired to work on an Emergency Relief Project at the college. The work was done on the library balcony and consisted of rebinding library books. We sandpapered edges, (theoretically cleaning them) and learned to sew together sections of a book. We lettered titles on new buckram, which was then glued to the book spine. Some simply couldn't do the lettering, so out of a dozen workers I was chosen to do all of the lettering. I liked that because I did not like the sewing. Although my fingers would get sore and tired, I was happy on the job and appreciated the Supervisor.

It was an afternoon in August when Dr. Uel W. Lamkin, President of Northwest Missouri State Teachers College, came to the project and took me off the job. Although I was frightened of him, (He was completely bald) I said I needed to stay on the job. He said, "People on relief must accept jobs when they are offered." I swallowed my pride quickly. He had a job for me in his outer office. In those days I was scared of anyone in a position of authority, even his secretary. I was not a skilled typist. I sat at a typewriter just outside the door to his inner office, and typed letters, the same letter over and over with numerous erasures on printed stationary listing names of officers of the World Federation of the Teaching Profession.

Following that nervous stint in the President's office in 1939, I got a student assistant job, ten hours a week, in the Registrar's Office, posting transcripts, sitting to the left of the Registrar, Mr. Raleigh Baldwin. We got along fine. I was not afraid of him.

During the summer, Mama decided that Dr. Crowson, our old friend back in Pickering, should loan me money for my senior year so that I could have the experience of dormitory living. I'm sure she wanted to be relieved of taking care of me. There was a strategic financial transaction. Dr. Crowson drove to Maryville and met me at the bank. It was a two hundred dollar loan to cover board and room at Residence Hall for the year, with the understanding that it would be repaid during my first year of teaching.

While writing on *The Northwest Missourian* I held a short term job preparing copies of the paper to be mailed to alumni. The work was done in the basement of the *Maryville Daily Forum*. Pieces of newsprint had names and addresses typed near the top of the slip of paper. Then a group of these were fanned out upside down on a table and brushed with a large paste brush. At first I messed up. One of the men in the basement helped me learn to do it. Once the paste was on it was necessary to work fast. Grab a paper, roll it up and roll the newsprint so that the name and address came out pasted ready for mailing. It was a dirty job with the combination of printer's ink and paste up to my elbows.

It took me so long that when it was time to close the Daily Forum for the evening I was not done. I had to complete the mailing. A kind man told me to stay and finish and climb out an unlocked basement window. By the time I got efficient, the job was given to someone else.

It was after one of these mailing jobs that I became a thief with deep-seated guilt. I went home and cleaned up. There was no one in all of Burr's "Castle" but me. I was hungry and there was no food. I ransacked the house. In the kitchen I found Billy's coin purse with a half-dollar in it. I took it thinking I could maybe replace it before it would be missed. Downtown at a restaurant I had dinner for forty cents. In a day or so I heard Mrs. Burr wondering what had happened to Billy's fifty-cent piece. No one ever asked me if I took it. It never got replaced. I was scared enough to never do such a thing again. I was desperate and really needed the dinner. The guilt never left me.

Students were scheduled for physical exams by Dr. Anthony, the college physician. When he checked my blood by looking through my eyes he said, "Do you feel all right? I have never seen anyone so anemic. How do you manage to get around?" I said I felt okay. He let me go. No prescriptions.

Dr. and Mrs. Dildine, famous scholars, former missionaries to China, built themselves a new house and held a Faculty Tea on a Sunday afternoon. Mama acquired the kitchen help job for herself and me. I disliked such exhausting work. It embarrassed me to perform servant roles in front of faculty members. It contributed to my sense of poverty and homelessness. Why were faculty so superior or why was I so inferior? I didn't like the way I felt. I was tired of other people deciding what I should do, and especially what I should do to make a little money. It didn't seem right. On top of it all I was physically fatigued as well as mentally tired of coping with the Depression and Mama's eccentricities. Why did I not have some rights of my own? Why was I not treated like an adult with a will of my own even if I did not have "a room of my own"? Why could I not assert myself? Was I some kind of robot for other people to shove around? When would I be treated like a mature individual with thoughts of my own, instead of a child of a "single" mother who acted as if she thought she was saintly when I knew she was not?

Marjorie Murray was a good friend. We met first at Christian Endeavor. Her folks were staunch Presbyterians with a splendid farm half-way between Maryville and St. Joseph. She had been teaching a couple of years on a sixty-hour certificate, and as many at Maryville did, came back to complete her degree. This was the year I used a typewriter in the office of *The Northwest Missourian*. Marjorie caught me in the hall outside the office.

"Hi, Helen. Do you have a free period?"

"Yes, why?"

"I'll give you a dollar if you'll write my English Lit paper. I have to go to math class now and next period I have English Lit with this paper due."

"All right, I'll see what I can do."

She gave me her text with the assignment instructions and rushed off to math class. I took her materials and produced what looked and sounded like a proper paper. I took it out of the typewriter just in time. She came, grabbed the paper, and sped off to English Lit. As soon as the class commenced the professor said, "Miss Murray, please read you paper!" Marjorie was reading her paper for the first time, just as if she had written it. She received commendations on the paper. She said I had been a lifesaver. I thought it was a good joke on the teacher.

In some respects moving to Residence Hall, the only dormitory for women, for my senior year, was good but far from perfect. My second floor room was a single with French doors to the left. Through those doors three students I did not know, and who had no interest in getting to know me, lived, held sorority parties, and led their noisy Greek lives.

I was happy in my work at the Registrar's Office and my Student Teaching of Biology got off to a good start. My students responded well. Miss Margaret Franken, the Supervisor, had an office with glass windows in an alcove at the back of the classroom. Although my detailed lesson plans had been accepted, she suddenly called me in and informed me "You will teach a unit on snakes and spiders." That would mean a whole new study and new plans. I couldn't understand this change. Why was she being cruel to me? Student Teaching was extremely important to me and I wanted to do my best. With my new living arrangement, new job, new teaching, and the strange newness of eating three meals a day, my life was radically changed. Some response to Papa's divorce was also still simmering in me. Something in my sensitive nature snapped. There was no one to talk to. I went to bed and stayed there a few days. I wasn't crying, I was simply staying in bed. The three roommates on the other side of the French doors ignored me as usual. On the evening of the second day, all curled up in bed, I received a visitor. Miss Truex, Assistant Dean of Women and dormitory direction, paid a "social visit." I suppose she came to find out what was wrong with me. I was both thrilled and embarrassed. I was a secret admirer of her poise and her beautiful clothes. She was wearing a red silk plaid accordion pleated skirt with a black velveteen jacket top, with starched white collar and cuffs. She came into the small room and sat in a chair by the side of the bed.

"We missed you at dinner," she said gently.

"Sorry, I couldn't make it." I was waiting for her to say, "What's your problem?" but she never did.

"So, you're working in the Registrar's Office now?"

"Yes." I hadn't eaten for two days and was weak. Student Teaching never came up. Miss Truex remained pleasant, never asking me where I hurt or why I was in bed. I was grateful for not being sent to a doctor. Whatever information she needed she must have obtained. I never had any idea how she knew about me, but soon after, my name came out on the Dining Table Roster to sit at the head table, her table.

It was my friend Marjorie Stone who got me back on track. She was psychologically stable, a Beauty Queen, (a blonde with black eyebrows and lashes) which was unusual since she was not a "Greek." Marjorie, who lived on the first floor, stopped to see me. She sensed my troubles quickly, went out and came back with a ham sandwich. I was starving; it was delicious. After her visit I decided not to have a nervous breakdown, I came to my senses and realized I must go back to see Ms. Franken.

I pulled myself together, feeling rested and fully composed, wearing a store-bought black suit handed down from Grace, I went to Ms. Franken's Office. It took lots of nerve, especially since I had not called in sick, just left her in the lurch. To my surprise she was nicer than she had ever been. She commended me on my "professional appearance." From then on I continued teaching biology, did whatever I was told, and struggled bravely to the end of the quarter.

For the second quarter and the remainder of the year I moved across the hall to be a roommate for Dorothy, a freshman. Seniors didn't usually room with freshmen, but I was glad to get away from the French doors. Dorothy and I got along well although we had little in common. The room was large with connecting bath for two freshmen in the adjacent room.

After a basketball game where I had been playing in a pep band, Ted Adkins, handsome college bus driver, took me out in his car. It was a second date. We went riding and drinking blackberry wine. It was delicious. It was a very cold night. We returned to the Residence hall entrance.

"I'll bet you don't even know how men are made." I didn't argue the point since he was close to being right. He took my hand and placed it strategically and that hand was no longer cold. He didn't realize that the dorm was closing. I said I had to go in so he let me out of the car, but I was five minutes late for dorm closing.

That wine had been good. Little did I know its potency.
I signed in and got up the stairs to the room. When the warm
air in the dorm hit me the worst possible sickness happened.
I threw up all over the bathroom, completely lost my
equilibrium, too sick to be embarrassed, too sick to clean up
the bathroom. The three freshmen ignored me for weeks. I
was campused for a week because of my late arrival. Ted
called me. I told him not to call again. He was an attractive
man. I was told he was divorced.

During the winter quarter I did Student Teaching in World
History. I had the class organized for group work as learned
in Professor Phillips' class, and it went quite well. The
Supervisor came only once, delivered a long boring lecture
and left.

One of the happiest events of my senior year was being
invited to go home for a weekend with Marjory Stone. She
was my strong supporter while I was vice-president of the
YWCA and vice-president of the Independents. Her folks had
a farm within commuting distance. She had a brother, a
sister, and loving parents. Saturday night they made ice
cream, hand turned, and topped it with a butterscotch and nuts
concoction, as if it were a celebration. It was an experience
I treasured more than Marjory or her parents would ever
know.

At Residence Hall seating charts for the evening meal were
posted weekly on a Bulletin Board. Breakfast and Lunch
were cafeteria style. Dinner was a proper, tablecloth, social
occasion. One entered one's chair from the proper side. Each
table had eight people with one designated as the hostess.
She was responsible for initiating polite conversation and
proper decorum. Table manners were taught. There was a

proper way to pass the dishes. It was easy to get used to, the food was always good, and the Dietitian was well liked. No one was free to leave until the head table signified it was ready. (I was never listed to be a hostess!)

Charles May and I played sousaphones in the band. He came to the dorm parlor a few times for me to critique a story he had written about a horse that entered a shoe store. NOTE: He wrote me from Camp Polk, Louisiana while I was in Luxembourg and sent me a recently published slender volume of poetry. Later I learned he had not survived the war.

When Thanksgiving vacation came, those of us who had no place to go were allowed to stay in the dorm. We were mostly foreign students. The Dietitian took good care of us. It was a good experience. For the Christmas break we had to clear the dorm. Mama had moved from Burr's "Castle" to a room in some other house. She rented a room for me in one of the approved college rooming houses. Ironically, this was the same room where I had sat on the bed with three students I didn't know very well, to look at a mail order book ("in plain brown wrapper") for which we had each contributed a dollar. It explained male anatomy and physiology.

Christmas was a miserable vacation in the room. My sense of homelessness was acute. It was good to get back to the dorm, getting three good meals a day where the members of the "Hashslingers Union" who served the food (mostly basketball stars) were friendly to me.

My final quarter for my degree came. I had never had an advisor that did anything other than sign a card on registration day. Mr. Baldwin told me I would have to declare a major and had to make a decision. We looked at my record. I graduated with a major in Social Science and a teaching minor in Biology.

Chosen

The Placement Office, managed by Professor Phillips, was another enclosure off the Registrar's Office. His secretary sat at her typewriter, directly opposite me. During the spring quarter she was laughing and engaging others in levity because there was a high school in southwest Iowa that wanted a teacher for band, social sciences and biology. I had no lead on a job and I was sure I could do that "funny" job. I quietly got the necessary information, applied for the position, was interviewed, and on May 23, 1940, the same day I received my Bachelor of Science degree, I was notified that the job was mine.

I was able to stay at Residence Hall for the summer session while I took music courses.

After signing my contract for Sharpsburg High School there was no problem about where to live. The decision had already been made for me. The room on the second floor of Mr. and Mrs. Young's house was across the hall from one where two other teachers lived.

When summer school was over, Donald Russell, bless his sweet, angelic heart, took me, my suitcases, the old Annell Typewriter inherited from Papa, and several junky instruments I had acquired, to my new living quarters. Donald was like a big brother. I loved him dearly.

Although my college life was fraught with hidden pain, fear, anxiety, poor health and general instability, I remember those four years with pride. I learned to stand alone and be myself as I moved successfully from adolescence into adulthood. I made remarkable growth from being an unfocused, giddy freshman to a serious senior ready to dedicate my life to the teaching profession.

I am ambivalent about the circumstances of my college life. If I had not had to work several hours a day and had not had family problems to plague me, I might have been a better student. However, the employment was necessary, was helpful to my graduation, and in a sense made possible my application for my first teaching position.

I was active in too many organizations. One Sponsor asked me, "Why do you spread yourself so thin?" How could I tell her, the more I can stay away from home, the better? My ability to get through my courses without serious study was both an advantage and a disadvantage. I felt just like I had felt during my childhood when I was frequently getting away with something, being deceitful, and burying feelings of guilt.

The break-up of the family disturbed me more than I ever wanted to admit—it made it difficult to focus my mind on assignments. I never worked for grades. "Just give me my credit so I can graduate" was my attitude. (That's why later when it was my turn to give credit I could easily tell which students were bluffing their way through school.)

The effect of the Depression, personally and politically, was a big factor in my physical and psychological health. Poverty is an evil demon to do battle with and my feelings of injustice were kept at bay, sometimes fully repressed, sometimes in the forefront of a lack of well-being.

The importance of perseverance, and self-esteem in times of difficulty, was an underlying motif that carried on into later years.

Helen Reed 1937-1938
Northwest Missouri State College
Football Game

CHAPTER 5

First Employment
Teaching and Show Business

Living conditions at Sharpsburg were near perfect. The Youngs were lovely people to live with. My room was comfortable and included a writing table and a walk-in closet. A woman who did my laundry brought it back and hung it up. The other second floor room was for Katie Cofer and Theoma Matthews. Katie taught English, Typing, and Business; Theoma taught grades One through Four. With Dorotha Richardson, who taught grades Five through Eight, and lived at the home of the Postmaster, we made a foursome to eat three meals a day at Mrs. Cook's home, halfway between the school building and Young's home. Mrs. Cook made her living cooking for "the teachers." We ate at a square table and enjoyed ourselves heartily. I began to feel better, physically and mentally. For once in my life all the problems of existence were adequately solved. It was great to be a teacher in rural Iowa.

The only other teacher was Mr. R. A. Collister, much older than any of us, who had many children, had moved frequently, and was definitely poor. He taught Math and Physics. As Superintendent he was serving his first year at Sharpsburg. He appointed me Principal. He was easy to work with and cooperative with creative endeavors, but behind his back we made fun of his eccentricities.

There were eighteen students in the high school. After pressure to consolidate, the School Board had held out to keep the high school. There were six freshmen, no sophomores, twelve juniors and seniors. My teaching assignment: a half year each of *Physiology* and *Vocations* for freshmen; a half year each of *Sociology* and *Economics* for the juniors and seniors, *Biology* for juniors and seniors; and the BAND, and of course my share of "keeping Study Hall". The day before the *School Opening*, Mr. Collister said to me, "Get the band out and have them play 'The Star Spangled Banner'." I went to look for the band music. Soon I knew the "band" was a band in name only. The students had been taught by an itinerant pianist who had a family band. They had been "taught" the Bennett Band Book I and some of Book II, and that was all. I was able to find a *Twice 55 Songbook*. Fortunately I had some manuscript paper. Overnight I wrote the parts for the expected instruments. The students came, read the parts, I conducted with a baton, and school was appropriately launched.

As inexperienced as I was, I could still cope with all sorts of academic/administrative problems. Many years prior, the school had offered Home Economics. There was a room in the basement with sewing machines, a sink, and good sized tables. There had been no Biology Lab. Since I was determined to teach Biology the way I was taught, I told Mr. Collister I could make a lab in the basement. There was no money in the budget. Collister was shy about asking for anything, but he wanted to encourage me so he took me to a Board Meeting. I went prepared with my listings, prices, catalogs, and my rationale for why I needed to buy items for dissection: earthworms, starfish, clams, and frogs. I would make my own dissection trays and tools at my own expense. I gave my plans and order to the board and everything on it was promptly ordered, including a microscope I had specified.

The lab worked out well. Both students and teacher learned. Students brought in large bullfrogs that we put in a tub with a heavy screen cover. I taped a frog foot over a slide so we could see the blood in motion through the microscope. Vivisection was done to show the frog lungs in action. I had never done such a thing and cautioned the students concerning the gravity of the act. The bullfrogs were expendable.

One Saturday morning while cleaning the lab, I put my nose into a large jar where I had left some cotton used in chloroforming the bullfrogs. I just wanted to see if it was still smelly. It was. I learned a lesson about sniffing gaseous materials. I came close to giving myself an unnecessary anesthetic and had to sit down for awhile until the effect of being chloroformed wore off.

Two white rats were ordered from the University of Nebraska, at my expense. I planned for the Biology class and the Physiology class to run nutrition experiments on the rats, something I had never done in college. The day those rats arrived at the train station, I think everyone in town heard about it. Such a thing had never happened before. Those white rats were celebrities. One day during class, I turned around from the blackboard in the lab to see the students all in subdued laughter as they saw Jack Blood with one white rat peeping out of his red flannel shirt. I laughed too, and instead of making a serious disciplinary problem, I gently said, "Jack, put the rat back in the cage before you give him a nervous breakdown." Jack, son of Fred Blood, President of the School

Board, was the star performer, the trumpet of the band. He was mischievous, not bad. The school custodian made a splendid two-room cage with exercise wheels for the rats. The old Home Ec room supplied a usable scale on which the rats were weighed regularly. They became like pets. They were so cute and at the close of the year went home with the young daughter of the custodian.

The freshman Physiology class had an excellent textbook. The four boys and two girls were 4-H Club members. When a hog was butchered, Harold brought in kidneys to prove the validity of the textbook. Rachel surprised me one morning by having on my desk when I arrived a complete alimentary canal of a chicken from beak to anus. (I recovered hastily from momentary nausea.) In that class I was the one that learned the most, all the while performing a proper school teacher role.

One evening after a big snow, Rachel's father took the class and me, the Freshman Sponsor, on a sleigh ride. The horse's harnesses had bells. After the ride, we were served hot soup at Rachel's house. It was very good to be a Freshman Sponsor for such fine students. (Rachel's family belonged to a sect that required arms and neck to be covered, no jewelry.)

When it came to teaching Sociology and Economics, I ordered lots of free literature and thought up several creative projects. With Mr. Collister's help we made field trips to several places: a Junior College, a greenhouse, a Coca-Cola bottling plant, and the local bank where Mr. Young showed us many details of banking procedures. I learned along with the students. For 1940 we were definitely modern.

My work with the band was my pride and joy. I made an arrangement of folk tunes with each part geared to the particular skills of each individual student's ability. The Band Concert in the spring was the highlight of the year. Many people praised me, but I especially valued the praise of my colleagues. They knew what I had done and the progress the band had made. Mrs. Young had a little in- house reception for me after the concert.

I also directed the Girl's Glee Club, without singing a note. One of the girls played the piano. Shortly before the concert, the band and glee club participated in a district music festival at a consolidated school in an adjacent county. Why was the Girls's Glee Club required to sing, "I dream of Jeannie with the light brown hair?" I can still remember teaching "All in the April Evening, I saw the sheep with the lambs, and thought on the Lamb of God." These were the required numbers. They still ring in my head. Who would have chosen these two numbers for Girl's Glee Clubs in public schools?

Shortly before the Band Concert, Jack Blood requested permission to sing in the Glee Club, so we dropped "Girls" from the title. Jack was serious and made a good contribution. No other boys would join him. Jack's mother commended me and was also pleased that I taught Jack to transpose so he could play his trumpet with her at the piano.

On the personal side, there were many happy moments as I fitted in with the other teachers. It was my first experience at being a full-fledged member of a real group. Katie, Theoma, and Dorotha included me on shopping trips to Clarinda and Shenandoah. Sometimes there were double dates to go bowling. Martin Moser, a local farmer and Sunday School Superintendent, was a steady date on Saturday nights. He wasn't my "hero," but he was available and well respected in the community.

One Saturday morning Katie said, "Helen, Theoma and I are tired of you always having to stop and pull up your stockings, so we are going to take you shopping for a garter belt."

"A garter belt?   What's that?" My ignorance was appalling.

"You'll find out. We'll help you."

They did and I was grateful although I could not hide my embarrassment. I was past twenty-one and still didn't know how to dress. It was as though I had no upbringing.

We rode with Mr. Collister to Des Moines to attend the 1941 State Teachers Meeting. His driving was erratic and scary, but there were no accidents. In Des Moines my friends went with me to DeArcy's Boot Shop, one of the few places narrow shoes could be bought and where I got two pair of British Tan oxfords that fit. I wore them for years. Before Easter the teachers helped me shop for a light blue suit that always made me feel well-dressed and I bought a blue wool jacket that I treasured. It made me feel very good. Several years later, Mama gave my clothes away while I was overseas without mentioning it to me. How could she do that? I miss those clothes.

My $100 a month salary paid off my debt to Dr. Crowson, sent Mama $15 a month and paid for room, board, and laundry.

When school was out it was discovered that there would be no more than eleven students for high school for the coming year.   The Board still wanted to keep it.   The Postmaster's wife was to become Superintendent. I was offered a contract if I wanted it. They understood I might not wish to return under the conditions.

I struggled with my decision. It seemed to me that if I

stayed I would still have to make the same decision a year later.

I applied for a music and social science job at Watson, Missouri (close to the river and Nebraska) and was accepted. Then I went back to Maryville for the summer session and took all music courses. Jean Fent, a teacher from Iowa, was my roommate at Residence Hall for the summer. Jean was dating Godfrey Hochbaum, a German refugee.

Martin Moser came to see me on weekends. Jean decided for us to do some double dating and for the four of us to spend a weekend on her folks' farm in Iowa. The farmhouse had two bedrooms upstairs. Jean and I slept in one, Martin and Godfrey in the other.

While at the farm, Godfrey insisted on Martin's camera taking pictures of him kissing Jean and then of Martin kissing me. Martin never got the pictures developed. He was either too pure or too puritanical.

I lasted only a half-year at Watson, Missouri. From Sharpsburg to Watson was from the sublime to the ridiculous. The faculty for the high school consisted of two men and two women including me. My teaching assignment was American History, World History, Band, Beginners Band and Elementary School Music. I carried a heavy record player across town to the Elementary School twice a week.

The day before school started the Superintendent came to me at my desk in the band room, picked up a book from a small bookcase there, one of Papa's biology texts. "You better take this one home." I replied he was welcome to use any of my books. He said, "Take it home. Don't want the kids asking questions." By that time I had noticed it was pictures of the progress of an embryo he found objectionable.

I took it home.

The band had about thirty-six students. Their former teacher had sat at the piano. They had no conception of key signatures. By Christmas the Beginners Band was the best so that band played for an all school assembly upstairs in the school house.

My living arrangements were within a stone's throw of the school. A second floor room with a bathroom had a wood stove on which to heat a kettle of water. I was the only roomer. Next door was the boarding house where some other teachers ate. Jane, who taught the first four grades, and John, who was the Principal and taught Math, lived there.

I suppose Mr. and Mrs. Bayless, my landlord/landlady, were nice to me, although I overheard a negative comment about my hayfever that made me feel estranged from them. I stayed in my room, not feeling sociable toward them. They were nice to Martin when he came to see me on weekends. We always went driving around in his car. He took me to Sharpsburg for weekends a couple of times. Once I stayed with Dorotha and once at Martin's home. His widowed mother tried hard to get me to become her daughter-in-law. She made the best cake I have ever eaten; burnt sugar cake with burnt sugar icing.

At Watson, the other faculty woman, Mrs. Clare Grundman, taught English and Business subjects. Her husband was band director in Rockport. She commuted to Watson just in time for her classes.

My history classes were organized for group work and I was pleased that they had caught on to how to function as committees. Also, I had been elected Senior Sponsor and had successfully managed a class picnic/wiener roast.

Then the trouble began. The Superintendent could not

imagine what was going on in my classes. According to him, they were completely without discipline. He said, "You will teach a chapter a day and assign ten questions to be turned in!" I tried unsuccessfully to do that. A football got tossed across the room. Yes, there was a breakdown in discipline.

I was called to attend a meeting of the School Board. I explained my philosophy of education rather well, I thought. I stressed the importance of individual initiative in creative group work and how good this learning experience was for the student's future citizenship. It all fell on deaf ears. The Board members (all males) told me I was to do what the Superintendent said.

I tried to do that and by Christmas vacation, I was having chronic diarrhea. I went to visit Mama in Maryville and was so sick I had to stay in bed. Was this my fault or was I a victim of circumstances? How did I do so well in Sharpsburg, then have this disastrous intervention in my career? Was some higher power telling me I was not cut out for teaching? (Was it as I had heard that these people were "river rats?")

Mama had become a cook and companion to Mrs. Bannister, a widow who lived in the upper half of her own home and rented the lower half to an English professor. Mrs. Bannister was nice to me. I sent a letter of resignation to Watson. Mama rented a cab to take it over and retrieve my belongings. She commented on how neat and orderly my things were and made negative remarks about Mrs. Bayless.

Mrs. Grundman resigned soon after I did. She wrote me that Jane and John had married and gone back to farming. There was only the Superintendent left to finish out the school year all by himself. I hoped he and the school board were happy.

71

Chosen

After two weeks in bed in January 1942, I read an advertisement in Mrs. Bannister's Sunday *Kansas City Star* that sounded good to me. The advertisement was very vague about what the job really was. I applied for the job of traveling producer and director of local talent shows for the National Producing Company (successor to the Redpath Chautaukwa) and received a telegram that I was accepted and should leave for Kansas City right away. At least I had not lost my self-confidence even though I had begun to wonder what I was put on the earth to do. The new Royal typewriter and new leather Gladstone suitcase, bought during Sharpsburg days, took off with me for Kansas City for an intensive two-week training period.

At the time I left for Kansas City, I had no conception of what was meant by "the war." Back in Watson, just before Christmas, a young man wearing an Army uniform walking very fast was telling everyone that Pearl Harbor had been bombed and we were at war. It was sort of a mystery. What he was saying didn't make sense to me so I passed it off thinking he had some form of mental illness.

The two weeks of training at the National Producing Company were taught by a young (30 something) man, Buddy Meyer. The class consisted of another woman and man, both older than I. We played all the parts of the show, *Swing Out*, danced all the dances, were given specific instructions about the materials in our advertising cases: tickets, billboard posters, play books, explicit instructions about four groups of six dance costumes carried in another large carton which also housed a Charlie McCarthy dummy.

There was detailed instruction about how to use the company's make-up kit. There was much to learn about selling newspaper advertising following a scheme used by the

72

company. It was also required for each town to have a baby contest—pennies in a jar at local establishments. How to set the price on tickets, how to set the time for the performance at an odd minute like 8:03 or 8:07 and start at precisely that time, how to choose the characters, how to plan and produce the specialty acts—in short, just as much as possible about the job we were to have. It was fun, but it was also scary.

Advertised in local newspapers as "A Home Talent Production" sponsored by a civic organization, *Swing Out* was a hilarious comedy-drama with music and dancing. A typical news item would read, "Miss Helen J. Reed arrived this week to direct the play. She has her BS in Education from Northwest Missouri State Teachers College and studied dramatic production under Buddy Meyer in Kansas City. Girls from the local high school will make up the dance choruses. The story of *Swing Out* is based on the Kissler family. Mr. Kissler is a successful, satisfied businessman who is pressured by a phony Frenchman for an advertising contract. When Mrs. Kissler is not trying to climb the social ladder, a lisping scatter-brained girl is laying a net for John, who runs the Arthur Advertising Agency. Rita, a friendly young widow who lives next door, tried to aid John to win the affection of Betty Kissler. Of course, there's Perkins, the butler. A theatrical agent, Gus Nelson, brings Edward Vergen and Charles MacArthur into the show. Annie, the maid, doesn't approve of Pierre Gaston, the Frenchman. In the third act, Mrs. Kissler gives a charity show. By this method each sponsor of the show can present local talent specialties."

I left Kansas City by bus for my first assignment, Union, Mississippi. On Sunday, February first, I arrived in Union to produce a show on Thursday and Friday, February 12th and 13th, 1942, under the auspices of the local Parent Teachers

Association. I was housed in the fine, white, southern home of Mr. and Mrs. Woodward. An upstairs bedroom was spacious with a four-poster bed, a *chaise lounge*, and other furniture. Breakfast was served there each morning by a black woman. I adjusted easily to all this. It was my privilege to keep to myself that this was my first SHOW.

It was also my introduction to the segregated south. One of the first mornings as I was walking to town, I met a black lady. She got off the sidewalk and stood still for me to pass. I greeted her with a very happy "Good Morning" and she broke into a gorgeous smile. I could not understand about her getting off the sidewalk. Later, I inquired of a man with whom I was working on advertising. He told me that was the custom. "She better get off." After that I didn't ask many questions about the customs of the region.

On the weekend Mrs. Woodward's niece and a college friend, were visitors. They were in school at Belmont College in Nashville. For Sunday dinner at noon when we sat down to eat, there was something strange at the place where I expected dinner plates. What was it? How was it to be eaten? How was the little pint-sized fork to be used? I looked around to see what the others did. Then I bravely admitted forthrightly that I had never before had a shrimp cocktail. They found that amazing. It was a dead giveaway that I had not been around very much. I liked it. Then the black lady came in from the kitchen and served dinner.

Union was a beautiful town with beautiful February weather. One could not have asked for a better place or more pleasant people to work with. So this is Mississippi! Truly delightful!

The planning for the drama production went very well. Most of what I had been taught in Kansas City was put into practice. The mornings were spent selling advertising for the newspaper, always accompanied by a local man. Afternoons the four dance choruses, of six girls each, were rehearsed with the designated pianist. "Shuffle step, two, three, shuffle step, shuffle step, two, three, etc., etc." I organized local committees for the publicity, the costume alterations, the ticket sales, the stage set and assisted them in the choice of characters. Everything went well. The set was designed by an Eagle Scout. Mrs. Woodward donated two cardboard mattress cartons that were used, after some ingenious artwork, as a "stone wall" at the back of the set. By the end of the day I was hoarse, soon learning to be careful in use of my voice during play rehearsal. Copies of newspapers attest to the success of the advertising and the SHOW. If only they could have sold more tickets, or at a higher price.

The contract made with the National Producing Company was not as clear as it might have been. There had to be royalty fees to G. M. Rouse, and ten dollars to Kansas City Printing for advertising posters. By the time the booker's contract was fulfilled, there was little left for the Director. From the highly successful SHOW produced for the Union Parent Teacher's Association, I netted $18. I was surprised it wasn't more.

Mrs. Woodward, who was a semi-invalid, got out of bed and came to the bus station to see me off. She presented me with a single long stem red rose and asked me how much I made. She seemed sad that it was so little. She had also given me a long black skirt. She said previous directors had been to Union and made a speech in formal apparel before opening. I explained to her that was not necessary. Then she asked me if this was my first show. "I thought so." But then she commended me on a job well done.

According to plan on the last day in Union, I received a wire giving the next location: Hornbeck, Louisiana. The bus delivered me at a railroad station. Hornbeck was a town in name only. It was a muddy place. There were no paved streets. My contact man told me in no uncertain terms that it was all a mistake. They had no intention of following through with *Swing Out*. I tried diplomacy; nothing worked. Through the kindness of a widow, contacted by the stationman, I got a place to stay. It was a slight hill up from the station. In my treasured British Tan oxfords from DeArcy's Boot Shop I carefully negotiated the muddy hill, keeping to the right while an approaching cow sensibly kept to the left.

I sent a wire explaining the circumstances to the company. It was Saturday night. There was no hope of a reply before Monday. On Sunday I went by myself halfway down the hill to a church. My landlady did not go to church. It was a primitive building, rough wood pews, a slightly raised platform in front and no lecterns. Some kind of Pentecostal group, I suppose. They could easily have been snake handlers. There was no church service of the type I expected. Each person gave a "testimony." As the time dragged on, I became aware of the fact that I was the only one who had not given a "testimony." The atmosphere became weird. Although no one greeted me or asked me to say anything, I got the message: no one could leave until they heard me. I was not going to say any of the things I had heard them say. I could not emote or speak in tongues.

I stood up, wondering to myself if *Swing Out* might, with its dance choruses, be considered "of the devil" and not appropriate to mention. I said in my best possible relaxed voice, "I'm a stranger in town, just passing through temporarily, but I appreciate the fact that no matter where I am I can worship the Lord with others and I thank you for the privilege of worshipping with you." That seemed to do it. They all became exultant, praised God loudly, and then sang something unfamiliar to me. I was a little scared. When I thought the service was over I left and went back to my room. No one was interested in getting acquainted or offering help. It was not a religious experience, hardly a social experience. I thought to myself, "So this is rural Louisiana!"

Monday the new assignment came through: Moreauville and Simmesport, Louisiana. On the bus everyone seemed to speak some kind of French, Cajun? What did I remember of my college French? *"Femer la fenetre."* "Close the window." That wasn't much help. The bus took me to Moreauville where it stopped at Bordelon's (liquors, drugs, cosmetics) next door to the home of Cecilia Gauthier where I was given residence and some meals. The house had a long, wide center hall with no furniture. My bedroom was large, delightfully furnished and heated by a fireplace, a new experience for me. A small boy built a fire with split pecan logs each morning and evening. Bathing was done in an annex at the rear of the house. A kettle of hot water was supplied when asked. In the backyard was a large black kettle under which a fire was built when the pot was used for washing clothes.

Across the hall from my bedroom lived the grandmother. She was ill and did not go out of her room so we all went to her room and sat by her fireplace while we listened to tales of her past or informed her of the current goings on. She was infirm, but not senile. Cecilia was in the SHOW. Thursday was scheduled for Moreauville and Friday night was for Simmesport. *The Bunkie Record*, a county newspaper, handled the advertising for the combined effort of the two towns.

Some of my meals were taken in the home of a woman who spent most of her time in the kitchen with a large pot of gumbo. That was the only time I remember having what I presume to be real gumbo. It had crawfish and other things. Once I saw her break an egg into the pot. I was so happy to be working that I nearly worked myself to death. One evening Mr. Bordelon offered me a shot of whiskey. He was disturbed that I would not drink it. "It won't hurt you." I was sorry and hated to not accept the gift, but I knew it was not wise. Other than that, I fitted into Moreauville and Simmesport. The specialty acts were superb. Everything went well. I adjusted to Cajun country, but made very little cash for myself.

On Friday, March 6th, the next assignment came by wire: Poplar Bluff, Missouri. This location was not as rural as those were in Louisiana. Riding all night long on the bus on a Saturday night as the only passenger, the driver had me sit up front and talk with him. It was a long night, but I felt secure. Right then I was feeling like a very successful Director in spite of not clearing much money for myself.

In Poplar Bluff things went well. There was lots of advertising. The men worked hard, but their ticket prices were too low; fifty cents was all they wanted to charge. A commendation was received from the National Producing Company and a pair of silk stockings as a prize for selling the most advertising of any director that week.

From Poplar Bluff, I traveled by bus to Gallatin, Tennessee. Once again, an American Legion Post sponsored *Swing Out*. By this time, I felt quite capable and was happy to get to the next job. The next experience was quite different. The home of Mr. and Mrs. Palmer was comfortable with city plumbing. For some unknown reason, my luggage did not arrive with me. What a disaster! Every day was important, every plan, every rehearsal. It would not do for me to panic. In less than two weeks, the show must go on. The luggage did not arrive for two days. What could I do without play books, advertising, dance costumes, and music? In the same clothes, after a good bath, I braved the situation. A meeting of the committee was called. They were told of the dilemma, just as if it were a minor problem that would soon be alleviated. (I certainly did hope so.) For the committee I played all the characters and talked my way in and out of all kinds of improvisations for these circumstances. It was a great relief when all the luggage showed up intact. We produced the show on schedule, April 9th -10th.

The contact man in Gallatin was a State Senator with a law office. He took me around to sell advertising. Everybody bought whatever he told them to. He also took for granted that anyone who had a show business traveling job was available for his sexual pleasure. He had not touched me nor been amorous in any way, but on the first day in his office he unzipped his pants, exposed himself, and used his hands to stimulate himself. I was shocked. I know now that he was anticipating oral sex, but at that time in my life I'd never heard of such a practice, nor did I know the word masturbation.

"Don't do that," I gasped. "Somebody may come in!"

He said, "Nobody's coming," but he quit what he was doing since I obviously was not going to be cooperative. He was important to the success of the show and the play took good shape. The sponsors and others were proud of their production.

As for me, my education in the ways of the world was

given a sudden boost by the Senator. He took me to dinner on Saturday night some place in Kentucky. It was not business; we had a date. On the way home he parked in a safe place. He held me tightly, pushed my head down into his lap. "Just don't bite me!" I didn't know what he was talking about. He did. Years later, I learned there was a practice known as *fellatio* (oral sex). It seemed really wild to me but I did not get excited, emotional or overly negative. The next morning he picked me up to take me to church. We both acted as if nothing had happened. After church we stood around and met people. The Senator had people thinking I was some kind of girlfriend.

Mrs. Palmer, my landlady, said she had never seen the Senator so happy and had never known him to date. She said I should hang on to him because he was a very eligible bachelor, a "good catch." She seemed to think he was about to propose marriage. I knew better but accepted her statements with objectivity. I did like him. But no, I was not in love. I was just doing my work to the best of my ability and it included keeping a cool head and keeping the committee of the local community happy. It was no time to upset people or the Senator or me.

After the day of the show, the Senator picked me up to take me to Nashville where, in the middle of the night, I would get the bus to Steele, Missouri, my next location. Steele is near the southeastern border of Missouri; that part of Missouri that might have been Arkansas or Tennessee, but for the river or politics. We drove to Nashville. The Senator was delighted that *Swing Out* had been so successful. As usual I did not make much more than my bus fare to the next place.

At about 9:00 p.m. after finishing dinner, we took my luggage to the bus station. Since my bus did not leave until after midnight he had a plan for us to relax together at a hotel. Here again, I was naïve, but not totally ignorant. I figured I could work my way through the situation.

He put five one dollar bills in my hand, told me to give them to the desk clerk and explain that I only wanted the room for a couple of hours rest before a long bus trip. Then he came to the room (I must have called the bus station.) When I opened the door saying something foolish he said, "Let me in before someone sees me." He took off all his clothes and told me to do the same. I caught on to what was expected and said, "No, I'll keep my slip on." After that we had a talk and he understood that not only did I not know the word prostitution, I was not about to have intercourse. He accepted that and saw me off on the bus to Steele. We parted friends. I felt somewhat older, slightly wise, and glad I had been smart enough to handle the situation without trouble. Later I wrote to him, and he wrote back several times. When I visited Mama on my return from Europe there was a letter on State Senator stationary. She was ready for me to marry and live in Tennessee. I do hope she had not unsealed the letter.

Swing Out in Steele was sponsored by the Junior Chamber of Commerce. Much of the newspaper advertising was done in Blytheville, Arkansas and in Caruthersville. That part of the country has its own dialect. On the bus to Steele, I had been mystified by some talk about *Crawsful*. Then I learned they meant the town of Caruthersville. When I got to Steele the Junior Chamber of Commerce men were educated and easily understood. Those energetic young men housed me in an excuse for a hotel, a rather primitive countrified place, but it served its purpose. Walking down the street in my blue jacket and pleated skirt, I was whistled at by men congregated on the street corner. I would just smile and keep moving. At age twenty-three, my perfectly proportioned figure was not hard to look at.

The play was definitely successful and the Jaycees were well satisfied with their production. There was not much profit for me. The booker (sales person who sold the *Swing Out* contracts to local civic organizations) "done me wrong again." I was sent to some rural community, not a town, somewhere in northwest Mississippi. The bus let me off at a house serving as a Hotel. It was very rural. When at last I made contact about doing Swing Out I was told, "No, we not doing that." Gravely, not too mean sounding, I cautiously said, "But didn't you sign a contract for a Director to come from the National Producing Company?"

"Nyah, we doin' a minstrel show of our own." I tried some more. It was hopeless. I wired Kansas City that *Swing Out* could not be done here. Kansas City wired back, "Play a show anyway."

That was the last straw. Because the war was taking the men and the money the job was harder. The Company seemed to be totally lacking in understanding as well as unfair, especially since I had given the company such a good reputation everywhere I had been.

I sent my resignation in a polite wire. There was nothing else I could do. The advertising case and the costume case were shipped back to the National Producing Company. By the time I paid my board and room where I was staying and the wire and the shipping costs, there was very little cash left in my pocket. I inquired about the bus. The first place of any size on the bus route was Memphis, so I went there. It was late at night when I arrived and I did not want to spend the night in the bus station. It did not seem to be the thing to do. Close to the station was a sign I could see, "HOTEL $1.00 a night." I should have known better, but being consumed with anger my thinking was not clear. I was tired, so I gave my last dollar to what was probably a *men only* hotel. I got in, took a shower in a place outside the room, and went to bed. It was a dirty place; there were ants in the room. In the morning I went out briskly with my suitcase and typewriter and lugged them one city block up a hill to Hotel Savoy. I walked in like I owned the world and registered for a room. My luggage certainly looked presentable and I was neat and clean. No problem. The lobby of the hotel had a duck pond with real ducks. The room was nice with Early American furniture. Settled in the room it was time to assess the situation and make decisions for the future. My injured pride was a problem, but not as great a problem as the immediate shortage of cash. Should I go to the Salvation Army? No, they'll think I'm pregnant. Briefly I imagined myself joining the Salvation Army and playing cornet or baritone on street corners. I didn't have faith that anyone would really understand me and my problems.

Down the street a couple of blocks was a Negro pawn shop. I took a white satin blouse out of my suitcase, sold it for thirty-five cents. With that I bought a loaf of bread and a jar of sandwich spread. These groceries I quietly took into my room, kept them hidden in a chest drawer, and along with hotel ice water, they sustained me for the rest of my time in Memphis.

Next, I went out for a walk. It was no time to sit and nurse my anger. How could I go about applying for a job? What job? Who would hire me?

The Hotel Savoy was only one block from a large U.S. Post Office. It was on the other side of the street close to the river. Of course, I wasn't going to mail anything or receive anything, but somehow (if I had a guardian angel, I may have been led) I went into the post office and started reading a bulletin board. There was an announcement of jobs available in Washington, D. C. for clerk-typists. Not that the job had any great appeal, but for right now, it looked like something to investigate. I read on. In two days there would be a typing test given in a basement room of the post office. Bring your own typewriter. Fine!

Back in my room the Royal Portable was put to work. It was good therapy. I typed and typed. More bread, more ice water, and more typing. The morning for the test came. When I got to the basement room it was large and already filled with women and their typewriters.

I found a place near the door. The testing monitor was a capable woman. She explained that the speed had to be at least sixty words a minute with not more than fifteen errors. The material to be typed was in a book, not difficult to read. When the signal was given, everyone typed like crazy. The much traveled Royal produced. At the end of the testing period—wonder of wonders, I was the only one who passed. At that I had 13 errors, two more and I would not have passed. The woman assured me that if I filled out her form, in ten days I would be invited to a job in Washington. She dispelled my skepticism with stories about the needs at the War Production Board. I was convinced, but not elated; there were too many questions. What had I done? What was going to happen next?

Mama received a collect wire from me that I had a job in Washington. She should wire me twenty-five dollars to cover my coming back Maryville to wait out my ten days. I had to use her address. At least there was a little pride left now that I could go home (?) with a job in Washington. She sent the money.

I paid my hotel bill and lugged the typewriter and suitcase to the bus station. They didn't seem so heavy now. All the way home on the bus I kept wondering why are so many things happening to me? Why do I get in so much trouble? Is it my fault? Then I said to myself, "Let me put the past behind me and think positively about the job. What kind of experiences are now in store for me?"

It was a long ten days of waiting, the letter did come, I got a bank loan enough to keep me from being destitute until my first payday. It was May of 1942, a very eventful year for many people, especially for a homeless twenty-three year old who needed to somehow, somewhere find a way to make a living.

Chosen

The Parent-Teacher Association of Union, Mississippi

PRESENTS

"SWING OUT"

A Hilarious 3-Act Comedy with Specialties

Under the personal direction of Helen J. Reed.

CAST

MRS. KISSLER .... MRS. GEORGE KURTS
ANNIE .... FRANCES GILMER
T. J. KISSLER .... LESTER WHITE
BETTY KISSLER .... LAVERNE VIVERETTE
PIERRE GASTON .... HOWARD HOUSTON
JOHN ARTHURS .... BOBBY FREEMAN
PATSY MILLER .... IVA LEE VANCE
RITA PHILLIPS .... MARY LOIS TAYLOR
PERKINS .... JERRY CLARKE
GUS NELSON .... CHARLES FREEBURGH

CHORUSES

MILITARY: Betty Gene May, Frances Osborne, Cecille Morrow, Bonnie Sharp, Lataine Houston, Darlene Moody.
FRENCH MAID: Martha Cooper, Chrystine Bean, Frances Service, Helen Bean, Marjorie Ozborn, Edna Earl Ozborn.
SWING OUT: Betty Ann Leeke, Coralyn McMahen, Shirley Alexander, Jurline Taylor, Elaine Jenkins, Shirley Howle.
WALTZ: Ruth Team, Bernett Vance, Jessie Webb, Marianne McMain, Mary Blanche Stribling, Thyra Mae Cleveland.

SPECIALTIES

Lillian Tucker, Betty Jean May, Sarah Jean Taylor, Fannie Bee Gardner.

Pianist—Miss Lucia Connerly.

SYNOPSIS

SETTING: The Garden of the Kissler Estate.
Act I—A Summer Morning.
Act II—Scene 1—The day before the Charity Show.
Act II—Scene 2—The next day.
Act III—The evening of the Charity Show.

"*Swing Out*" Program

First Employment - Teaching and Show Business

J. R. BEACH,
PRESIDENT

$\mathcal{N}$*ATIONAL* $\mathcal{P}$*RODUCING* C*O.*

PHONE
WE 3353

Super Shows

3005 HARRISON AVENUE
KANSAS CITY, MO.

July 16, 1942

Miss Helen Reed
616 N. Buchanan
Maryville, Missouri

Dear Miss Reed:

Several times this summer we have spoken of you
and wondered what you were doing. I sincerely
hope that you are busy and I hope at least as
comfortable as one can be in this hot weather.

We are making our plans for our fall plays.
It maybe you have the urge to do some shows
this fall. If so, let me hear from you and
know how you are getting along.

Sincerely,

J. R. Beach

JRB:BK

Letter from National Producing Co., July 16, 1942

87

Chosen

J. R BEACH,
PRESIDENT

NATIONAL PRODUCING CO.

PHONE
WE 3353

Super Shows

3005 HARRISON AVENUE
KANSAS CITY, MO.

August 5, 1942

Miss Helen Reed
Canterbury, Apt. 37
704 Third St., N.W.
Washington, D. C.

Dear Miss Reed:

Glad to have your letter of the 29th and know
that you are doing your part in keeping the
wheels of progress turning in Washington. It
takes a lot of wheels, doesn't it?

Our work is coming along nicely. The weather
has been favorable for us. Since you are busily
engaged there, of course, we'll have to "worry
along without you." But when they throw you out,
then you drop me a card and we'll start entertaining the world again.

Sincerely,

J. R. Beach

JRB:BK

Letter from National Producing Co., August 5, 1942

88

CHAPTER 6

War Production Board
Working in Washington, D.C.

It was a long trip by bus from Maryville to Washington. Once there it was necessary to locate a place to live and I found a room in a home way out on Longfellow Avenue where several other government workers lived. After some washing and ironing, the process of getting myself into the machinery of civil service employment was started.

I was not the only one being shifted from office to office in this process. In those few days of getting fully employed and organized for work there was a woman who seemed to be going to all the same places I was. That is how I got acquainted with Cleo.

Numerous clichés would apply to descriptions of Cleo. She was Mrs. George White from Corbin, Kentucky. Her clothes were more colorful than necessary and she wore too much makeup.

When questioned about her marital status Cleo said, "No, we are not separated. George knows I have to run off every so often. He loves me and understands that I need to come to Washington to help the war effort."

Cleo and I were an "odd couple." She was everything I wasn't. She had been around the block. I hadn't been around nearly as much. In spite of our very considerable difference in backgrounds, she respected my way of thinking. We were in similar circumstances and having similar experiences. We laughed a lot together about the things that were happening to us in the various offices.

We were both assigned as clerk-typists in different units of the War Production Board with offices in the Social Security Building.

Cleo set out to find us an apartment. I shall be forever grateful to Cleo for getting us the apartment at the Canterbury, 3rd and G Streets, NW: kitchen, small living room, large bedroom and bath. It was fine. This saved money as well as calming our frazzled nerves. We could walk to work, straight down the street for about five blocks.

Each evening Cleo apologized for the use of two small silver rods she stuck up her nose swabbed with special medicine to take care of sinusitis, or an allergy, or something. She would sit for a while, talking to me, with these two little silver rods sticking out of her nose.

The Alcohol Unit of the Chemical Statistics Division of the War Production Board was where I was to work. My desk was on the aisle of an enormous corridor of many, many desks. Behind me sat a group of Statistical Clerks. One other typist, a delightful young married woman who drove in each day from Manassas, Virginia, sat on my left. Typing consisted primarily of rows and blocks of figures. No one knew what they were typing. It was to be done quickly on ditto masters, inky purple things. About thirty copies were run on the ditto duplicator. Running the machine soon became part of the job. It wasn't hard, just messy. During the first week I typed hard and fast. Then "Manassas" let me in on a secret. It was legal to take a half-hour break each morning and afternoon. It was a necessary fact no one had told me. There wasn't much briefing about the work. Just type what you were given in someone's handwriting.

The first week or so I started having a peculiar sensation. Was I sick? No, I couldn't afford to be. What was happening to me? When I was a little dizzy someone noticed me and said, "Don't worry. It's the air conditioning. After a while you will get used to it."

One of my first dates in Washington was with Gilman, a fellow I met at work. He was about my age, seemingly naïve and innocent. He took me to a picnic in Rock Creek Park. We were having a good time around a camp fire until the group started singing songs I did not know in a language I did not know. Gilman didn't know either although he knew members of the group. In my ignorance I asked one woman a question. She was horrified. "OH, you're not Jewish?" It was as though the group had been defiled. Gilman and I left soon. We had several dates, but when he disappeared he was not missed.

After a few months at work an unusual opportunity presented itself. There was a "dollar-a-year" man who had a sketch he had drawn that he wanted someone to reproduce with mechanical drawing tools. He could not find anyone to do it. It related somehow to the work of the Alcohol Unit. Why could he not have done it himself? I have no idea. I volunteered to try. I drew up the *still* of his sketch and he was quite pleased that it looked the way he wanted it. I was gratified, but I was still a clerk-typist. It did not raise my status or pay.

About this time, my immediate office moved from the Social Security Building to the Municipal Building. I was promoted to Statistical Clerk. The new office was managed by Mr. Phil Clark, a young man who was running his bowling alley supplies business, on the side. There were only three of us. When we moved I took the largest desk so I got to give out the work to the others. During this time, I made beautiful charts and was called to another much larger office to draw lines with a ruling pen on large typewritten pages of blocks of figures. These pages were about two feet or more square. They had been typed on long carriage typewriters that I wished had never been invented. The chief of that "program" section could not find anyone who knew how to use a ruling pen until he found me. What made me so brave? I had Mechanical Drawing in college.

The work was done at a drafting table with a large T-square and India ink. It was a job that did take skill. If one of those pages had gotten messed up it would have been a catastrophe. Luck was with me. The pages looked great. The program chief told me he would get me assigned to his unit and get me promoted to a higher salary. By that time I had found that I was eligible to take a civil service examination to get a Junior Professional Rating on the basis of having enough college credit in biology. It seemed like that would be more interesting. I took the exam and got the rating. It would pay much more than a Statistical Clerk, but unfortunately there were no openings in biology at the time.

Cleo got me to go along with her on the purchase of a Stenotype Machine and go to night school to learn to be a Court Reporter. She said Court Reporters made twice as much as we were making. Each of us decided after a few lessons that we were not destined to be Court Reporters. Cleo got somebody to buy our machines. It was an interesting learning experience.

Cleo and I each went our own ways but we did lots of

sightseeing together. She was a "culture vulture," feeling that while she was in Washington she should visit every possible museum and landmark. Every weekend was culturally occupied. Cleo informed me that she had studied voice and performed at a Conservatory back home in Kentucky.

Cornelia Otis Skinner was performing in *Candide* at the National Theater. Cleo said it was something we must not miss, but after buying the tickets we were out of cash. We ate peanut butter and lettuce sandwiches until payday. When we were running out of toilet paper, Cleo would always bring some home from the office restroom. She had her own ways of being resourceful. We did enjoy that *Candide*.

In spite of her marriage, Cleo thought nothing of dating available men. She thought she was doing me a favor the night we picked up two GIs from Ft. Belvoir where they were in Engineering Training Camp. Those fellows would be given forty-hour problems in the field, during which time they could not sleep. Instead of going to bed then they would come into Washington and live it up. After a night of running around town, including an Amusement Park in Silver Spring, Maryland, we took the men back to our apartment. Then Cleo and her fellow went out to get hamburgers to bring back.

Alone in the apartment, with William S. from Alabama, I was comfortably feeling the effects of a recent Martini. In those days we did not know the expression "date rape," but that is what happened. His timing was perfect. What he did was well done. I was not hurt and after that I knew about the satisfaction of desire.

Cleo and her friend came back with the hamburgers that were quickly eaten and the men left.

I told Cleo what had happened. She laughed, quoted George White in an obscenity, then got serious and said that

I must take a douche. "But I don't know how to take a douche," I wailed. She took me across the street to a drugstore to buy me some equipment. Back in the apartment she gave me a lesson on how to take a proper douche. It was embarrassing, but I was grateful. Now I was scared while I waited two weeks to know that I was NOT pregnant. My adolescence was over. Cleo took off for a weekend trip with a man she knew from her office. William S. showed up that weekend. I was not afraid of him. He seemed relieved that I said I was not pregnant. He was not attractive and I suggested calmly that he put more attention on his training at Ft. Belvoir. We never corresponded. There was no need. End of dramatic episode.

Cleo decided to go back to Kentucky—or George White told her it was time to come home. He picked her up from the apartment, a friendly man who seemed nicer than I had expected from a used car salesman.

Agnes Wunderlich, a Statistical Clerk, with a desk behind mine in the first office I worked in, was delighted to share the apartment. Agnes was nothing whatsoever like Cleo. She was tall, thin, dressed conservatively and had been engaged for twenty-five years to Austin Boelter. (At the office we laughed behind her back.) She was from St. Paul, Minnesota and went around carrying love letters with her name in large fancy script. She had been a church organist. She and Austin wrote music and lyrics for popular sheet music songs. They didn't get married because he lost all his money in the stock market, but they were going to be married soon. Agnes moved in with me. Soon she brought her mother who slept on the couch. The dear old lady kept out of the way. She was frugal. She cooked. Agnes was so concerned with bargains she would take a streetcar for miles to save a nickel. She was a very good friend with genuine concern for me as a person. Each night when we went to bed Agnes would kiss me goodnight. I liked that; it was new to me. She mothered me and I needed that.

An item in a Washington newspaper stated a need for a tuba player to join the WAAC Band at Daytona Beach, Florida. The tuba was my instrument so I went to see the Recruiting Officer. "Yes, you should definitely apply. With your background you could probably became an Assistant Director." Now that was talking my language. There was not much information available about the Women's Army Auxiliary Corps, but what little I knew appealed to me. In addition to my patriotic fever, the idea of wearing a uniform, not having to worry about board and room, might provide a type of discipline I needed. My life needed a change.

My application was filed. A group of us took some exams: Mental Alertness and Mechanical Aptitude. I breezed through Mechanical Aptitude with a total of 149 out of a possible 150. (It would have been perfect if I hadn't called an awl an icepick.) The Mental Alertness would have been better had it not been for the woman on my right, a "Slovakian" who did her arithmetic in a loud whisper that disturbed me. A physical exam was given at Walter Reed Hospital. There was a waiting period called a ten-day waiver. I thought it was because some of those doctors had considered my tracheotomy as chronic hoarseness, sore throat. When the waiver came through it was on my feet: bi-lateral curvature of the great toe, both feet.

I was accepted and on December 30, 1942 in Washington, D. C. A group of women assembled at Union Train Station and left for Daytona Beach, Florida. After seven months with the War Production Board I felt it didn't really need me and put it behind me. I had no idea what a complex future was ahead of me.

CHAPTER 7

World War II – WAAC and WAC

Our group of women from Washington arrived at Daytona Beach at four o'clock in the morning. The next few days I lived on the fifth floor of Hotel Clarendon (now the Plaza). The hotel had been stripped of all rugs, furniture, decorations, and elevators. Running up and down stairs was exhausting. There were eight of us in a regular hotel room with army cots. We had no way of knowing how many thousands of us were there altogether. Strangely enough the "Slovakian" who had irritated me at the recruiting station was one of the eight. She seemed uncouth and I tried to avoid her.

I had come with a special notebook in which I planned to keep an account of my life (at least my life) in the Women's Army Auxiliary Corps. Through the door of the hotel bathroom I heard the "Slovakian" talking about me, making fun of having seen me writing in my notebook. She had come from a job in a bookstore. "She's crazy for thinking she can write. Only a published professional writer could write about the WAAC." I was shocked that she knew so much when she was so uneducated. Anyway, it was impossible for me to write during the time in Florida. We were kept busy, fatigued, and the climate contributed to the need for sleep. It was all I could do to get to my bunk, go to sleep and get up the next day.

Basic Training was four weeks of drill, films, interviews, learning about Army Regulations, making beds properly, and doing what we were told, including calisthenics which I hated at first, but began to feel it was doing me good. I was not athletically inclined. When we finally got to have individual interviews, I explained to a WAAC officer that I had been recruited to play the tuba in the band. The officer said, "Why you couldn't possibly play in the band. You have not had professional experience." It seemed I should have played with someone called Phil Spitalny in New York. I felt that I would have to talk with someone with more understanding. "Well, all I want is the chance to try out." I was still confident that I was there to play in the band. The officer said, "In the Army you do what you are told. You don't tell us. We tell you."

Public Law 554 had been passed on May 15, 1942 after lack of enthusiasm in Congress. The first WAAC Training Center was opened in July in Des Moines, Iowa. There was much difficulty in getting the Center organized and properly militarized. To give you an idea of what Daytona Beach was like during the early days of the Second WAAC Center here is how military historian, Mattie E. Treadway, described the difficulty of finding a proper base.

"It had been known since summer that a second WAAC Training Center would be required to meet the expansion program directed by the General Staff. The only site offered the WAAC was that of Daytona Beach, Florida, where it was proposed to train women in leased city buildings, rather than to dispossess the occupants of any established military post... Director

Hobby appealed to the Service of Supply for any other location stating that a military atmosphere and reasonable discipline could not be inculcated at any such establishment. The town itself was a resort area, with streets perpetually crowded with sailors, soldiers and coastguardsmen from nearby military stations. For barracks, it was proposed to house the WAAC Trainees in a number of scattered hotels and apartment houses, ranging in capacity from 37 to 600, as well as auto courts, inns, and villas; and a 6,000 woman tent camp was to be built in a cantonment area. For classrooms there were to be provided the Methodist, Baptist, and Presbyterian Churches, a golf course, several garages and storerooms, the City Auditorium, the Fifth Avenue Gown Shop, a Theater, and other business houses." Mattie E. Treadwell. United States Army in World War II, Special Studies. The Women's Army Corps. Center of Military History, United States Army, Washington, D. C. 1991. First printed 1954. Page 77.

After several weeks in civilian clothes we were issued cotton uniforms: khaki shirts, skirts, caps and brown shoes. My clothes fit just right, but not my shoes. I kept getting leg cramps. On *sick call* a GI medic taped my legs from ankle to knees, but it didn't help. Eventually I got a slip of paper from a medical officer stating my right to wear civilian shoes. I kept it in my shirt pocket, but I was never questioned. Fortunately, I had an appropriate pair of oxfords. I was afraid someone would look at my record, see the waiver on my feet and discharge me, something I had no intention of letting happen.

Chosen

I had been in the WAAC for three weeks and began to understand that just because I had been recruited to play in the band, did not mean that the army would place me in the band. My patriotism began to dwindle, but I learned how to take pride in being a soldier, in being a member of a group all of which dressed alike, and did the right thing at the right time. After all, this was a soft easy life. All of our thinking was done for us. We had not to worry for the 'morrow wherewith we should be fed or clothed' for the 'morrow' always took care of itself. (So why was I so exhausted?) After we learned, we just relaxed and let mental stagnation set in.

One evening my morale was very low. We were still housed in the Clarendon Hotel. Suddenly a whistle blew. Someone yelled, "Company 8 assemble on the ramp. Lt. Burkholder has some announcements!" I can see us yet, some still in civilian clothes, all huddled together, eagerly anticipating the current pronouncements. After other announcements, the Commanding Officer said that the company bugler was leaving immediately for Officer Candidate School and "Can anyone here blow a bugle?" I waited until everyone else had a chance to volunteer. A bugle was a far cry from a tuba, but then I could play a cornet also, so finally I raised my hand and timidly asked if I could try the bugle.

That evening, during our free hour, I got the bugle from the Orderly Room. Hurriedly, with a sneaky feeling I went down by the beach. It was so unusual to be alone I felt guilty as though I were committing a crime. There was a tunnel down under the boardwalk near a bandstand. Maybe no one could hear me if I went down there. The first few seconds were bad, but I persisted and soon they were better. The next day a Lieutenant showed me the official army bugle calls in

100

the *Soldier's Handbook.*

The first morning I tried to blow *First Call* for the company there was no resemblance to a military bugle call, but no one could possibly have gone back to sleep. The former bugler did not read music so that company did not have high expectations. One afternoon, I was invited to bugle for a WAAC retreat. It was not yet part of a regular schedule. A Captain explained what I was to do and where I was to stand.

I had not yet mastered the art of bugling and I knew it. My stage fright was obvious. I couldn't remember the calls, but I solved those problems by holding the bugle in both hands, the music hidden on a small card in the right hand. We were on the beach behind the Clarendon Hotel with the companies facing the ocean. At the proper signal, I started to sound *Retreat.* In my nervousness I thought I could feel the ocean coming up on my heels, so I took a big step forward. The entire performance was lacking, but on another day I was asked again and the second performance was much better.

Whenever we were given a break during drill, or between classes I studied music for the bugle calls from small cards I kept in my shirt pockets. In the midst of regimentation so new to me, I enjoyed this new means of retaining a sense of individuality. Before I became the bugler I had been deeply irritated by the rude awakening, hurriedly jumping into clothes and rushing madly about to get to *Reveille.* Now I enjoyed getting up earlier, dressing quietly in private, being able to have my bunk all made and have a few minutes of calm before breakfast while bedlam ensued in the barracks. What did it matter if I got into the habit of waking up at four o'clock each morning!

By the end of Basic Training I was offered the opportunity

to attend Officer Candidate School. This I refused knowing my voice could never drill a company, one of the main things I had seen WAAC officers do. I was assigned to attend Army Administration School for the next six weeks.

We still had to pull KP (kitchen police). During basic training there had been rumors that a WAAC had to go to the hospital after her day of KP and she did not come back. When I was on KP I was determined not to let anyone know I was fully fatigued. When I was sent to help unload a meat shipment off a truck, a man looked like he was going to dump half a cow on me. I quietly walked away. No one seemed to know the difference. The next morning it took all the nerve I could muster to get my tired bones out of bed. Eventually I learned to say that because I was a bugler I was not to be listed to pull KP.

During the six weeks of Army Administration School, those doing the teaching were inexperienced and immature, most of them recently out of the First Training Center. Sometimes they would admit forthrightly that they didn't know something. A poor befuddled Second Lieutenant was teaching map reading. She came to a point where she should have explained physical geographical markings that indicate the nature of the terrain. She invited help. Since I was the only one in class who knew anything about it, I blithely announced that I had *Physiography* in college and then proceeded to show I remembered nothing from the course. We all knew it didn't really matter.

Army Administration School, the Florida climate, with marching and army food three times a day, easily put me to sleep. I thought I had learned to sleep discretely, but one afternoon a young WAAC Second Lieutenant came to my chair and table at the back of the room, and said, "My supervisor is coming today so would you *please* stay awake."

After six weeks of Army Ad School our company arrived in Philadelphia on March 20th. Our insignia was bright red AAA for Anti-Aircraft Artillery. We were housed on the fifth floor of the Bellevue-Stratford Hotel. The rooms had been stripped to simulate barracks. Some members of the company were experienced Filter Board workers. (Aircraft Warning Service—fear of invasion). The rest of us were assigned to a motor pool or to clerical work at a regimental headquarters in south Philadelphia.

As soon as we got settled I went to a music store and bought a U.S. regulation bugle. At the store, I met J. Frankel, a veteran band direction (WW I). He was old enough to have been my father. He had me play the calls for him, then taught me to play them faster, coaching me on how they should really sound. To my amazement he sent a dozen red roses to the hotel for me, and they were delivered to our Orderly Room. We were not to have any suck things, but our Captain was sympathetic, so they were housed in my room. It was embarrassing.

By rolling up a pair of socks and stuffing them in the bugle for a muted sound, I could practice the calls without being heard outside the room. Somehow word of my work on the bugle got to the Commanding Officer, Captain B_____. Instead of having the First Sergeant blow a whistle for First Call, she decided for me to blow my muted bugle. Every morning I opened the door of each hotel room and did the best I could with a bugle full of socks. Then we would stand Reveille in platoons in the hall across from the elevators. The members of the company didn't think much of the idea and I was not popular with some of them. The comments some women made on being awakened in the morning were not music to anyone's ears.

I was in the group assigned to clerical work in the AAA Eastern Defense Command regimental offices. The enlisted men (GIs) that were teaching us the work were not eager to be replaced. They were not sold on the idea of women in the army.

While we were still living in the hotel, our company was asked to send an honor guard to East Lansdowne, a suburb of Philadelphia, for the funeral of a Waac who had been stationed in Syracuse. I was asked to go along as part of the guard and to play *Taps* at the interment. This was a truly new experience for me. I had never played *Taps* and had never been at a graveside service. It was a cold April day; there was sudden unexpected snow. We shivered and shook, but I put my heart into playing *Taps* as best I could. (I cracked a note when the mother started crying aloud. Later I learned that I had stood at the wrong place.)

Gradually we were becoming accepted by the men. They didn't know whether to treat us as civilians, as ladies, or as military personnel. We tried hard to please them and to learn military procedures. On certain afternoons the men with whom we worked left the offices early in order to pick up their gear and rifles and prepared to "stand Retreat." One afternoon the Major who was the Commanding Officer of the regiment, came into our office carrying a bugle and said, "Where is that Waac they told me could blow a bugle?"

He said the bugler was on special detail at Bethany Beach (Coast Artillery Anti-Aircraft Lights) and asked if I could bugle for Retreat. I said I could play the calls, but needed briefing about regimental Retreat. The Major was kind and thorough with his explanation. (He had no idea how scared I was. I didn't have the slightest idea what regimental Retreat was.) He said I was to sound *Attention* after playing *Retreat* before starting *To the Colors*. This I had never heard and had not seen in print. The Major said, "Oh, that's just Ta ta, Ta ta." What that was on the bugle I had no idea.

At the appointed moment, assuming extreme military posture, I marched to the flagpole and looked out over a sea of GIs and rifles. The Waacs were all watching from the office windows. Before I left the office, they made me feel I had better do a good job. I was already nervous enough. Women in the army were not fully accepted and each little opportunity to show how useful we could be was looked upon as a significant challenge by all concerned. As I waited to sound *Retreat* I felt as though the future status of all women in military service depended on what I would do at that moment.

It was a cool, clear day and the air was still. It seemed like a long, long time, but then from way down the block the Major's command to sound *Retreat* came. The bugle sounded perfectly, with a beautiful clear tone. I played with ease, invigorated by release of the previous tension. I just blew something for the "Ta ta, Ta ta," I was to do for *Attention*, and proceeded with *To the Colors*. By this time I felt rather good about the whole event and the call had snappy rhythm with real spirit behind it. The regiment was dismissed and I returned to the office building. The Major was waiting outside for me. My salute was halfway up, but he interrupted with "Lady, you got yourself a job."

For the rest of the evening, I was the heroine of the day. The entire company, including the officers, heard about the Retreat and all expressed pride. I was slightly embarrassed about all the publicity, but it still felt good. The favorable comments from GIs were especially appreciated. The next day the GI bugler came into the office and gave me his Army Field Manual on Bugling. When I saw what I should have blown for *Attention* I was embarrassed, but laughed at the difference. From then on, when notified, I bugled for Retreat.

Convinced that women were here to stay, the army built us barracks and proper military headquarters in League Island Park, not far from a large Naval Hospital, close to AAA regimental headquarters. Now the women stood Retreat along with the men. It was like camping out. I was fortunate to be assigned to a cadre room at the end of the barracks. Frances, from Virginia, was my roommate. We got along well. Even before we left the Bellevue-Stratford Hotel, the Commanding Officer of our company took a special interest in me. In the army, officers were forbidden to fraternize with enlisted personnel. When she made bed check, I would communicate with some witticism. After the move to the barracks she occasionally left me a letter under my pillow, mostly about the beauty of nature. Once she had me meet her in Paterson, New Jersey to attend the Dutch Reformed Church where her father was minister.

As a typist in the regimental office I interviewed soldiers for GI insurance and prepared their application blanks. In May I was appointed Manager for the WAAC PX (Post Exchange). A WAAC Lieutenant who knew no more about the job than I, was my supervisor. I was in charge of purchase orders, a daily work sheet, personnel, banking and financial details. Just when PX management seemed to be going well, a problem arose. There was a mystery in the bookkeeping that was solved when a GI confessed he had climbed over the top of the cage at the front of the store in the Dayroom, and had stolen cigarettes. In the meantime the books were audited, I was questioned at length, and depositions were taken. The officers could not find anything the matter. I asked to be released from the PX job and became Company Clerk.

First Sergeant Adams left due to illness. I could have done the First Sergeant job, but no one considered me. If I had been more assertive I would have asked for it. Financially I should have. Not only was I not assertive, I was ignorant of how army rank functioned or how it was obtained. I was lacking in self-confidence. As I look back on that situation, the most honest I can be about it is to say that I think I was just plain stupid.

Captain B., our Commanding Officer, was transferred to Ft. Oglethorpe. She invited me to meet her in Chattanooga, on my furlough, and take a bus trip to Monteagle, Tennessee where we spent a weekend in an Inn on top of Cumberland Mountain. Due to the regulation that enlisted personnel and officers were not to fraternize I understood that we were not to sit together on the bus. She had made the arrangements at the Inn. When we went to bed, I unfortunately asked if we could have a "goodnight kiss." I was shocked when she not only rejected the idea, it infuriated her and she refused any further conversation. The next day we hiked on the mountain all day long in the rain without talking. It was a miserable weekend. On Sunday morning while she stood in the window of our room reading her Bible, I said, "How can you do that right while you are being cruel and unchristian to me?" She still would not talk. I could not understand how something so simple could cause such trouble. I was deeply pained and took my heartache back to a room at the Read House Hotel in Chattanooga where I spent three days locked in my room in deep depression. Over the phone I sent her a wire to phone me and she did. I came to my senses and went back to my company in Philadelphia. She wrote to me while I was overseas. She had married and had a baby. Soon after I was discharged she invited me to New Jersey to meet her husband and baby. She then explained that she had been attracted to me and at Monteagle had a fear of becoming a homosexual.

Lt. Frankel took me to dinner at the Doylestown Inn, and once to L'Aiglon, a small French restaurant in Philadelphia. He took me with him when he conducted an old army band (WW I) that played for an "E for Excellene" award for Container Corporation.

One of my friends in the Philadelphia Company was Taylor, a talented artist. Her drawings of people in Lancaster were delightful. We went into town to dinner a few times. Once she prepared a pot of beans on the stove in the Dayroom, and invited her friends to a party! She was unmilitary, a delightful young woman. She did not elect to stay in the WAC.

Nancy Hedges became a good friend. Our officers drafted us to spend Thanksgiving dinner with a family in Germantown. Their invitation could not be refused because part of the WAC mission was to keep up civilian morale. It was a strange experience. The "family" knew more about the war than we did. Several were inebriated by the time we sat down to dinner. Half of the items on the table were also full of alcohol. It was an awkward experience, but we survived.

Nancy had never seen a coin operated washing machine. I had to show her how to work it. Back home in Charlottesville, Virginia, where her father was a famous eye surgeon and Professor at the Medical School, University of Virginia, it was a black lady who did her laundry. Before the breakup of the company in Philadelphia, Nancy took me home to meet her family. For me it was a trip to the Old

South. Later, on a pre-overseas furlough I visited Nancy in
Grand Rapids, Michigan where she was in Army Physical
Therapy School. She told me confidentially that she had
failed the course, but out of consideration for her father (that's
what she thought) she was given a second chance. In my
hotel room I drilled her on "the muscles," and told her she
could do it. By the time she was commissioned a Second
Lieutenant as a Physical Therapist, I was overseas. She was
stationed at the VA hospital in Swannanoa, North Carolina.
She contracted strep throat and died suddenly. Dr. Hedges
wrote me two letters about it.

While in the company at Philadelphia, Lt. Machen, a
native Philadelphian, took me to her doctor. It was against
Army Regulations; she could have been in serious trouble.
We were not provided with medical service. I had an inability
to get over diarrhea. The cure the doctor prescribed: two
weeks flat on my back, no food, drinking only grapefruit and
orange juice. (Was there no Kaopectate in those days?) Sgt.
Kravitz, the Mess Sergeant, took a personal interest. Her staff
took care of me. It was against Army Regulations to be sick
in quarters, but we got away with it. Near the end of the two
weeks I asked a Waac, when she went out for the evening, to
bring me back something to eat. She brought a hot dog and
a devil's food cake. It was good and I got better right away.

In August 1943 we were sworn in to the Women's Army
Corps. Not very many women took the opportunity to "quit."
It was much better to be in the Army rather than an Auxiliary.
Auxiliary status interfered with military operations. In March
1944 our Philadelphia Company was disbanded.

I spent two weeks at Hotel Collingwood on 34th Street in
New York City. (It was torn down when Lincoln Center was
built.) New York City was new to me. A WAC officer sent

me to a building, which I was to reach via the subway train. She gave me scrip to exchange for tokens, told me which train to take and where to get off. Never before had a city been so big and I so little! When I got to the token booth, I was already scared, but I got on the right train, got off on the wrong side of the street, panicked a little, and got to the right building. New York City was so very different from Philadelphia!

I worked at AAA Eastern Defense Command Headquarters as a clerk typist for two weeks before being transferred with a WAC battalion to Fort Oglethorpe for overseas training.

At Fort Oglethorpe I was asked to bugle *School Call* through a big tin suspended megaphone. That excused me from KP. What a blessing! We crawled on our stomachs (i.e. abdomens) in mud under barbed wire. We climbed up rope netting. We lifted duffel bags much too heavy. We were given pelvic exams, psychiatric interviews, furnished with gear, belt, canteen, First Aid Kit, gas mask, musette bag, utility coat, and mess gear.

Films were shown on the Holocaust. I closed my eyes some. Overseas Training was a test of the survival of body, mind, and soul. As far as I know all of us in that group went to Camp Shanks for overseas shipment.

I didn't know anyone. There was no opportunity to get acquainted. (Was it intentional that our psychiatric exams came immediately after what some of us considered a brutal pelvic exam with cold forceps?)

After a few weeks of what could have been "stamina testing" we were sent to Camp Shanks to be shipped overseas. While there, we were able to go to Orange, New York where we established bank accounts. There was an attempt to be sure everyone had GI Life Insurance.

Helen Reed
Bugling on roof of Clarendon Hotel (now the Plaza)
Daytona Beach, Florida
January 1943

Chosen

112

CHAPTER 8

Overseas – World War II

After a few days at Camp Shanks, we boarded a train that took us to the New York harbor. Going overseas was a serious, solemn event. Most of us had never left our native land before. We were a group of five hundred Wacs and had been ordered to be quiet. We found our seats on the train and didn't say a word. Time passed, but the train didn't start.

We had learned the art of patient waiting, but the silence grew more and more morbid. Some looked tearful. A WAC officer came through the train, saw my bugle and said, "Say, can you play anything besides regular calls?" I nodded and she said, "Play something." I played several pieces including *"You're in the Army Now,"* to get the group singing. I took for granted they knew the words, *"You'll never get rich by digging a ditch,"* but they sang loudly *"you son-of-a-bitch."* I wanted to correct them, but it was impossible. The music was a catalytic agent—a new feeling of togetherness prevailed on the train after the singing.

In New York we boarded the U.S.S. Argentina where we lived in a series of rooms furnished with hammocks. I was in a group of thirty-six with hammocks six deep. I took one at the bottom. There was barely room to move around. In the morning we took our mess kits to the serving line for breakfast of mush, boiled potatoes, hard boiled eggs, and coffee. The serving line was reached by climbing down a rope ladder into the hold and while I was learning to keep my fingers from being stomped on by the one above me, the GIs in charge of food service were yelling at us to speed up our exit from the ladder. Then we ate standing up at tables secured to the floor.

Because I accepted an opportunity offered by two Chaplains to work in the ship's library, I escaped calisthenics and that also caused me to miss the first boat drill. Since I didn't know where I was supposed to go, I hid in the library or was busy being sick in a latrine each time the signal for boat drill was given. Thirteen days on the ocean in one pair of army fatigues was miserable. In spite of our crowded conditions, we changed to Class A uniforms to leave the ship.

As we passed between Scotland and Ireland and up the Firth of Clyde, we were thrilled to see beautiful, green and gorgeous land. On Sunday, May 14, 1944, we landed at Gourock, Scotland. Early in the morning we got on a ferryboat and waited an hour or more. A visual memory that will always be with me is the tremendous welcome the Scottish people, hanging out of apartment house windows, gave our group of women as we marched a short distance to board a train to some countryside in northern England. I was grateful that my legs were capable of marching. They were still "sea legs" and felt a little unstable.

My group lived for a few days in "goat-shed" English barracks and were introduced to "biscuits" (English army three-piece mattresses), and gray, mohair, scratchy blankets that kept us from freezing. For several days we were assigned to a large mail unit, with card files and many pieces of mail for American military personnel to be re- addressed to places in England and on the Continent. It was our first work overseas and we worked hard and fast, knowing already the importance of mail from home.

From that isolated place we were transported, first by train and then in army trucks to Cheddington where we were housed in a former pub. Cheddington, Headquarters of the Eighth Air Force Composite Command, was our introduction to the 8th AF men. Some were congenial and talked to us, but many were inclined to avoid us. After our first meal in the Mess Hall with them, one woman said, "What is wrong with these men? Why aren't they glad to see us?"

Someone told her, "They resent losing office jobs to women so they can be sent to the 'front line'." A few weeks later the fellows warmed up and received us with normal friendliness. Months later at least two of our group married 8th AF men. We were approximately one hundred women and three hundred men, including men who had spent a year stationed in Ireland before coming to England.

As soon as we located our bunks on that first day, we received instruction about the nightly alerts that would warn us to go to air raid shelters. We were to take our helmets, gas masks and blankets. Our arrival in England was several months before D-day. At night there was complete black-out. German buzz bombs were expected to land anywhere at any time. Some nights there would be several "purple alerts", meaning go to a shelter, a brick wall maze not far from the barracks, and we would be tired or sleepy the next day. We were all wearing ankle high "field" shoes. Since I had to wear three pair of socks to fill up my shoes, I slept with them on to expedite urgent exits to air raid shelters.

My work assignment was in Statistical Control at the headquarters offices. The harsh reality of war was brought home to me more than once as I happened to see files of letters and wires from parents who could not yet believe that their sons had been shot down over Germany. We worked with Tables of Equipment and Tables of Personnel which were in constant flux before D-day.

At Cheddington we were issued bicycles. They were a real joy for most of us. Those who had not previously ridden learned quickly, especially after the English hand brakes threw them over the handlebars. We rode to Tring, Aylesbury, and other places where there were movies, pubs, or shops to browse in.

From this Eighth Air Force WAC Detachment I formed lasting friendships with Joan Faller from Montana, Marge McClelland from Ohio, and Jean Smallwood from Tennessee. I think they were all more comfortable in army life than I was. Joan was the best educated, a sensitive, intelligent woman who associated with others with ease. Marge saw good in most people and had a wonderful sense of humor, as did Joan. Jean always had a steady date and could be depended on for the latest rumor information. She and I always bunked next to each other. It was wonderful to have friends to bicycle with.

As a result of my bugling I was invited to play second trumpet in the *Sad Sacks*, a Special Services (recreational unit) dance band. At first I was skeptical about having one Wac in a GI band, and also unsure of my ability to play the trumpet since I still thought of the tuba as my instrument, but Captain Marjorie Hunt, my Commanding Officer, was all for it and the fellows were wonderful to me. We played two or three dances a week at Red Cross Clubs, Officer's Clubs, and Aero Clubs, in addition to our regular day's work. At last I played in a band and I was helping to keep up morale. The

Wacs were proud to be represented in the band and they loved to dance to the *Sad Sacks* music.

Playing in the *Sad Sacks* was a personal advantage, especially after we were issued carbines. I had no difficulty in taking the gun apart, cleaning it and putting it back together. The thought of shooting it came in some other category and I wondered vaguely if it was really legal to ask Wacs to shoot. I was afraid I could not cope with the kickback and furthermore I had no intention of ever shooting. On the day my group was told to go for target practice, I excused myself—I had to get ready to play in the band.

Around this time there was a humorous incident at work. We had learned how to work and how to conduct ourselves in the offices and we were well aware of our subordinate military status. However, after a few weeks, we encountered an unusual, non-military circumstance.

The officers, who had previously enjoyed having tea served every afternoon by British women, decided that the Wacs should perform that service. That seemed improper for us as American women with military rank. One night this was discussed in the barracks. Eight women agreed that if we would all stick together we would not have to serve tea. Yes, we would all stick together. I had not been invited to serve tea, but I agreed that we should not do it. One Wac was especially loud-mouthed. I never knew what precipitated it, but soon after our decision, we were called to the office of the ranking officer. We were lined up in front of his desk. He started from the left and asked each Wac if she had anything to say. The first one, who had been most adamant in the barracks discussion, said, "Nothing to say, Sir!" Each Wac was questioned in turn and each repeated, "Nothing to say, Sir!" It was all I could do to keep from laughing. The incident was closed, but tea serving never came up again. The episode was like a page of comedy. *"Tempest in a Teapot?"*

After spending spring and summer in Cheddington, the entire command moved to Watford, about an hour north of London. At Cheddington we had been amazed at the long evenings. At 9:00 p.m. the sun was still high, but at Watford in the winter where we lived in a camp formerly occupied by the British, about ten blocks from our work place, it would be dark by the time we left work. Many of us worked at a headquarters stationed in a former school for boys. Each office had a fireplace that burned coke that did not heat. It was so cold we tried to type wearing gloves. Much of the time in Watford we anticipated moving to the Continent following D-day. We named our barracks "Tipperary" because it was such a long walk from the train station. We could take the train into London for an evening of theater or concerts and return to Watford by midnight. This meant that dating became more important and couples could go to pubs together.

We were issued new winter clothing. M-31 jackets and pants were green with separate brown wool jackets and pants that fitted inside the green material. We were also issued leggings. They took awhile to lace up. I don't remember wearing them, but apparently we did because I have a picture of my bugle and me in that outfit.

To most of us the replacement of our Class A uniforms (that none of us liked) with gold-khaki Eisenhower jackets, skirts and slacks was an important event. They were made of comfortable Scottish wool, with flaps and buttons at the back to make a secure military fit between jacket and skirt. At last we felt good in our uniforms and were proud of them.

At Watford we lived in a series of barracks with sixteen to

twenty women in a building. One evening I fell asleep and didn't play *Taps*. A Wac from another barrack came over and said, "Aren't you going to play *Taps* tonight?"

I looked at my watch and said, "No, it's too late. It has to be done at 11:00 p.m." She wouldn't take **no** for an answer.

"You'll have to do it anyway because no one in our barracks can go to sleep tonight until we hear it."

This appeal was irresistible. I went out and played the call gently with tender feeling.

Soon after our Command moved from Cheddington to Watford, the *Sad Sacks* played for a benefit dance in the Watford Town Hall. It was a large affair with many British civilians and military personnel and the band was a big hit. People raved about it.

Our barracks was heated by a small, black iron potbellied stove. We had a wire coat hanger we could lay on top of the stove to toast bread we had taken from the Mess Hall—English wartime, gray bread. Once someone in our barracks received a package from home that included a can of tuna fish. We had a delightful little party around the stove with tuna on toast.

From time to time we were told to pack our duffel bags for imminent departure to the Continent. When we would not move we would wait with low morale for the next order to pack. Because I worked in statistics, I posted a cartoon chart on an unused bulletin board in the barracks with the names of each Wac. Then I made a line representing each person's morale. Some lines went down off the chart and off the board. It was a momentary diversion, serving as entertainment. I soon took it down, not wanting anyone to take it too seriously.

One early morning in Watford, as we prepared to go to

work, there seemed to be an unusually quiet atmosphere, an eerie feeling. We asked the fellows what had happened. A robot bomb had landed not far from camp. Later some Wacs and GIs went to the landing place to pick up some shrapnel. They collected their war time souvenirs!

I didn't need to collect shrapnel. It was enough for me to remember observing at close hand the experience of bombed out civilians. Taking the train back to Watford from an Underground Station in London, one evening we saw that the subway platform provided a series of double deck cots with wire springs, no mattresses. A woman I observed carried an attaché case from which she took a small blanket and prepared to climb to an upper bunk. It was a scene to be viewed as one of courage in extreme difficulty. Later when I would see people in London carrying a similar attaché case I would wonder if it provided a blanket for a cot in the subway, and I remembered the crowded restroom at the subway station where several women were performing their ablutions.

After watching and listening to the sound of bombers, finally the anticipated D-day was over and on February 22, 1945 we left Watford for France. Two days later I started keeping a journal, an activity I had planned from the onset of my military life, but had never been able to accomplish.

At our first station in France, writing about ordinary happenings helped me keep my sanity during a period of intense vocational frustration. When I was happy I didn't need to write. The excerpts from my journal, viewed after many years, still bring back an intense emotion, but now serve to remind me that it was an unavoidable period of transition. In later years there were many occasions during which I could be grateful for the learnings of that period of time. Learning to be patient in periods of transition was an art and skill that served me well when years later I encountered several types of transitional periods in civilian life.

Excerpts from my journal describe our camping out on the grounds of an old chateau near Ognon, France.

Journal Excerpt 24 February 1945

Last night we built a good fire in our little stove. Army cots are not very comfortable. On awakening we all moan and groan about aching joints. Yesterday morning we slept late, spent the rest of the morning carrying wood and whittling slivers to start the fires. After mess we had a speech from Major Rosen, the Post Commandant. He told us we were in an area which had been occupied for four or five years by the Germans, for that reason we must stick to the beaten paths as the surrounding area has not yet been completely cleared of "booby traps." They expect it to take about twenty years to finish the job. Our Mess Hall and offices are in the chateau.

Our tent area is between two long greenhouses. We are not allowed to enter them. Behind the chateau is a woods in which valuable statuary is still standing. This area is also off limits. The chateau is a few hundred years old and belongs to a family six hundred years old in France.

To the right is a building housing French personnel of the estate and said to house relics of antiquity. Also off limits. We are allowed to go to the village of Ognon. The hotel, with Trois Canards Café (Three Ducks) is about all that is there.

Last night Marge and I walked some little distance in both directions. This morning we policed the area, mostly raking leaves. The area looks rather nice. We have gravel paths and some unauthorized, ungravelled.

There are ten of us in a tent and we cooperate well on wood detail. It is quite a sight to see us all sitting around the stove whittling shavings and slivers for kindling. My hands are sore this evening. Tonight we are all sweating it out wondering where we will be assigned, what about our jobs.

Journal Excerpt 25 February 1945

We are debating the possibility of hot water at this point. We have a "watering trough." When there is water one can take one's helmet and wash in ice water. When a few individuals cooperate, a tank behind the building can be heated. Someone must stay and operate a regulating handle. The GIs use used it prior to WAC occupation say it regulated "Hot-Cold-Off."

Journal Excerpt 26 February 1945

Yesterday I made out my application blank for a correspondence course in *Statistics* from the University of Chicago. Marge was transferred to Glider (9th AFSC Hq) today. I was a little saddened. Joan will be going, too. It is said there will be only about fifty of us left here. Joan is poking the fire. It has to have constant attention or the green wood goes out. Probably it is about time we went on wood detail. Right now I don't feel much like going. A fine attitude! And just after we read Emerson's "Essay on Self-Reliance" aloud in the tent. Joan started it and asked me to finish. As one of the few bits of reading material I brought with me, "Self-Reliance" has certainly proved worthy of repeated reading. Just heard some detonations of something close by.

Here I sit sniffling away in a set of dirty combat clothes, scarf, 4 buckle artics and scarf and sweater underneath my jacket. Watford seems like a soft life by comparison.

After supper we had a formation. Just an apology for keeping us waiting around all day for the inspection and very few assignments, mostly Signal personnel. Capt. Hunt hopes to be able to tell us something tomorrow. Marge left for Glider today and already I miss her. She has a wonderful attitude toward most things. I wish we could have been together longer. It will be simply terrible with Joan gone too. Would that I had been some individual of the Gastropoda—that I might retract my body into its shell and save the more delicate portions of my sensibility from the intrusions of foreign substances.

Journal Excerpt 27 February 1945

This morning when we were raking leaves we ran on to several "booby traps." All but one had been unscrewed. A Staff Sergeant took them to Ordinance for checking. We didn't get any news today and morale around this area is pretty low. This set-up is

really a mess. What a life! Another day of ennui
might kill me.

Journal Excerpt 28 February 1945

This morning Joan and I volunteered for detail. We
had the honor of filling the Lister Bag. After we filled
the bag, we borrowed a wheel barrow and carted a
load of wood. It looks like a few more mornings of
detail and afternoons of loafing. I can see how we
will spend our days here: hauling wood detail every
morning from 0800 to 0830, after which you are all
dirty at the last minute when you are cleaned up for
work. Work, work, what a word with so many
connotations!

This was payday and lots of the fellows were drunk
at supper this evening.

Journal Excerpt 1 March 1945

Joan and I had a serious discussion of the futility of
despondence in spite of our seeing little to brighten
our outlook into the future.

My morale hit rock bottom last night. Seventeen
Wacs are being transferred to Glider tomorrow. I will
miss Joan, but perhaps we will all be seeing each
other.

This suspense is terrible. The agony of prolonged
waiting. Who knows how many stored up abilities are
lying dormant in this WAC Detachment? Who knows
the big job I am capable of doing and never got the
chance? Oh to be a real Statistician with a real job.

Much of my journal for the month of March records the difficulties of keeping warm and clean and my continuing negative attitude about not being employed in serious work. There was an occasional bit of typing to do for an officer and on the 8th of March I went into Paris with another Wac. One afternoon and evening gave only a hazy impression. We were grateful for the Red Cross Club. After the usual tourist things: walking down avenue Champs-Elysee to the Arc de Triomphe, saluting the unknown Soldier's Tomb, and resting our feet in a theater, we walked to Napoleon's Tomb. After supper at the Red Cross Club, we went to a dance at Rainbow Corner. I danced with fellows from Germany who had not seen American women for months. The fellows enjoyed talking about their station and mission. We saw several incidents that were unwelcome reminders of the horrors of war, especially a fellow who was standing up for his buddy who couldn't stand, and yelling, "His CO got a Silver Star for what he did." The MPs came up with a "Black Mariah" and took some of the fellows away. I didn't get back to camp until 0200 because our driver took an hour to find his way out of the city. Jean had moved my bed for me because we had orders to move together so there would be no excess tents.

Journal Excerpt 6 March 1945

This afternoon "Cotton" (a part-Indian Wac from Arkansas who drives a Jeep), asked if I would like to go on a run to Glider (Creil, France.)

Coming back just the other side of Chamant we saw an interesting peddler's wagon. The people who owned it were off on the side of the road hunting edible weeds or something. So I had my first experience in French bargaining.

"*Combien pour une petite baskettes?*" They were all dirty looking things. "*Cette baskette pour moi.*" That worked and I had bought a little basket for "*Cinq francs.*"

Then the old lady wanted something to eat. At first I thought she wanted me to buy something to eat, then I soon understood **she** wanted something to eat. So "Cotton" gave her a stick of gum.

Journal Excerpt 10 March 1945

It looks now like we would be here until the middle of next week, another week of having people take baths and brush their teeth right in my face, just a few inches from me. Why couldn't we have stayed in the other tent? They didn't need to take it down.

We did finally have inspection today. I spent most of the afternoon skimming through a couple of books on Political Science and Algebra and did some figuring in an arithmetic workbook. Anything to keep occupied and thinking something other than what one is bound to think. Latest word after Major St. John's visit today is that it will be ten days or more before we move. I wouldn't mind so much if we hadn't had to move into a different tent. I don't have room to breathe. It's so repulsive, this way of existence. We are sitting around the stove griping and offering constructive criticism about the army and its organization. Soon it will be six weeks since I have really worked! What a gruesome thought.

Overseas - World War II

Journal Excerpt 17 March 1945

Shades of St. Patrick! The saints be with us. We moved to Glider this morning, and is it different! This semi-privacy is delightful and it is good to be back with Marge and Joan, and I don't know anyone I would rather bunk with than Jean. We now live on the fourth floor of the Glider building, which is Headquarters for the 9th Air Force Service Command. The building was formerly the entire accommodations for a girls school.

We live in "cubicles." They resemble beauty parlor stalls. Two bunks, upper and lower to a compartment, one wall locker inside the cubicle, one outside. A lavatory and bidet to each cubicle. We put a box over the bidet. There are showers in the basement which we use.

Though at first sight this place looks like a chicken coop-guinea pig existence, we are quite comfortable, especially by comparison with tents, stoves, helmets, and an "8-hole latrine on a higher plot of ground." It is not the pioneer existence we have just emerged from. Instead it is climbing hundreds of steps tens of times a day. It means never going out of the building except to wash mess kits if one prefers. There is no place to go anyway except on courier and liberty runs. One has to be released from one's section and signed up for the truck into Paris several days in advance to be sure of a pass of Paris.

Chosen

Journal Excerpt 23 March 1945

Went over to Chantilly (5th AF Hq) this afternoon on the Ice Cream Run. That is we took the courier over and had ice cream and coke at a Service Club. It is an interesting town, not as bombed out as Creil. We bought a few postcards and did some window shopping. While we waited for the courier, a Jeep driven by a Major came by. He offered us a ride home, so we had a very successful afternoon. We spent the morning writing letters. Once in a while a very small job comes up and is quickly disposed of. I think we are gradually becoming so accustomed to no work in the offices that our feelings about it are rather deadened.

Journal Excerpt 31 March 1945

Yesterday spent the day in Paris. At the Cathedral of Notre Dame we accidentally got in the wrong line and had to kiss the bones of some saint. We didn't know what it was all about, but there was a priest there so we did what the ones in front of us did, and we did not laugh until we were out of the Cathedral. We took a bus tour in the afternoon. We feel quite free to travel around Paris now.

Journal Excerpt 8 April 1945

Have been trying to compensate for vocational frustration by increased social life with some success. Went to Paris to a symphony concert with two GIs and had an awfully good time. Friday night we enjoyed a concert of sacred music at the church in Creil and Saturday night eleven of us former Tipperarian Wacs had a big celebration. We did a lot of drinking, mostly wine.

Journal Excerpt 1 May 1945

On the 29th of April, we left Headquarters in Creil, France at 1730 enroute to Airstrip 81 to depart for Luxembourg. On arrival we landed on a field covered with wire mesh, waited some time for a truck, drove all over Luxembourg and finally arrived here at the "seminary," formerly occupied by German soldiers, much earlier by monks. The building is said to have been built circa 1832.

The WAC has five floors of one wing, two Wacs to a room. Jean and I have No. 89 on the fifth floor. Next door are Joan and Marge. The rooms looked like they hadn't been cleaned since shortly after 1832. We scrubbed everything, even the walls that had pin-up girls drawn on the plaster. The room furnishes us a sink, two German lockers, two stools, a chair and table we salvaged from a vacant room and two army cots. We moved in by candlelight, but the electrician came the next morning. We were only entitled to one light, but Jean told the man that her roommate was studying nightly so he put in a ceiling light also.

We have to use a latrine either on the fourth floor or go into another wing on this floor. Our only source of hot water and bathing facilities consists of two bath tubs in a large room in the basement. Last night I went down and queued up for a bath. The line for a tub was so long I went into another basement room, used my helmet for a sponge bath, washed my hair and nearly froze in the unheated basement.

Joan and Marge joined us for a K-ration party last night and then slept in our room because it was warmer. I don't know what is wrong with us—we haven't stopped wise-cracking and laughing for three days.

Journal Excerpt 11 May 1945

May third, twelve of us Wacs sent out and celebrated our year overseas. We had a good time, living it up with a lot of wine. Yesterday afternoon we marched in our first VE Day parade and did "eyes right" to the officials of Luxembourg.

After the parade, several couples of us went to witness the civil ceremony of Joan and Frank's marriage. It was an interesting procedure and when the official got his pronouns mixed up and referred to Joan as "he," not one of us even smiled.

Journal Excerpt 30 May 1945

We had been in Luxembourg for several weeks when I decided to get my hair fixed. Without an appointment, I managed to get accepted to be given a permanent at a salon. With my limited French and the hair stylist's slight knowledge of English, we arranged for my new "coiffeur." Due to a shortage of soap and water the hair was not washed. Curlers on a machine were heated electrically and then placed on the hair, which was soaked with lard.

When I returned to quarters, the lard was dripping. All I could think of was how soon I could get a shower and shampoo, but before I could do that someone told me I was to report to our Commanding Officer, Captain Mims, immediately. Embarrassed as I was, there was no alternative but to go. She told me I would be sent on TDY (temporary duty) to London. This was most unusual. I was surprised and hardly knew what to make of it. I was to go with a male Captain I would meet for the first time at the airport.

I didn't know whether to be happy or sad, whether to be scared or thrilled. All I knew was that I was going to be alone in London. Oh well, at least they speak English and I do know my way around in London, more or less.

I got busy and fixed my hair, washed and ironed, packed my Musette bag, and tried unsuccessfully, to sleep. What did this mean? What did this TDY portend for my future? How did I happen to be the one chosen? How do "they" know I can do the work? What if I can't do the work? (I probably can.) After all my impatient waiting to be assigned work in France now I am singled out to go back to England with a male Captain? What if I don't like him? (I probably will.) Many questions.

From June first to June 21 I was on Temporary Duty with the Foreign Liaison Section of **Disarmament** in London. The Captain, whose name I don't remember, had little to do with me. It was a good job and I enjoyed it. We were hiring aliens for interpreters to serve in Germany during the occupation: Austrian, German, Czech, Polish, Russian, Hungarian, all sorts of refugees—interesting people (all men), quite a change in work for me. The interviewing was an education in European geographical history.

Each form I filled in had only one blank for the alien's country of origin, but many of them told me enough to fill a page, about the various borderlines and changes of names their country experienced. It was hard for me because my knowledge of European history was slight, but I was able to evaluate the relative homelessness of the aliens, as well as to judge their ability to converse in English.

"Ah, but it was good to be in England." It was the best time I had had since I had been overseas. Because of the blackout, concerts and plays began at 6:00 p.m. I was able to go to an event almost every night. Following a concert one night, a young American Second Lieutenant offered to walk me to the Red Cross where I was billeted. He was overjoyed to see and talk to an American woman! He was not conscious of the rules about "non-fraternization of officers and enlisted personnel." I don't remember that we even told each other our names. We did not exchange addresses. We discussed the concert, a Haydn quartet for four violins. We were both very polite and I felt a deep sense of security, escorted by an American man as we walked along the street in the blackout. There was no effort at affection, without touching we appreciated each other. I never saw him again. It was a brief, unusually satisfying episode.

During my second week of living at the Red Cross, a group of Wacs from Accra, Africa, came and shared the floor space. There had been three plane loads of Wacs from Africa to London. One plane had disappeared over the ocean. The survivors were in subdued grief. One told me in a whisper, as she reviewed her shock, "My best friend was on that plane." Many of these women had yellowed skin, said to be the result of anti-malaria pills. In a few days a memorial service for the missing Wacs was held somewhere in London.

The concerts every evening, good food, good bed, the hot baths—it was as good or better than a furlough. On June 21 Captain Mims wired England for Foreign Liaison to send me back to Luxembourg immediately to replace the Company Clerk who was being sent home to be stationed with her husband in the states.

Journal Excerpt 25 July 1945

I like working in the Orderly Room. There is plenty of work. I was Acting First Sergeant for the past three days while Capt. Mims, Sgt. Farrar, and Cpl. Liles went to Erlangen, Germany to check out our new quarters. Also was Acting First Sgt. and mail clerk while they were on furlough for eight days. I enjoyed it heartily. Major St. John was here last night. I had to fix up her bunk, etc. I certainly like her. We are due to move to Germany on the twelfth of August.

Journal Excerpt 2 September 1945

June, July and August were about as happy as any three months in the Army. I was sorry to see Sgt. Farrar leave, but I certainly enjoyed taking over her job. First Sergeant seemed more like the job I was cut out for than anything else in the Army.

133

Chosen

We moved to Erlangen, Germany on 12 August as
scheduled. These are the best living quarters we have
had and they still are not modern. We live in
apartments that have bathrooms and kitchens. For hot
water we build a wood and coal fire under a tank at
the end of the bathtub.

While I was serving as First Sergeant of our Detachment,
Capt. Mims took a WAC baseball team to Heidelberg to play
in a tournament. There were no other WAC officers so while
she was gone, I was in charge of the company.
A GI Sergeant from an outfit stationed on the Czech
border came to see me in the Orderly Room. He was
planning a party or dance to be held in a Castle his group had
liberated and asked for my help in bringing American women
to the event. I asked many questions and agreed to bring a
group if I could get a bus load to sign up to attend. Twenty-
four of us elected to go. I think the main feature of the
evening was the drinking.
I drank some kind of "boiler-maker" with a quick ice-cold
beer chaser. Both men and women had a good time and as far
as I knew we had all behaved with dignity. Most of the time
the men enjoyed talking and showing pictures of their
families back home.
When it came time to load the bus to return to Erlangen, I
called off my roster. "Jake" (a platinum blonde, oldest
woman in our group) was missing. What was I to do? I was
worried about her and embarrassed about keeping the driver
waiting. Two Wacs volunteered to go look for her. I was
grateful for their help. After about twenty minutes the two
searchers and "Jake" showed up. I sensed it was best to
minimize the incident. I said nothing to her and she said

nothing to me. We all took our seats on the bus and the tired Wacs were quiet with many eyes on "Jake." Her face bore a look of successful martyrdom, perhaps slight shame, or was it that "swallowed a canary" look?

When we got home and everyone had signed in at the Orderly Room, the two who had located "Jake" told me they found her flat on her back in a field. They said, "She was in action with one fellow and three more were lined up getting ready." I thought perhaps I was expected to have a discipline case, but I didn't wish to get involved. I didn't know whether to laugh or cry. It seemed ludicrous. I visualized the scene including the three disappointed soldiers who didn't get their turn. I imagined that "Jake" could have been a hooker before joining the WAC. I figured the less said about it the better. The incident was over.

In late October, First Sgt. Melansen, who had been with our company in Cheddington, arrived in Erlangen and my job reverted to Company Clerk. I was granted a furlough. Teresa, a Wac I did not know from the 9th Air Force, went with me to Lake Annecy in France where the Army had engaged a hotel for R & R. (Rest and Relaxation)

Teresa and I soon found we were not compatible. One evening I went with her and two burly GIs in a Jeep to an "off limits" country roadhouse. When we got out of the vehicle the two fellows strapped on their pistols, saying they were preparing for trouble. I thought wearing pistols and going to an "off limits" place was trouble enough. We sat in a booth, the two women opposite the men, and had drinks said to have been made from fermented potatoes, very potent. I sipped a little, gently.

A Frenchman came over and invited me to dance. The GI opposite me, a hefty fellow, told me, "Don't you dare do that!" So I pointed to my foot and said, "*Merci beaucoup, mais J'avez une mal au pied.*" I hoped that I said, "Thank you very much, but I have a sick foot." That saved the day and was the last time I went anyplace with Teresa. Her friends were not my type.

Andy, a good-looking 8th Air Force GI with a Greek background, was also on furlough and we became well acquainted—we rode in a boat on the lake, we visited a cafe on the lakeside, we had fun just enjoying each other's company. One night, in an area between the back of the hotel and Lake Annecy, there were leaves ready to be raked up. Andy recounted how as a child we had enjoyed rolling in the leaves and these leaves were inviting. He held me close as we rolled together, we kissed, we were happy. It was very dark; there was no one around.

When we stopped rolling and stood up, Andy said, "I'll have to go change clothes."

I was surprised. "What do you mean?"

"You just caught me just right."

"Oh, I'm sorry. I didn't mean to do anything wrong!" I was about to cry.

"You didn't do anything wrong. It was fine. I'll slip up the back stairs and be right back to take you into the hotel. You stay right here."

I was nervous while I waited in the dark, but he came back quite soon in a black coverall flight suit and took me back to my room. We were friends from then on without any discussion of our rolling in the leaves.

It was about two o'clock in the morning as I was entering the parlor that divided Teresa's room from mine. We each had a bedroom and bathroom; her's much larger than mine.

Here came two GIs carrying Teresa. She had had too much to drink and had passed out. They knew I did not know her very well. I said, "Is she sick?"

"No, not really, but she will be in the morning! Where shall we put her?"

I took them to her bed and they stretched her out. I loosened her shirt collar and tie, went back to my room and worried about her the rest of the night. In the morning she was okay and acted as if nothing had happened.

Andy told me that the fellows had tried to keep Teresa out of a men only party, but she insisted and got drunk. He also said that people said I was a nice woman, but Teresa was not. I was beginning to wonder if I might be falling in love with Andy. When I made a subtle reference to marriage, he made a definite statement that after discharge from the Army he would marry a Greek girl. We remained friends. A few days after my furlough, Andy told me he and Harry (his buddy) were making a trip to Ansbach and I was invited to go along. We would be back late that night. I had never been on the *autobahn* before. It is many miles of a straight expressway, no curves, no speed limit. Andy drove a military vehicle. It was scary, but safe. I enjoyed the trip. I never even knew Andy's last name.

Journal Excerpt 10 November 1945 LeHavre, France

This notebook has served its primary purpose—a book to write little words in at a time when nothing else could be done. My spirit is elated at the thought of the approaching discharge!

Helen Reed
Blowing "Assembly" at camp in Watford, England
Winter 1944
(Leggings, jacket/pants with wool liners.)

WAC DETACHMENT
VIII AFCC & IX AFSC
Luxembourg - VE Day 1945
(Rare Photo)

Chosen

CHAPTER 9

Leaving Europe—Back to Washington, D. C.

At Camp Philip Morris, LeHavre, France on the tenth of November, 1945, the WAC Detachment from Erlangen, Germany awaited a signal to board the U.S.S. George Washington. I know that on 17 November I was on board ship, but remember very little about it. The diarrhea I had in LeHavre got worse and a WAC officer I did not know got me to sick bay. I believe I had fainted. I woke up with intravenous feeding in my arm. Getting off the ship at Boston Harbor on 23 November we were met by people giving us coffee and doughnuts. It was thrilling to get home to our native land.

I was in a group taken to Camp Miles Standish for physical examinations and sent on to Fort Dix. It occurred to me that it would be more convenient for me to stay in the army at least for a short time because I did not have a job to go to, nor a place to live. I found a WAC officer and asked her about staying in the army. She said, "Demobilization is for the convenience of the government. You will be discharged here." That was the end of the discussion. At Fort Dix we were divested of most of our gear. I got to keep a battle jacket, extra skirt and shirt, a utility coat, the shoes I had on and three pair of socks. We were told to turn in our duffel bags and purchase luggage at the PX. I did not know any of the Wacs there. It was the most unclean place I had ever seen in the army and I was glad to be leaving. In late afternoon, on the 29th of November 1945, I was "honorably discharged from the military service of the United States of America." I was like someone who needed a halfway house. There I was at Fort Dix, New Jersey with no place to go, no reason to go except the necessity to leave. It was terrifying. Then I remembered that I had mustering out pay, that helped. The next bus that came went to Philadelphia. I was so glad I was familiar with Philadelphia and went to the Bellevue Stratford Hotel where I had lived during earlier military days. When I registered the Desk Clerk told me, "This is only for tonight. We are all booked up because of the Army-Navy game."

I went to the hotel dining room for a good dinner. It had been a long time since I'd had one. In the doorway of the dining room, waiting to be seated, standing tall in my overseas uniform, I felt that my first night on my own could at least be comfortable. A woman came through the lobby and came up to me saying, "I left my glasses here last night. Would you..."

"Madam, I am a member of the United States Army." The woman turned hastily and left embarrassed.

The next morning I took stock of possibilities. It seemed best to go to Washington. Once again it was difficult to get a room. I got one at Meridian Hill Hotel, just for that night. I went back to my old address, the Canterbury Apartments, at 3rd and G Streets, NW, Washington, D.C., to see if Agnes Wunderlich and her mother still lived there. Agnes had married Austin Boelter and they were there and glad to see me. They told me to see Mrs. Toone, the landlady, about getting an apartment.

Mrs. Toone and her husband were the landlords for the apartment house. They were both very small people, originally from Ireland. Mrs. Toone was in charge; Mr. Toone did the mopping of the Lobby and other cleaning chores. She remembered me from the days when I delivered the rent from Cleo and me. I'm sure she was an "angel." She picked up a set of sheets and towels from her apartment and took me in the elevator to the fifth floor. She explained, "I'm taking you to an apartment which is very temporary. In a few days I'll have something suitable for you. The woman who lived in this apartment died in the hospital. In about a week her family will be here to take care of her belongings. In the meantime, it's illegal to touch any of her things, so please don't tell anyone your address. You can count on me to take care of you." I thanked her quietly.

"You're very kind. I appreciate your help." I had no alternative but to accept this offer. I felt very strange. Certainly I did not want Mrs. Toone to get in any trouble and wondered about my role in this "illegality." She quickly made up a cot bed and left me. I resolved to spend only nights in the place. Before the week was over Mrs. Toone gave me a splendidly furnished first-floor room with bathroom access down the hall and kitchen facilities in the basement. I was assured that in a few weeks an apartment would be available for me.

I discovered I was eligible to go back to work for the successor to the War Production Board—the Civilian Production Administration. There were no openings for a Junior Professional Assistant in Biology, the rating I had obtained that would have given me much more pay. As a Statistical Clerk, I worked in a small office with a Dr. Haney and several others. He was nice to work for. My job was to audit molasses and alcohol records. The work was not hard, nor vital. Using a Monroe Calculator I did find numerous errors. Just when I was beginning to experience vocational frustration, once again as I had in the army, a genuine call to service came. Dr. Haney had me work with him on allocation of streptomycin to hospitals. This was an important assignment followed by some work on strategic allocation of chemicals for production of plastics.

From the announcement in the army paper *Stars and Stripes*, I had assumed the GI Bill either not true or not applicable to me. When I realized it should be taken seriously I enrolled in three courses at George Washington University. A full time job and three courses was too much so I dropped a Psychology course that had already taught me that Psychology would not become my life's work.

Mrs. Toone enabled me to move to a second floor apartment which I furnished. Mama came to visit. I suppose I must have invited her. She had no desire to go sightseeing in Washington; all she wanted to do was cook.

After a couple of days of Mama's visit, I was seated at the card table working on my pawnshop bargain flute. She was preparing dinner. When dinner was ready she issued a direct order to come at once. I was busy with a tricky spring and didn't hop right into the kitchen.

"I will come when I have finished what I am doing."

She said, "You come now." Her voice was sharp.

I kept my cool as I said, "This is my home. I pay the rent here. If any orders are needed, I will be the one to give them."

Mama sat down at the table. I stopped what I was doing and joined her at the table. We ate silently until I said the food was good. Mama had nothing to say. The next day she left on the train from Union Station. I thanked her for her visit.

My decision to prepare for professional work was not made lightly. I studied college catalogs at the Public Library and the Library of Congress. I took a day off work to walk alone all day in Rock Creek Park in deep meditation. I searched my past, studied my failures, concentrated on my successes. What had I done in the past that was virtuous, helpful to people and within my abilities?

Everything pointed to school band directing as my chosen profession. Graduate school at Columbia University offered the best opportunity to study toward entry into that line of work, and I had no difficulty in being admitted based on my undergraduate record.

I processed my GI Bill papers, got a room at Whittier Hall (a hotel for women at Teachers College) and made the transition from Washington to New York City. It became a turning point in my life, successful in more ways than I could ever have dreamed.

Chosen

CHAPTER 10

Getting Acquainted with Columbia University and New York City

Life at Whittier Hall and Teachers College, Columbia University, was calm, organized and studious. I was focused on my goal of becoming a school band director and since I did not have an undergraduate major in music, I was permitted to take whatever courses I elected. There was no mention of working toward a master's degree. The professors all seemed to understand about me, including my need to be excused from the "Sight-Singing" section of my *Harmony* class. One day in *Harmony*, my assignment paper was held up as an example of excellent music manuscript. To my embarrassment it also had the professor's adequate supply of red ink. I enjoyed my other courses, all geared toward instrumental teaching. Sometimes I lunched with an "in-group" of music students, feeling inferior because I could not sing with them.

Because my background demonstrated ability to play and teach brass instruments (my opinion at the time), I thought I should choose the clarinet as a representative woodwind instrument for private lessons. When I learned these lessons were a part of my GI Bill credits, I was overjoyed. My previous experience with the clarinet was in a woodwind

147

orientation class at Maryville, the summer before Sharpsburg. Mr. Henry Christman, a Juilliard instructor, became my teacher. He too, was very understanding about my lack of background and my reasons for taking clarinet lessons. Most of my lessons were given in a studio at his home in White Plains, a few at Juilliard. He was an ideal teacher for me—I had never known the discipline, the rigorous practice and the intensive attention that was now expected. At first, after each lesson my lip would be so sore I could not practice the next day. He then introduced me to using a lip saver. In a few weeks he took me to a music dealer in lower Manhattan where he had already negotiated the trade-in of my clarinet for a new Buffet. I still have it and today Buffet is still the highest ranked brand. A new clarinet today would cost ten times what I paid!

The practice rooms were provided on top of the Teachers College buildings. They also provided some "get-acquainted" space. I had a couple of dates with Ken M. from Kentucky who also played clarinet. On my last date with him, he asked me to spend a weekend with him in a downtown hotel. I refused the invitation and soon after he was dating a more mature woman who lived down the hall from me. Ken called her on the phone in our corridor. I had to tell him, "The sign on her door says she will you at Hotel Commodore." I could hardly keep from laughing.

During the second semester, I had a date with a black fellow veteran I met in one of our classes and we became better acquainted in a practice room. I did not understand why he preferred to meet me in the subway, but he patiently educated me on the importance of understanding race prejudice and why it was necessary to take precautions. He took me to a nightclub in Harlem where we had ham sandwiches and milk and heard a black man sing in *falsetto*. We sat in a park for a while afterward. We were good friends.

By the beginning of the second semester, I was working hard on the clarinet and using Oliveri reeds which were in short supply. It occurred to me that Lt. Frankel's store might have them, so I wrote asking him to send me some.

Lt. Frankel showed up at Whittier Hall without warning on a Saturday morning, saying he brought reeds (not the ones I wanted) and was in town for the weekend expecting to take me to dinner. He had me meet him at his hotel where he had engaged a suite of rooms and planned to have dinner in the room. I was angry about that and convinced him to have dinner in the Dining Room. He explained something I did not understand about getting a special rate. That was the last time I saw Lt. Frankel.

Taking the train back from White Plains one day, the man sitting beside me started gently fingering my initials on my briefcase. When I got off the train, he got off and gave me his card: Franz Karl Joseph Keuker, Ph.D. It seemed wild to be meeting a man on the subway. I let him visit me several weekends at Whittier Hall, take me to expensive dinners and give me fine jewelry. He had a need to talk and I was a good listener, as I wondered how much of his story was true and how much he might be making up. He was born in the Netherlands, interned during WW II in Indonesia, studied medicine in South Africa and discovered a cure for Tuberculosis in the Himalayas. He held a Ph.D. in Business from Columbia University and was currently in the jewelry business.

Later he said he was separated from his wife in the Bronx; she lived upstairs, he lived downstairs. Although he had not

demonstrated any affection toward me, he told me he had
enough money to buy me an apartment "so that he could have
someplace to lay his head." Now that I knew he was married
and had a need to "lay his head" I returned the jewelry and
told him goodbye. He insisted on my keeping two items to
remember him by. I still have a delicate gold filigree pendant
and a silver pin, made in India. I never saw him again and I
still wonder about him.

One more happenstance of living at Whittier Hall was my
friendship with the young black woman across the hall from
me: nineteen year old precocious Johnnie Parker from
Atlanta, a Ph.D. candidate in Musicology at New York
University. She lived at Whittier Hall because her folks felt
she was too young to live in "The Village." We went to
dinner at "Toffeneti's" on Times Square occasionally. Our
conversations were mostly about our studies. Because I was
taking a course in *Orchestration*, Johnnie got me invited to do
some orchestrations for a show at the Harlem Boys Club
entitled "One Wheel Chariot." In the end, they used two
pianos, but I still have a "thank-you" letter. Its plot involved
a young girl, a second instance of the Virgin Mary.

At the end of the second semester, I enrolled for
Foundations of Education, a course occupying the month of
June; primarily to be sure my GI Bill check would continue
without interruption and tide me over until regular summer
school.

A. Helen Reed   B. Albert Trobian - 1946

Chosen

CHAPTER 11

Marriage to Albert Trobian
M. A. In Music Education

Six hundred and eighty-nine graduate students had assigned seats in McMillan Academic Theater on the campus of Columbia University for the June 1947 "Foundations of Education" course. On the last day of class, Professor Rugg invited several students who had attended optional luncheon meetings (I did not attend) to join him on the stage to make comments. "And you come up too, Mr. Trobian," he added, almost as an afterthought.

When Mr. Trobian got his opportunity to speak, we wondered what he was saying. He was slender, boyish, self-composed, with brown wavy hair and a soft baritone voice, unassuming, but trying hard to give the audience a message. As he drew pictures in the air illustrating his ideas, members of the audience having no idea what he was trying to communicate, became rude and started shouting, "Get him off of there!"

His voice was not very strong, but I was curious to know what he was trying to say, especially since he used his hands so artistically. There was some indescribable attraction for me, yet it was not emotionally activated. What were these ideas?

Soon a break was announced, the last one before the final session of the course. During the break I went to his seat to ask if he would be at Columbia for the regular summer session.

"I don't know. I don't have any money." I ignored that answer.

"If you are, I'd like to talk with you sometime about your ideas. Here's my name, address and phone number." Neither of us acted excited. That was Friday and the course was over.

To my surprise, he called me on Saturday and we spent the afternoon talking in Whittier Hall parlor. He did most of the talking, describing his family, and sketching his background as an elementary school teacher, and a conscientious objector in the Medical Corps of the Army. I related briefly my role as a Wac in the Women's Army Corps and the Army Air Corps. Near suppertime, he said he should leave and we said goodbye without making any plans to meet again.

I responded positively to his experience as a conscientious objector and his explanation of teaching being his "calling." He was the only man I had ever dated who had such spiritual qualities and could express them so firmly. I liked that. It was in keeping with my own vocational orientation, but I had no need to voice my views. Whatever response I made to him was no more than a neutral friendship. I don't think we ever got around to the explanation of what he wanted to say when he spoke on the stage in the auditorium.

Sunday morning the phone outside my room rang and with no preliminary remarks, Albert Trobian said, "Don't you think we ought to go to church this morning?" I had just gotten up.

"Well, I guess we could go to Riverdale Church, it's close."

On that special Sunday, I wore a distinctly feminine outfit inherited from Grace: black taffeta skirt and jacket with three-quarter sleeves, georgette blouse with jabow, white straw hat bound in black velveteen ribbon. It felt good to be dressed up and going to church with a man. He was wearing a gray wool herringbone suit with vest, despite the summer heat.

After church we went to Sunday dinner at a Stouffer's Restaurant on the sixteenth floor of an apartment hotel close to Whittier Hall. It did not embarrass Albert to be my guest. He was at ease taking everything for granted. Afterward we went to Riverside Park. There was no silly sentimentality and no parkbench lovemaking. It was as though we had known each other for years. There was none of the traditional romantic "I love you, will you marry me?" nor did he ask me if I loved him. I didn't know if I loved him so I let him talk. Just as his invitation to go to church was made without any previous small talk, he said, "I will complete my degree, get a job, build a house, and we will be married." I thought, "Is this a Latin Lover Italian approach? What about me? Shouldn't he ask me?"

Since he was so direct and so secure, I thought I would be that way too. I made a matter-of-fact cool response. "If you're going to marry me, what makes you think I'll wait that long?" Was I playing hard to get? No I was just being realistic. For me it was now or never, yet I felt that things were moving out ahead of me, as if I were a bystander looking on Albert as the leading man in this drama and I was here just to complete the scene. Is this what falling in love is like? What is this strange attraction to this unusual man? By midnight we were engaged to be married as soon as summer school was over. I was in a daze and wondered if this was really happening. Could it be that some higher power was in charge making plans for us?

The realization that I was going to be married caused me to hastily re-evaluate my work at Teachers College. I wanted to be ready to be a breadwinner as soon as possible. I went to Professor Church, my advisor, and asked, "What do I need to qualify for a Master's Degree?" He looked up my record, immediately enrolled me as a candidate for an M. A. in Music Education, and scheduled me to play a recital on clarinet. Another requirement for my degree was to pass a piano exam. Miss Merrill, who administered the exam, knew me from the "Recreational Piano" class where I had been a good student. She also knew my dislike of the piano. I played eight little pieces and passed the requirements. Had I been examined by anyone else I believe I would have been so frightened I would not have passed.

My clarinet recital, planned with Mr. Christman's help, was juried by Professor Church and Professor Harris. I was tense, but performed without calamity. After I played, Professor Church came up to me and said, "How long have you played the clarinet?" I thought, two semesters would sound like a joke and wondered, "Oh, what is he going to do to me?" Then he said he could tell I had not played very long, but added, "Anyone who could develop that beautiful tone in ten months deserves to be congratulated." In a few days, Ken M. came to see me after his recital and said, "They wouldn't pass me. They told me to find out who your teacher was. I'll have to stay in school another year."

My friend, Mary Gertrude Brown, a kindergarten teacher from Independence, Missouri, lived down the hall from me at Whittier Hall. Albert went with Mary Gertrude and me to a concert in Central Park. During intermission he went someplace and came back with three ice cream cones. After we got back to our rooms, Mary Gertrude said, "Where did you get that innocent child?" She was surprised to learn that I planned to marry him.

Albert was radically different from any of the miscellaneous men I had dated. He seemed aware of who he was without being pretentious. For a thirty-year-old man, he was young with genuine sophistication. I was twenty-eight that August and still conscious of being homeless. His folks came from Italy; mine had been Mennonites. He grew up in Pennsylvania while I was moving around in Kansas. How different our backgrounds were, yet we had similar visions of the future—a need to be useful and to be helpful to others through a call to the profession of teaching. Somewhere, deep down underneath our exteriors and our backgrounds was a mutual hunger for a stable foundation for our lives. Albert represented that for me, and much later I learned that I represented that stability for him.

One afternoon enroute to class, a strange feeling overtook me. A loud voice of reality said, "You will soon be a wife." I felt weak. What was going on? Was this me? I went home to bed. The next day excitement was still in the air, but my normal ability to cope with ever-changing circumstances returned.

When Mama got my letter telling her I was engaged to be married, she wrote back, "No, don't do that. I will buy you a car so you can drive me around to visit relatives." I did not answer that letter. The date for the wedding was set and I did not invite Mama. I used her name on the wedding announcements.

Albert's twin brother Paul, and his sisters, Irene and Lucy, came to New York for the weekend of the wedding. On Saturday we took a ferryboat to Coney Island (why we went there I have no idea). It rained and things in general were hectic. I felt a little strange that Albert's family was here, but mine wasn't. I was grateful they didn't ask me too many questions. They were very surprised that Albert was getting married in such a short time. I wondered if they thought I had seduced him.

Irene asked Albert what he planned to wear for the wedding.

"My good old blue suit. I taught school for four years in that suit." That was unsatisfactory to Irene so she took us all shopping to buy Albert a new suit. We all agreed on the suit while Albert submitted like a patient lamb to trying it on and being measured, accepting it graciously as a wedding gift, but not too happy about all the fuss. When the store clerk said it would be ready on Monday evening, Irene said, "Oh no! He's going to be married in that suit at nine o'clock in the morning." Although it was time for the store to close, the sleeves and pant cuffs were tailored immediately, while the five of us waited. I was amazed at Irene's powers of persuasion. She had taken for granted that Albert would let her buy him a suit. Now she had spoken with authority. How did she do that, especially in New York City? It made me wonder what kind of noble family I was marrying into.

The wedding ceremony was scheduled for nine o'clock on Sunday morning in the Pastor's Study at West Park Presbyterian Church, Amsterdam Avenue at 86th Street. All of that running around on Saturday had left me exhausted and it was close to eight o'clock when I woke up. The new navy blue suit I had bought needed to be pressed. I rushed to the ironing room hoping to find a warm iron, which I did. My left hand smacked against a hot iron. My hand was burned, but there was no time to worry about it. I pressed the suit and hurried back to my room. Irene and Lucy called from the lobby to see if I needed help. "No, please stay downstairs." We took a cab to the church and on the way passed Albert and Paul waiting for a bus. It seemed silly not to pick them up, but we didn't.

At the church, the ceremony was performed by a substitute minister, a hospital Chaplain. The regular minister was on vacation. Irene and Paul stood up with us while Lucy stood in a corner with a camera. The minister kept trying to joke with us, but Albert and I ignored his humor. Why was he being frivolous on this holy occasion? We were serious.

After the ceremony we walked to Haddon Hall, a hotel close to the church and to our apartment. The preceding week we had signed for the first floor at 125 West 85th Street, between Broadway and the river, a newly renovated one room and bath apartment with Murphy Cabronet (one unit stove, sink, fridge, and cabinets). We had shopped for furniture: a tan colored couch with small floral pattern that could quickly be turned into a bed, a buffet type chest, a desk and chair, and a dinette table with four chairs. We were lucky to find a first floor apartment in a good location with brand new facilities. I thought that was a good omen.

We quickly adjusted to each other's desires. Mating came naturally to both of us. Albert had secretly paid a visit to the Margaret Sanger clinic. He said he just wanted to see if there was something he should know to be sure he didn't hurt me. He wanted us to take a shower together, which we did. Many nights in the afterglow of sexual satisfaction, we would regale each other with stories of our childhood. Albert's parents, Luigi Lori and Mary Mecozzi had married at age seventeen in Italy and had taken off right away for America "where the streets were paved with gold." Luigi Lori worked in a coal mine, caught influenza, and died when Albert and Paul were three years old.

Two years after Albert's father died, his mother married another coal miner, Sam Trobiani. Due to a strike around 1921-22, the family lived in company barracks and for that reason Albert and Paul did not go to school until they were seven years old. After that they lived in a company house in Russelton, Pennsylvania. The children spoke Italian until they learned English at school and from other people.

Albert could tell many tales about the coal miners. I was always intrigued about old man Bessetti who put on all of his suits of underwear, all his clothes and then jumped out a window and ran away to avoid altercation with his wife's lover. Or Kiki who got into a duel, and a man's fiancé coming over from Italy after the man who sent for her had been shot, but the fiancé managed well after she go there. Or the stories about his mother who had never been to school, yet superbly ran a boarding house to support the family along with the production of wine and whiskey. Or the "Pittsburgh Man," the vendor who served the village. I could never keep the stories straight and I could never get Albert to write them down. They were like fiction to me. It was so much fun to hear Albert recount the coal mining settings. My stories were about moving each year from one parsonage to another.

Several times during the first six months, I gave Albert a tongue-lashing, usually over nothing—he didn't replace towels on the rack, and he forgot to come home for dinner at 6:00 p.m. When he wore a tie I didn't like with a green shirt, I picked up my keys and went down in the park figuring he would come after me, we would make up and all would be forgiven. When after a few minutes he didn't come, I hurried back and found him in tears. When I saw myself behaving like my mother, it frightened me and I resolved never to let it happen again. I realized I was childish and irritable, selfish and inconsiderate. All I could say was, "Please forgive me, I'm so sorry. Don't cry honey, I'll do better. I won't nag you anymore." He was the considerate one—kind and loving. Once I said, "The men I went with always pulled out the chair for me at a restaurant. Why don't you do that?"

With a sly grin he said, "Because you didn't marry any of them!" He explained that he did not consider chauvinist behavior to be respectful to women. He also told me that I should know that the word *divorce* was not in his vocabulary.

We both realized that our behavior was a natural result of two very different persons learning to live together. Neither of us ever questioned our love; it was always taken for granted. When it rained we would put on our raincoats and enjoy ourselves strolling down West End Avenue eating apples.

We had become members of West Park Presbyterian Church. The two of us were assigned together to teach an intermediate grade Sunday School Class. Soon the Presbyterians brought out their "New Curriculum," and the class was divided. I had the early adolescent group and felt that the "New Curriculum" was not appropriate for my students, so for the summer of 1948, I enrolled in courses at Union Theological Seminary to see if I could learn what and how to teach my Sunday School Class. I enjoyed the summer at the seminary so much that I enrolled in Religious Education courses in the fall.

On Sunday mornings, I came down from the Tower Room where my class met, to find Albert who came up from the basement where his class met. He sat on a straight chair in a hallway reflecting a deep inner peace. A little girl, about five, stood at his knee. They were communicating, quietly understanding each other. It seemed irreverent for me to interrupt. Then the child's mother came looking for her and Albert and I went to the Morning Worship Service.

There was a group of elderly ladies at the church who were attracted to Albert and wanted to elect him a trustee and usher. When I told him what they said, he assured me he could never wear those "fancy pants outfits." The tradition was for ushers to wear formal morning suits, tails, striped pants, and cravats—they looked ready for a wedding.

During an incident in the apartment when I was displeased about some insignificant thing, I called Albert a worm, then quickly told him it was a term of endearment. Soon after he gave me a greeting card on which he had drawn a little "worm." "That's me," he said. We laughed and laughed. From then on whenever I was not in agreement on something, I would say, "All right, you worm!" He would grin happily as though he had been complimented. Without any protocol we established that neither of us would call the other by a first name. He did not like to be called "Al" except by his sisters. We called each other Bunch and Bunchie, short for "Honeybunch."

Late one afternoon, after about three months of marital bliss, we were standing together by the front windows of the apartment. I experienced a slight attack of nausea. Albert was immediately excited. "You're not. . .?" His face wore a smile as beatific as a heavenly angel. He was obviously thrilled by the prospect of an offspring. Up to that time we had had no discussion of potential children. At any rate I was not pregnant, but it caused me to imagine a scene on a college campus where I was wheeling a stroller with a beautiful baby boy up the campus walk to meet the Professor of Philosophy at the end of a perfect day!

We went to see Katharine Hepburn on Broadway in the *"Taming of the Shrew"* and had a wonderfully good time. In the *Playbill* was an advertisement of a bra-top white silk slip. It looked so special that I remarked I wished I had one. It was just idle talk, little did I know he would go to Best and Company on Fifth Avenue and buy me one.

"How did you know my size?"

"I took the *Playbill* ad and found a clerk who looked your size."

"Well, for future reference, I am a perfectly proportioned size twelve." It was a lovely gift I wore for many years. I'm still surprised that a shy guy like Albert could buy me that gift.

Albert landed a job as interpreter for an Italian marine company. It turned out he did not know the necessary technical terms and the job was not possible. I had taken an equally miserable job with Merit Protective Service, working as an "incognito shopper." I shopped at Sterns on 42nd Street and Best on Fifth Avenue. I was taken on a trip to New Rochelle where a woman who had a special knitting store that was under investigation for possible stolen skeins of wool. The crew chief told me I was to tell a story about how my sister from the south was trying to find a match for a particular color. It was all a farce. On that assignment I was so nervous and performed so poorly, I was reassigned to the office, typing reports. While quitting our jobs, going to school and the excitement of being newlyweds, we enjoyed, as many couples did in those days, window shopping on Fifth Avenue and getting a bag of roasted chestnuts to eat on the

163

street before they cooled—a fond memory of a younger American before cyberspace took over.

After six months in our nice, clean, new apartment, we realized (i.e., I realized) we could no longer afford to pay $125 per month for rent. Albert said we could move, but I had no idea how that was going to be done. He found Mr. and Mrs. Samuels on 86th Street who ran a rooming house with music studios. They took our furniture in return for the renting of a room on the fifth floor (no elevators). The room had a sink and a bathroom down the hall. We became friendly with Mr. and Mrs. Samuels.

One day I came down the last flight of stairs, quietly sniffling and shedding tears. Mrs. Samuels came out to the lobby.

"Oh, what's the matter?"

"I'm married to the sweetest, most lovable man in all New York City—and the one with the least sense."

The trouble was that our room had a gray ceiling and gray walls.

Albert said, "The color of this room is not a healthy influence. Our personalities must not be subjected to so much gray."

"I know, I just ignore it."

"Well, I have arranged with Mr. Samuels to buy the paint and paint it myself."

"You sure you can do that?"

He was sure. I went off to school and work and came home to find Albert standing on a chair in his shorts, happily painting. The ceiling and walls partially down were light blue. In the morning he painted the remaining walls peach. It was a splendid job, well done. What a difference it made! His happiness was evident and it made me happy too, but I had to let out my feelings about his skipping school.

"Why must you skip school? That's not right." I wanted to cry.

"I know, but it's more important to live in harmonious surroundings."

I learned that Albert would always be good at "feathering the nest."

The Samuels' gave up their landlording, retired and moved to the country. We moved to a room on 76th Street where the landlady did not like that we did not "go to business." After much hunting we found a second floor furnished apartment at the corner of 97th and Amsterdam for $80: one room, dining room, kitchen and bath.

While I continued at Teachers College and Union Theological Seminary, Albert took philosophy courses. Sometimes to save money, we walked home from school. Frequently we would stop at Shlumbum's and spend whatever we were saving. By this time we had more understanding of each other. I had learned what not to say and that nagging need not be done since it didn't work anyway.

I began to realize that I was married to an exceptionally companionable person and an unusually thoughtful husband. I loved him more than I could ever have imagined. Being married was wonderful even if we didn't always agree on every little thing. I thought that he should dress for summer heat more like other students, instead of always a suit, white shirt and tie. I bought him a half-dozen pastel colored short sleeved, open neck sport shirts. That was a mistake. They were donated to Seaman's Institute. I ironed nine white shirts with stiff short collars each week and fully understood that he made his own decisions about what he would wear. He didn't fight about it, just gave me his explanation. I was grateful beyond measure that we could disagree peacefully.

In 1948, I got a job working as a receptionist for Dr. Finkelstein's Ophthalmology office on the third floor of the Paramount Building on Times Square. While he taught at Columbia, I managed his office five mornings and three afternoons a week, taking appointments on the phone. It was understood that I could study since the pay was only $14.00 a week.

Most of my taking appointments went well with one exception. Mrs. Goldberg told me when she wanted her appointment. That time was taken. I told her what was available. She became angry, but I held firm.

"Young lady, do you know that I am Judge Goldberg's wife? I can get you fired."

"I'm sorry, but those are all the available appointments." We both hung up. This episode had worried me and I think my handling of the problem gave me a new feeling of confidence since at first I had to master my fear of the telephone. I explained what had happened to Dr. Finkelstein. He said I had done right and remarked, "Some of my patients do not have manners commensurate with their so-called social rank. You did right so don't worry anymore about it." Dr. Finkelstein's comment surprised me and I was grateful for his understanding.

Being happily settled in the apartment on 97th Street, after a few months I found out it was possible to go downtown to the Housing Authority to find out what should be paid for an apartment. I talked to a man who said I only had to pay $50. Next payday I told the landlord I had been to the Housing Authority. He was infuriated, but from then on our rent was $50 instead of $80. I was learning my way around New York.

The next year I became a candidate for the Doctor of

Education with major in Religious Education. It was not an original plan of mine, but when Professor Harrison S. Elliott invited me into candidacy I was so flattered I had to accept. Mostly I thought it would show me the path to help Albert through a doctorate.

A half-time job was offered by the Church of St. Matthew and St. Timothy (Episcopal) on West 84th Street. Holding the title of Director of Religious Education, I ran the Sunday School, typed letters, ran the Annual Bazaar and did some of the pastoral calling. The Reverend Mr. Burgess, and I got along well and were friends for years after we left New York.

Albert finished his Master's. I completed my Ed.D. and we were available for college teaching positions in the spring of 1950 and registered with the Teachers College Placement Office.

Without previous contact, the President of Payne College in Georgia showed up at our apartment and demanded we join his wife and three sons at a picnic in Riverside Park. He was interested in possible employment for Albert, but not in anything I could do because I "would just get pregnant." We concluded that interview with mutual understanding that we were not candidates for that college.

In August we made a trip via Greyhound to two colleges in West Virginia. Soon we were certain that *Davis and Elkins* was not for us. At *Salem College* we were interviewed at the President's home and accepted two skimpy contracts for the academic year, 1950-51.

Albert was to teach education courses and direct student teaching. I agreed to teach music education courses, education and psychology courses, night courses in Religious Education, and private lessons on wind instruments. We had reached our goal—we were employed together in one college where the need was evident. We soon learned how complicated that need and that particular professional life was at Salem College.

A.-B. Albert & Helen Trobian - Wedding Day
August 17, 1947, New York City

Chosen

albert   mama   Helen

A. Grace K. Smith (Grace Reed) with Ron and Phil - 1949
B. Mama in New York City with Albert and Helen - 1948-49
C. Albert Trobian - 7 years old - 1926 (First Grade)
D. Albert Trobian - 1927

CHAPTER 12

Salem College, Pittsburgh and Greyhound Travel

At Salem, West Virginia, there was no problem about where we would live. We were told that we would live in the house that served as a dormitory for women, with Miss L. as the resident landlady who would collect our rent. Our kitchen, part of the original house, opened into a spacious room with a library table, two chairs and two cots. A shower bath was tacked onto the outside. Our entrance was reached by climbing up a hill. We referred affectionately to our living quarters as the "shack on the back." Each night we were up 'till two o'clock getting ready for our courses.

With our busy schedules, when to do the laundry became a problem. It could not be done on Friday night or Saturday because the college belonged to the Seventh Day Baptist Church. The Sabbath was strictly observed from sundown on Friday to sundown on Saturday. There was no Presbyterian Church, so we were "obligated" to attend the Methodist Church on Sunday. In a small hill-country community, little things like this take on an amazing importance. We were in luck when we found a laundry in Clarksburg that came to pick up and deliver.

I enjoyed the transition from New York City to rural West Virginia. Regretfully the same could not be said for Albert.

On Registration Day he and Miss Van Horn, the Registrar, were both in tears. I never knew exactly why. There was some problem connected with scheduling Albert's student teachers. When I finally learned what was bothering him, I offered to help and worked out a solution.

He said, "All this time I suffered and you knew how to do it."

"No, I just looked at the situation and figured it out."

There was also a problem with a student in one of Albert's classes. We had both been indoctrinated with the virtues of open classroom discussion and it was perfectly natural to set a class in a large circle so everyone could see and be seen speaking. It showed respect for the individual, that everyone was equal and that the teacher was a leader, a guide and a facilitator, not a dictator. That seating arrangement did not convey any such philosophy of education to one native West Virginian who gave Albert a rough time. He announced in no uncertain terms, "I came to college, not to kindergarten." He was talked to kindly at length, but the damage was already done, he still didn't want to sit in a circle and continued to cause trouble.

One of my most vivid memories of that first semester in Salem was a faculty meeting requested by Albert so he could make a presentation proposing a few changes. He sat at a table up front with the Dean and the President. He was the cleanest and best dressed man in his white straight collar shirt (Chinese laundry), silk tie, beautiful blue suit with fine herringbone weave with a single red thread delicately woven in. He was a beautiful picture in too great a contrast to other faculty wearing old clothes with the elbows out. His clothes were different and so were his ideas. He was in advance of his time and of this place with these people, but he was here to "educate." I was apprehensive about the meeting and wondered how I could best help Albert and still stay in my wifely place. Sadie S., an elderly refugee professor of German, who was sitting next to me, suddenly got a nosebleed. I went out to take care of her. As we left the room, I heard Albert saying, "You can't get anything done by talking to the Dean or the President..." and I didn't hear anyone laugh. I felt it providential for me to leave, all the time hoping Albert was not digging a hole for himself and would emerge intact. He didn't achieve anything at the meeting, but President Bond invited Albert to accompany him to a meeting in a college at Fairmont, W. Va. He delayed the President's car until he had cashed his first paycheck and wired it on to my father's wife who had written us about Papa's illness and asked for financial help.

Miss L., our landlady, was a typical "old maid." We were no more friendly than necessary. Once in our kitchen, Albert was quietly telling me to be careful what I said because she was listening right outside the door. I told him, "That's just your imagination," and flung open the door. She nearly fell into the room with her heavy alibi. After that I trusted Albert's intuition more.

In spite of my vocal difficulty and a tendency to stage fright, we accepted several invitations for Albert and me to speak in local churches. There was a panel at the Methodist church where it was obvious to everyone that public speaking was not our forte. There had been no time to prepare. Later at an EUB (Evangelical United Brethren) church for a World Day of Prayer program, I spoke and Albert was to enhance my speech by intermittently giving word pictures of life in various countries he had visited around the world. It was a good plan, however he had long periods of silence. I would then get up and say, "He has given you time to meditate and to envision..."

One evening, Miss Van Horn took me to a Business and Professional Women's meeting where I spoke effectively as a member of a panel. I was so glad she was proud of me since I wanted to heal any wounds left from Registration Day. After that I had a reputation as a public speaker and had to politely refuse invitations. My self-confidence was raised and every so often I needed to puncture my inflated ego.

By the end of the first semester Albert was thoroughly miserable. Just before we left New York his dentist had removed two front teeth and given him a temporary plate. It was removable and he was in constant fear of it falling out. After careful consideration, we decided for him to be on leave from Salem College for the second semester while continuing his studies toward an Ed.D. He had already been admitted to doctoral candidacy at Columbia University. This would permit him to return to his dentist to complete bridging in the missing teeth. My heart was heavy at his departure for New York, both for him and for me, but I bravely carried on. It was agreed with President Bond that I would add Albert's courses to my load. On Wednesdays I taught from 7:00 a.m. to 10:00 p.m. When President Bond decided for me to also teach a Freshman English course, I told him, "I don't have the proper qualifications."

"But you could do it, couldn't you?" He pushed.

"No, not with the overload I already have." I also refused the Methodist Church request to teach a Leadership Training course on Monday nights. My limit had been reached and I had learned to say no.

During the second semester, the senior class sponsor, a Biology professor, came to me with tears in his eyes. The

English professor refused to direct the senior play and he was desperate. He could not do it himself, would I do it? Discussing the forthcoming Easter break, I learned that he and his family planned to go to Wheeling to "play the ponies." I agreed to direct the senior play in exchange for transportation to and from a hotel in Wheeling, where Albert could come to be with me for the break. I chose a play and the seniors were wonderful to work with. (I had experience. Ha!) After the much praised play some older women said to me, "And it was such a nice clean play." I wanted to say, "What did you expect?"

After a few lessons, I put my three clarinet students together as a trio, bought them new music as they progressed, and soon they were playing all over West Virginia on their own initiative. When I found they were skipping their English class to practice, I had to step in. I was surprised, but gratified to see how popular they were.

With a few brass students, I formed an ensemble that played at the cemetery on Memorial Day. The first episode with this new group was a disastrous performance on a chapel program. I didn't know until afterward that the first trombonist was drunk. After the fiasco I was devastated. My disappointment was so intense that Mrs. Sobak, a woman from my Wednesday night class, took me home for lunch and stretched me out on a couch. It didn't seem to bother anyone else. I had to learn to take such hurts in stride.

Dean Ash sent me to represent Salem College at the Third Annual Allegheny Regional conference held at Bethany College, March 22-23, 1951. On Friday afternoon I participated on a "General Education for Women" program. I don't remember what I said, but I do remember Dr. Florence Shaper, a Sociology professor from West Virginia Wesleyan

175

saying that my comment made the whole conference worth while. There went my ego again; it was my first professional conference and I was pleased with myself.

At the end of the semester, Albert came home and we sat together on the Commencement stage. I was so excited to have Albert home that enroute to the faculty marching line, I forgot my MortarBoard. It was too late to go home for it. A newly appointed vice-president of Salem College, Cecil Underwood, said, "Here wear mine, I don't want to sit on the stage anyway." I wore his hat gratefully. A few years later he became Governor of West Virginia.

Miss L., our inquisitive landlady, had bad timing at our door the day Albert came back from New York. On a cot in full view of the kitchen door, we were being spontaneous together and things were happening. Just when interruption was totally unwanted, Miss L. knocked and called from outside the kitchen door. We both jumped off the cot. As I yelled, "Just a minute," I hastily got into my floor length housecoat and she never knew the situation I was in when I opened the door with semen running down my legs.

At Salem, students had been taught by rote memorization. Albert endeavored to teach them to express themselves and to think about what they were saying. In an in-group culture this was looked on as heresy. No freethinking allowed. For an examination, he wanted each student to ask him a *significant* question. These students felt he should tell them something they could reiterate on an exam paper.

It was impossible for Albert to adjust, therefore impossible for me. We decided not to continue at Salem College. We looked for hours at maps, without any criteria for a decision as to where we should go next. We thought it might be a good omen to go from Salem to Winston-Salem, North

Carolina and sent our one trunk, but when we got there we were surprised at how hot it was and how permeated with the smell of tobacco. Before we found a place to live, we got a letter telling us that my mother was in the hospital at Knoxville where she was visiting her brother John F. Good. We paid Aunt Estelle and Uncle John a visit. We had been there once before when Mama had taken us to see "the old home place" down in the country south of Knoxville. We visited Mama in the hospital and were told that her diabetes was under control and she would soon be discharged.

It was time for us to move on. Uncle John drove us to the bus station. He asked us where we were going, but we didn't know. We planned to figure it out in the station. He thought we were lying and parted from us coolly, but we couldn't help not knowing. He was a rich uncle, but not the kind one tells troubles. In the station, we decided to go to Philadelphia where we exhausted ourselves looking unsuccessfully for an affordable apartment.

Albert said, "Let's go to Cheswick for a few days to see my mother and brother." That was fine until the second day—Albert and his mother had a noisy disagreement, shouting at each other in hill-country Italian. I had never seen Albert so close to violence. My inquiry concerning the trouble was never answered.

"It has nothing to do with you. We are leaving on the six o'clock bus in the morning." He was extremely tense and I felt sadly left out that he couldn't even share the problem. I did not nag or probe, but prepared to depart, at the same time wishing I could tell his mother goodbye, knowing it was not possible. She and I did communicate despite our language barriers. She called Albert *Umberto* (ooum-bear-to) and me *Elena* (A-layna). We went into Pittsburgh where we left our luggage in lockers at the station. Across the bridge on Northside Pittsburgh, we found a room with cooking facilities. There was a pay phone in the hall and a window overlooking a park where a band played an occasional concert.

It was summer of 1951. We were unemployed, homeless and moneyless. I took my flute I was carrying around, to a pawnshop, and retrieved it later. Albert got a job in a mattress factory and after two weeks got me a job in the same place. His third week was his last, as was my first. He had given the foreman a suggestion on how to do the work better. I had been on clerical work until the last day when I was put to clipping labels with a large, heavy paper clipper. I worked steadily until I almost fell over. We were not sorry when the mattress factory told us both goodbye.

Sometime in August, we were notified that Mama had passed away (as they say in the south) in the hospital. A wire had been sent to Cheswick where it laid in a mailbox for a week. Albert cried loudly at length blaming his family because we had missed Mama's funeral. I was so concerned with calming him down, telling him he wasn't to blame, it wasn't anyone's fault and that it was all right to miss a funeral—that there wasn't time to grieve, or he had done it for me. We couldn't have gone anyway; we were broke.

One of the last times I saw Mama she told me she had put three thousand dollars in a savings bank in Chicago and named me as beneficiary. In my "don't talk about dying" mode, I did not get the name of the bank or any details. Uncle John settled her estate and I received a check for seven hundred dollars. The bank we went to in Pittsburgh would not cash it because we were "unknowns." Albert's sister,

Lucy, was living in Pittsburgh with her husband Tony, and baby son, Richard. She came to our rescue and got the check cashed.

On September first, we got on a Greyhound bus and continued to ride buses for the next three months without any specific destination. Sometimes we ate in bus stations; sometimes we bought fresh fruit. We were looking for a desirable place to live. We walked around at various bus stops, but always got back on a bus and enjoyed the scenery.

When Albert talked about setting up a gift shop, I talked about getting a job. Neither of us had any precise references to a future, yet we seemed at peace. At least Albert did and I had an occasional little flash of reality telling me this bus riding was not a terminable way of life, but was meant to take care of us for the moment. In my mind I always knew there was a "tomorrow." What, when, and where was a mystery that was not ready to be disclosed.

We rode the bus like happy vacationers; I felt we had earned a vacation. We saved money by riding the bus all night. We stopped overnight in Asheville and continued as far south as Coral Gables, Florida. Down there they were having a sixty-mile an hour gale with a terrible cold wind full of tiny frogs and debris. It was gruesome; we headed north.

Somewhere on that bus trip, I have a memory of a philosophy discussion with Albert. There was a point at which we communicated on a high aesthetic plane. We were both conscious of an "Intellectual Thrill." It was a beautiful, indescribable experience.

Chosen

Memorial Day Service

I. O. O. F. CEMETERY

Wednesday, May 30, 1951 — 10:00 A. M.

"Star Spangled Banner" _____ Lead by Clyde Spurgeon
(See Words on Back of Program

Pledge to the American Flag, Lead by Comdr. A. M. Swiger

"I pledge allegiance to the Flag of the United States of
America, and to the Republic for which it stands, one
Nation, indivisible, with Liberty and Justice for All."

Scripture Reading and Prayer _____ Rev. Buren Dowdy

Pledge to the Christian Flag ____ Lead by Rev. Buren Dowdy

"I pledge allegiance to the Christian Flag and to the
Saviour for whose kingdom it stands, one brotherhood
uniting all mankind in service and love."

Tower Sonata No. 2 _____ Pezel
Brass Ensemble
Directed by Dr. Helen Trobian

Address _____ Honorable Cecil H. Underwood
Vice President of Salem College

Tower Sonata No. 3 _____ Pezel
Brass Ensemble

Taps

Sponsored by
Salem Business and Professional Women's Club
Program, Compliments of The Fox Printing Company

SALEM COLLEGE BRASS ENSEMBLE

Trumpets: Charles Harris, Bill McMicken
Horn: Gareth Greene
Trombones: James Breen, Glenn Hemminger
Baritone: Roy Burdick
Tuba: James McCarty

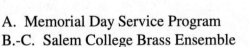

A. Memorial Day Service Program
B.-C. Salem College Brass Ensemble

CHAPTER 13

Cincinnati and Back to New York

Toward the end of November, we found ourselves in a bus station in Cincinnati. Winter was coming and we would soon be out of cash. With Dr. Finkelstein and Teachers College as references, I applied for a position advertised as "Assistant Accountant", at Christ Hospital. I was hired and we rented an apartment within easy walking distance of the hospital. The job paid $140 per month for working on a team with a staggered schedule. Mornings were spent on a large machine, recording each patient's bills for medicines and services received. In the afternoons we figured hospital insurance bills. As a member of a team, other duties at intervals included typing reports of surgical procedures for the Industrial Division, getting statistics from the blood bank, changing the tape on the cash register in the Pharmacy (that was tricky), counting the $500 in change from the Front Desk, and *balancing the day's accounts.* If any mistakes were made during the morning recording, it would cause the team to have to stay overtime. They were proud of my quick learning and accuracy, no overtime. I was lucky, but I made a special effort to concentrate.

I was anxious about the job because I knew that when my references came through the employer would wonder about my background. That did happen, but I survived by using the "married woman" reason for my lack of professional employment. After I started the job the weather got colder and I had to go to work wearing a combination of two spring coats, one inside the other, and was careful to always take them off together. I didn't want to have to explain the story of my homelessness. I was easily embarrassed by the coat problem. Albert was relieved that we had a source of income and happy that I could work in what I described as a congenial environment. The staggered schedule enabled me to take a few lessons at the Cincinnati Conservatory from symphony men who were also on staggered schedules due to out-of-town concerts.

At the time I started to work at Christ Hospital, Albert embarked on a new career. Paul had encouraged him to learn more about the construction business and to go to Pittsburgh to learn plastering and brick laying. We knew this would be temporary for a few months. During the bitter cold winter, he learned a little while he lived in a basement where he was miserable, so he came back to Cincinnati where he applied for work with a construction company.

I received a phone call at work. "Is he for real? His hands are soft. What's the score?" I defended Albert as a good working man and talked the employer into hiring him. On the day he was to show up for work, Albert went to the railway freight station to receive our trunk from storage. There were complications that took all day, so he didn't continue his effort with the construction company.

Soon Albert was hired to work for Natorp's, a large landscaping company. He came home from work muddy, tired, and happy that he was earning pay and enjoying work, although he said some of the men made fun of him. One of the tree trimmers lowered a quart milk bottle onto his head and everyone laughed. He would rush home from work, take a bath, have supper, and we would go to the Conservatory for a concert. He would sleep through the first half, wake up for intermission and get enormous enjoyment from the remainder of the concert. Perhaps the construction company job was not really a good idea. The landscaping company provided a job more natural to Albert's interests. He loved planting.

Mrs. Cooper, a team member at Christ Hospital, invited Albert and me to her daughter's wedding reception. Albert wore dark blue pants, light cream jacket, narrow red tie, and he was tan from working outdoors. In the office one day Mrs. Cooper said to the other team members, "You should see Helen's husband; he's cuter'n a bug's ear!"

Albert began to feel that he should be doing work more commensurate with his mission in life. He was interviewed for a position as teacher of an elementary special education group in Hamilton, Ohio, just north of Cincinnati. He was not hired.

We read in a newspaper about a man in Omaha, Nebraska who had advertised for people who wanted to start a new school. That sounded interesting. We were willing to help and thought it would be good to be in on the ground floor of a new school. The newspaper had sparse information so we took a bus trip to Omaha and found the man. He was in construction and wanted someone to give him money to build a new school building. You could say the trip was "a joke on us." When we returned to Cincinnati, we decided to go back to New York for Albert to once more work toward his doctorate before his admission period would expire. In New York we rented a tiny apartment on Cabrini Boulevard at 181st Street.

During my initial period of searching for employment, I paid a visit to the wife of my major professor. As a graduate student, I had met her in their home at the Seminary. Dr. Harrison S. Elliott had passed away while we were at Salem College. Mrs. Grace Loucks Elliott had for many years been the Executive Director of the National Board of the YWCA. I told her I thought Dr. Elliott would have been proud of my work at Salem College. He was a pioneer in group discussion methodology and I was dedicated to his processes. We had a nice talk without my dwelling on my need for employment. Earlier that day I had stopped at Union Theological Seminary's placement office and had been advised to try "Ruth's Employment Agency." The next day when I went to "Ruth's", I was told not to fill out forms but to call Mrs. Elliott around five o'clock at a number I was given. At five o'clock I called from a pay phone on the street. Mrs. Elliott had already made arrangements for me to become director of a special project at the National Board of the YWCA. The Ford Foundation's Fund for Adult Education had given a grant to the YW, the YM, and the 4-H clubs for a national project—"development and testing of new types of materials and processes for adult group discussion."

I was overjoyed and at the same time apprehensive since the actual work was not spelled out. It was a one-year project that I hoped vaguely might lead to something else. Albert was very pleased and did not mind my having a traveling job. He was sure I could do it. At the time I thought, "Good, now Albert will have long stretches of uninterrupted time to work on his doctoral project seminar."

At 600 Lexington, headquarters of the National Board of the YWCA, I was given a large desk in a room just off the elevators, formerly used as a library. Futami Hayashi was hired as my secretary. She was more than competent and I was always grateful.

Eighteen local Associations throughout the United States had been enlisted to participate in two program series 1) Great Men and Great Issues in Our American Heritage and 2) World Affairs Are Your Affairs. Reading an essay before the meeting and seeing a film gave members of each group a common background for discussion of the issues. Some Associations had two groups. It was my job to visit each group to be certain the process was adequately started and to return later to conduct evaluation.

Futami Hayashi booked the films, handled correspondence, and booked my flights and hotel rooms. I went twice to each of eighteen groups, with the exception of Billings, Montana, where I went only once. The other cities were: Allentown, Lancaster, Reading, and Wilkes-Barre in Pennsylvania; Binghamton, New York; Decatur, Illinois; Detroit, Michigan; Madison, Wisconsin; Toledo, Ohio; Asheville, North Carolina; Greenville, South Carolina; Knoxville, Tennessee; and Montgomery County, Maryland. It was a good job with a good salary and no limitations on the expense account.

Futami Hayashi prepared calendar information with hotel addresses so Albert could send me letters. It was great to check into each hotel and receive mail, even though some of the letters were written while I was still at home. He and Futami were good resources for me. Once on the job there was no room in my mind for any long-term goals. The job consumed my mind.

I arranged with Mrs. Elliott to start an adult beginner's orchestra for staff personnel at 600 Lexington. She was all for it. I worked with potential members after hours. The orchestra rehearsed on the lunch hour. The members were eager to learn and each made definite commitments to the group. When I was out of town, Futami kept the group rehearsing. Albert helped carry instruments from Metropolitan Music Company when they were bought for members of the orchestra. He was always a strong supporter for such musical ventures.

In addition to the strings I started, we had a clarinet and a horn, and then I started a flute. For a petite Asian woman, I found a proper size cello. Albert unearthed a viola in a lower Manhattan junk shop. I think he took more interest in my experimental adult beginner's orchestra than he did in focusing on his own embryonic project.

It was an unusually successful experiment. Although the orchestra was just expecting to furnish background music at the national Hobby Show held at 600 Lexington, a blue ribbon was given me for the orchestra. When I left the project the group of seventeen held a farewell dinner for me at Johnny's Keyboard, a restaurant down the street. They gave me a card each had signed, and a gift of $25. I was thrilled.

The discussion project closed at the end of the school year. My article in *The YWCA Magazine*, January 1954, summarizes the goals and results.

My chief concern this year was to help Albert focus toward a doctoral project. He seemed to have ideas in his mind that could not be put on paper. It seemed impossible to set up a plan for a doctoral seminar. Many nights I would be up until four o'clock as I tried to help.

At one point he had a vague idea of writing something on "philosophy for children." I would say, "Good. Let's focus on that."

"No, not yet, I don't have it ready to focus," and he would

dart off into upper bracket philosophy language and leave me bewildered. Occasionally I would try to help with references from John Dewey or William James because I knew he knew them well. That only resulted in his going off on a new tangent.

Frequently I would have to take a cab to the airport around six in the morning and sleep on the plane.

Albert took me with him for an appointment in Professor Raup's office. Raup was supposed to be his major professor, but they could not communicate. I think Albert was brighter than he was. Something he said provoked Albert to anger and Raup retorted, "Well, I'm glad to see you can stand up on your hind legs and talk." I was embarrassed and angry with Raup and we left before I could give vent to **my** anger.

Later Albert had me go with him for an appointment with Professor Childs who had become his new advisor. On a previous registration day, Dr. Childs, talking to me about Albert, had said, "It is obvious that the world of ideas is very real to him." This time Childs suggested he consider doing a dissertation on George Albert Coe. He had been a mentor for my major professor, and I was sure Albert could analyze his ideas.

It was not possible to influence Albert. If he couldn't write his own philosophy, why should he write about someone else? His attitude never changed. For many years, I wondered what I might have done. Finally it came to me that it was no fault of mine. I always felt that he had something remarkable to say to the world of philosophers if he could ever put it in coherent language and I soon found that it was not to be achieved by quoting from any other philosopher, dead or contemporary. All I knew at the time was that it might have some subtle reference to non-violence, to his army experience as a Conscientious Objector (which was not to be mentioned, background only), and that he was not an agitator or crusader for any particular school of thought or belief system. I began to regard him as a genius with some deeply buried jewel of thought so profound it would take a lifetime to discover and after trying unsuccessfully to help, I felt that my best role was to learn to live graciously with it, and not to be forever nagging him about it. Albert was better off just the way he was without the degree since such artificial measurements were not necessary for a man of his creative depth and sensitivity. He had no need for superficial rank. He would never have "sold his soul" just to give him rank and access to remunerative employment. I loved him just as much, was proud to be his wife, and my love felt personal pain as I learned about the kind of pain he suffered.

The Leadership Services Staff of the YWCA sent me to two one-week summer camps; Camp Sequoiyah near Weaverville, North Carolina and Forest Beach, Michigan, across the lake from Chicago. I led film discussions in the mornings and in the afternoons I taught YWCA Executive Directors to make and play "Shepherd's Pipes." I came home from Forest Beach with mosquito bites that refused to heal. The slightest scratch would turn into a red saucer-size welt. Was I allergic? In desperation I went to a physician who gave me an injection of streptomycin. My body turned red and swollen all over. The cure was worse than the malady.

Early the next morning, I was awakened by Albert's gentle application of olive oil to my skin—all over like a baby.

"Be careful, don't get that on the mattress," I whimpered.

"Be quiet. I'm giving you a treatment," he spoke gently, but with authority.

After the olive oil, he put me in a full tub of hot water with a pound of Epsom salts. He followed the tub with another round of olive oil massage. Within twenty-four hours, I was healed and felt that my life had been saved by Albert's care and the wisdom of his special healing powers.

While I was finishing my job at the National YWCA, Albert went on one more bus trip. In Parkersburg, West Virginia, he found an "inexpensive" building that housed a music store and an apartment. His brother, Paul, encouraged him to buy it.

Albert had never given up an idea he had expressed during our long bus trips of having a gift shop, and in the not too distant future, he visualized "Trobian Institute," a school of our own.

I talked to Paul on the phone in the Parkersburg Hotel. "But, Paul," I said, "it could be three years before we would be self-supporting."

Chosen

CHAPTER 14

Parkersburg, West Virginia—Belpre, Ohio

"Oh, don't worry about money," Paul said, "Albert started me in business; now I will take care of whatever is needed. I'm turning over $50,000..." I was still skeptical as I put down the phone, (Paul was in real estate, construction, insurance, and a lumberyard) but if it was what Albert wanted, I would put my heart and soul into it. With Paul's down payment the building was ours.

We took a room at Pete's Motel down the street from our new address: 1816 East 7th Street, Parkersburg, West Virginia. It was the winter of 1954 and ice formed on the motel windows, but Albert went right to work on remodeling. Paul sent men from Pennsylvania to put down an oak floor. Albert's vision of a store, concert hall, and living quarters took shape. His plans were superb; he had a genius for space utilization and he supervised every little thing. The idea of Trobian Institute was a contribution to his lifelong dream of having his own school. There was a library room for instruction and discussion. The new store front, the piano and organ room, the concert hall with platform stage, two tiny restrooms and drinking fountain, the one hundred chairs with red velveteen seats, the new heating-cooling unit, the transfer of a bathroom to another space, all of this and other details were accomplished. The concert hall had beautiful lights and the reception room (also for the sale of pianos and organs) with its indirect lighting, dogwood panel, rose and green walls, was a decorator's delight. Many salesmen stopped and one New Yorker said to Albert, "Where do you think you are, 57th Street? This is West Virginia."

We moved from the motel to our own bedroom. Paul's funds ran out; the money I had saved ran out. During that hectic time when we were out of cash, Albert sold the kitchen table for a few dollars. What was left in the kitchen was an ironing board with adjustable height, on which we laid a piece of sheetrock to serve as a dining table. On an evening of intense frustration about our situation, the last bit of food available was a can of split pea soup. I had put water in it and as I stirred it I started to cry. I had not been complaining. My tears irritated Albert. I can't remember what he said, but it angered me so much that I kicked the improvised table and violently upset both bowls of pea soup. They were airborne and the soup painted the kitchen. If I had tried to paint I could not have covered more. I had never before given vent to anger. This should happen when we were hungry for our last bit of food?

It was no time for a battle of words. I crawled into bed thoroughly ashamed, took a fetal position, felt suicidal, hating my soul. I expected Albert to say more infuriating things. I was wrong. He quietly went about cleaning up the mess the soup had made, and he never again said anything to cause me anger and shame. We ate from a little garden Albert made at the rear of the building.

As had happened before when we were near desperation, there came a "guardian angel." Mrs. Garner and her husband came over from Belpre, Ohio, just across the Ohio River, knowing nothing about me except our radio ads for Trobian Music Company. She offered me the position of Choir Director at the First Congregational Church in Belpre for five dollars a week with transportation furnished. How we did stretch that five dollars!

I told Mrs. Garner I did not sing and did not play a keyboard instrument. She said Mae McAfee, a high school student, would continue as pianist and organist. The fact that I had no choral experience bothered me, but not Mrs. Garner, so I figured this was meant to be and accepted the job. Mae McAfee was a fine musician and understood my methods; we made a good team. I planned every second of each rehearsal and was pleasantly surprised at the results.

In the meantime we were living in our own building and continued to anticipate Trobian Music Company and Trobian Institute. The one hundred red velveteen concert hall chairs were in place and the stage was ready for a curtain. Dorothy Bailey, who lived in the corner house on the next block, came to see me about cello lessons. It was soon obvious to me that she was already a competent cellist. I described to her my preference for conducting over playing and that I had music available. She and I immediately conceived the idea of "The Little Orchestra" when she said, "Mrs. Staley will play, she's been a concertmaster, Mrs. Cruikshank will play viola, and Mrs. Greene will play violin." Other violins were added and our chamber music group of women was formed. A woman from Belpre requested string bass lessons, so she was added to the group. We had one rehearsal in the Trobian Institute concert hall and Albert was radiant with delight. The acoustics were fine.

193

Chosen

As a result of my work with the church choir, I was offered the music position in the Belpre Public Schools. In August before school started, I organized the band. I was not completely a newcomer and students and parents received me well. Each morning I walked across Parkersburg, across the Ohio River, across Belpre and worked with the marching band. It was necessary to get ready for an outdoor performance at a township fair. The band had uniforms discarded by the famous Parkersburg "Big Red Band." I fitted into one of the majorette jackets and had a white flannel skirt made with a red silk stripe sewn down each side. At the fair, I spent a little time showing off by playing cornet with my left hand while I conducted with my right, as I had seen my high school director perform.

From then on my job was totally time consuming day and night. There was no time to worry about our company or the Institute or Albert or me. Trobian Music Company was Albert's idea, not mine. Profits from the store were expected to provide funding for the institute. Looking at our advertisements after more than forty years, I can't help feeling that we were both demented, yet it led to my church choir job and the music position at Belpre, Ohio. The salary was enough to sustain us, but not enough to make payments on the outstanding bills.

During my first month on the job we were out of cash and had no idea what to do about it. Earlier I had been refused a loan at Household Finance where I was castigated for the situation we were in about our building. Once again it was Mrs. Garner who turned into a "guardian angel." Walking home after working with the band one day, I stopped at the little local library she operated. Without my asking or even hinting, Mrs. Garner said, as she delved into her bosom,

"Let's go to the First National Bank,"and drew out a handkerchief enclosing four ten dollar bills. That forty dollars saw us through to my first paycheck when she was promptly repaid.

Albert was taken to court by electrical and construction creditors. They had been paid weekly, but now they were not being paid. On Thursday, the first day of March 1955, the store was to open, but instead it closed. That was the day the property was put for sale by the Circuit Court of Woods County, West Virginia. We had to find new living quarters quickly or be evicted. We got temporary "light housekeeping rooms" in someone's house. In a few weeks we moved to an apartment on Market Street, close to downtown Parkersburg.

I was not aware until long after that my name was on the bank loan for the building. Albert walked over to the Belpre Band Room (a separate building) to tell me the news that the building would be offered for sale on March 31, 1955. I was never called to court. I treated the entire episode as if I were looking on as an outsider. Albert was quietly emotionally distraught. Because they were already paid for, it made him happy to give the 100 concert hall chairs to the First Congregational church.

After settling in our new apartment the next important episode in our lives was my purchase of an automobile. It was picked out for us by the skilled mechanic husband of a favorite waitress at Pete's Motel. For $300 I bought a 1946 deluxe edition, light green, Plymouth club coupe with a choke and throttle. Mrs. Crawford, a friend from the local YWCA board taught me to drive. The clutch had to be replaced after my learning period, but from then on we had a reliable car. After all my walking, it seemed miraculous to me to simply be seated while crossing the Ohio River. Albert made it clear that it was my car, not his, and he had no wish to drive it. Later he did maintain his driver's license for many years, out of fear of an emergency. He explained his lack of interest in driving.

"Paul and I had acquired a Model A. I was driving behind a hit-and-run driver who hit a child. I stopped and took the child to the hospital for examination. The child's parents accused me of having hit the child. There was minimal injury to the child and the case was dropped. Nobody believed that I had seen the other driver. After that I never wanted to drive again."

Albert busied himself with volunteer work for the Parkersburg YWCA, painting and cleaning the living quarters for transients or any women who wanted to stay at the "Y". He was good at making the place more livable.

My second year at Belpre was even busier than the first. "The Little Orchestra" rehearsed in the Belpre band room. Before Christmas, a Band Boosters concert was given and the orchestra played for the operetta at the high school in the spring. We were invited to present a concert in November for *The Women's Club* of Sistersville, West Virginia. For that program, in addition to conducting, I played clarinet on a Mozart Quintet, and horn on my own arrangement of three Bach chorales. It was an auspicious occasion; we were proud and rightfully so. I was grateful to Mrs. Staley and Mrs. Bailey—they had made the group possible, but it was my choice of music that made it so enjoyable.

Although a community orchestra had originally been Albert's idea, the women of the orchestra were the nucleus for the formation of the Mid Ohio Valley Symphony, conducted by Joseph Perkovic, director of the Marietta High School Orchestra. This group was formed right after we started

inviting men to play with our women's group. I played First
Horn, some people wanted me to conduct (which I would
have loved) but I played it cool, no need to push.

The Methodist church offered me $10 a week to direct
their choir. I declined, but coached a local woman to do it.
Word got around; the Congregational Church raised my pay
to $10. On Good Friday, the choir presented a cantata for the
worship service. We were all very pleased with it. The choir
sang one night at the local television station; television was
just becoming known to the general public.

There were all sorts of events to keep me busy. As an
Associate Member of the American Guild of Organists, I
played trumpet on one of their programs. The county music
association named me president-elect. Band members were
taken by bus to several Saturday workshops at Ohio
University. There were several parades and football shows,
and new uniforms in school colors were purchased by the
Band Boosters.

It was good that I now had my car because the Junior High
students moved to a building several blocks from the high
school.

For the final county music event of the year, a band and
choral festival was held on Saturday in the Marietta College
Field House. Each of our band directors had chosen a
selection for the "Select 500 Piece Band", the final
performing group. I had chosen a piece I felt would work
well for a large group; *Brass Band Blues* by Charles
Hathaway. In my rehearsal, I had first checked on a possible
problem in the trombone section; "First I want to hear the
trombones at letter A. Remember that's B-natural in fourth
position, not B-flat." The rehearsal was excellent.

That evening Albert had taken a bus to Marietta and met

me for dinner at a hotel. I was well dressed in my good black conducting dress and black pumps. Douglas Hess, the county music association president, introduced me (the only woman) with "We have saved the best 'til last." That made me feel great. Then the entire band stood up. Everything felt really fine. My conducting of that "Select 500 Piece Band" was done with a flair and provided thrilling entertainment for the audience. I received many compliments—a once in a lifetime triumph never to be forgotten.

That was the spring of 1956. I realized my overly busy life was neglecting Albert, and that for his health and well being he should get away from Parkersburg. I resigned my position at Belpre, signed up Albert and myself in employment agencies, and helped Albert study job openings.

A group of band parents came over to our Market Street apartment with a petition to get me to stay another year. In reality the job and excessive community involvement (I was an officer in nine organizations) was wonderful, but I began to feel that another year would be bad for both Albert and me. I was physically exhausted and Albert was vocationally frustrated. We both needed a change.

Parkersburg, West Virginia   Belpre, Ohio

THE WOMAN'S CLUB
of
Sistersville, West Virginia
presents

The Little Orchestra

HELEN REED TROBIAN
Conductor

NOVEMBER 29, 1955 — 8:00 P.M.
THE FIRST METHODIST CHURCH

Program

I

ine Kleine Nachtmusik — Serenade..........................W. A. Mozart
heme from Piano Sonata in A
inuet from Don Giovanni
legro from Symphony No. 12

II

uintette in A — Clarinet and Strings ....W. A. Mozart
    Allegro, Minuet, Trio
iree Chorales — Horn and Strings..........................J. S. Bach
    Jesu Meine Freude
    Christ Lag in Todesbanden
    Ach Gott, Wie Manches Herzlied

INTERMISSION

III

Concerto No. 13...Charles Avison
    Allegro
    Amoroso
    Allegro
Sinfonietta in D..W. A. Mozart
    Allegro
    Andante
    Molto Allegro

IV

Andante Cantabile...Tschaikowsky
Music from *Kismet*..........................Wright - Forrest - Borodin
To a Wild Rose...Edward McDowell
String Quartet, Opus 48...I. Pleyel
    Allegro

THE LITTLE ORCHESTRA

VIOLINS
    Mrs. Seva Wise Stealey
    Mrs. Winona Squires
    Mrs. Wheaton Shearman
    Miss Florence Adams
    Mrs. Faye P. Greene
DOUBLE BASS
    Mrs. Dee Keenan

VIOLA
    Mrs. Dwight Cruikshank
VIOLONCELLO
    Mrs. Gordon Bailey
WIND INSTRUMENTS
    Mrs. Albert Trobian

199

Chosen

Little Orchestra
Parkersburg and Belpre - 1955

CHAPTER 15

Happy Chicago Years

In the summer of 1956, Albert had a lead on a job in Cook County, Illinois, so we left Parkersburg and loaded the car for a trip to Chicago. Albert's interview did not achieve the desired result, so we visited employment agencies in Chicago and for the next three years both of us were "satisfied" with our employment situations. Albert was hired for a low level job at the National Safety Council where he unloaded paper at the dock, wrapped packages of leaflets, ran a film projector for meetings and sometimes mopped floors. I was employed as an assistant to the Purchasing Agent/Office Manager at MusiCraft where my work consisted of routine clerical chores. I had an unusually fortunate scheduling arrangement; I could punch the time clock on my particular schedule or work full time whenever I preferred. From 8:00 a.m. to 10:00 a.m., I practiced on instruments in a rented studio at the Fine Arts Building on Michigan Avenue. I took short-term lessons from symphony personnel on flute, horn, cello, trumpet, and oboe reed making. I seemed to be preparing for an unknown future as my work and my continuing studies fell comfortably into place.

Our first living quarters were undesirable, but fortunately we were able to move to a tiny apartment in a building next

door. One night in that place during a siege of flu, I fainted.
Albert humped up all the bed covers and rolled me over them
to bring me back to consciousness. He then ran a few blocks
to a small private hospital and came back with a refugee
doctor who took one look at me, prescribed vitamins, and
said, "You sick, you stay in bed, you owe me ten dollars."
We laughed about that for years and would repeat it if one of
us sneezed. In the same building, when a desirable apartment
became available, we moved to it and enjoyed decorating it to
suit ourselves.

At the Loop Center YWCA, I organized a small chamber
music group. An old unoccupied church in our neighborhood
was leased (or given) by the Methodists to a Nisei group, with
the understanding it would serve the community. Albert and
I and one other white couple represented the "community."
Albert became a volunteer sexton and I was drafted as a choir
director. This time I had experience. We became members
of the Official Board of the *Christian Fellowship Church
(Methodist)* on Sheridan Road. Albert spent all his spare time
cleaning and fixing up the church, which had not been
occupied for some time. We enjoyed our friendship with our
Nisei church members. Albert even made **gnocchi** to take to
the Wednesday night church supper. Everybody liked it.
Chicago was a delightful change of pace for us. We both got
our jobs right away and stayed on them for three years even
though they didn't pay much. We each had community
service responsibilities. Albert was in excellent physical and
mental health. In my case, after being treated for everything
except a fibroid tumor, my cello teacher recognized my need
for medical attention by taking me to her doctor. I wound up
in the hospital with a hysterectomy. When I came back to my
room after time in the recovery room, the nurse held a little

pan to my lips—Albert turned green and bolted for the Men's Room where he told me he threw up. Neither of us ever discussed our inability to have children. We simply took for granted that it wasn't meant to be.

A highlight of my music studies was being sent by my horn instructor, the famous Max Pottag, to play in the horn workshop led by James Chambers (New York Philharmonic) at the 1958 Meeting of the American Symphony Orchestra League in Sioux City, Iowa. At the workshop (we all played double horns) I was thrilled when Chambers commended me as the first one who could demonstrate tuning both horns together perfectly. Our lives were full with our work and the things we were doing for the church and the "Y". We had many friends and were respected as a capable couple.

I have a vivid memory of a special evening downtown. Albert and I had agreed to meet at the Palmer House. He was to go home from work, dress in his new suit, and meet me at the stated time. I went to the Palmer House entry and watched the subway exit. He appeared, all dressed up, exuding virility and happiness. He waved with magnificent exuberance. He was wonderful. At dinner Albert started telling me about Garibaldi, and in contrast to his usual demure demeanor, he sang a little. The other diners were not disturbed. They seemed to enjoy our happiness with us.

Settled in the new apartment, Albert began to feel that his mission in life was not being served by his work at the National Safety Council. The Council bought new typewriters and made a number of Royal typewriters available free to employees. Albert brought one home (It was given to the church later).

We prepared a one-page abbreviated resume letter with our pictures printed in the upper left-hand corner. We bought a

Directory of Colleges and Universities and checked the ones
we planned to send our letter. Albert sat at his second hand
Royal and diligently typed the envelopes. I said, "Don't make
envelopes for Texas, I don't think I'd like it." He did anyway
and that is where I spent the happiest four years of my
professional life!

Wiley College was one of several schools that our church
contributed to and was one of the very few that responded to
the letter. We went to the Sheraton Hotel where there were
telephone booths and a long distance operator to serve the
public. Albert called the president of Wiley College in
Marshall, Texas and I didn't need to talk at all. There were
two jobs for which the two of us were qualified. We received
a wire confirming our employment.

I had to renew my driver's license after not driving for
three years. In Chicago it was better to take the bus. I had to
go to Evanston where I practically failed the test due to my
lack of attention to one-way streets, something Parkersburg
and Belpre had not had. The examiner said, "Well, I'll pass
you, but for goodness sake, be careful!" We loaded the car
and took off for Texas.

CHAPTER 16

Wiley College, Marshall, Texas

We arrived in Marshall, Texas on Friday, September 11th, 1959. After we checked into Hotel Marshall, the only hotel in town, we made an exploratory trip to Wiley College so we would know where to go for the faculty conference the next day. I just drove around until I found it. Saturday morning we left the hotel at 7:30.

The conference was held on the first floor of the library, the faculty sitting at tables. As the only faculty of non-color, Albert and I were seated conspicuously where we could be observed by everyone. Many long, boring speeches were read until 12:30. There was no break, no interaction, and no opportunity to ask questions. We were told to have lunch in the cafeteria. When we broke for lunch, we were greeted congenially, especially by Mr. Fred Tillis of the music faculty, who made immediate arrangements for all music majors playing wind instrument to take private lessons. After lunch there was nothing to do but go back to the hotel.

Sunday morning we went to the Methodist Church next door to the hotel. Before the sermon all guests were asked to stand and introduce themselves. Albert told me to introduce us. I announced,

"We are new members of the Wiley College faculty." We

sensed a peculiar feeling in the congregation, which I thought was strange because Wiley was related to the Methodist Church. At that time we did not know that the relationship was distant—the "Central Jurisdiction" was the Methodist segregated bureaucracy for all the black churches. At the close of the service when the minister was shaking hands with the departing Methodists, he deliberately turned his back and walked away from us. We were naïve, but not totally ignorant of race prejudice, so we left quietly. It had not occurred to us that we would meet prejudice at this level.

The next Sunday we attended the First Baptist Church, sat near the rear, and made a hasty exit. As we were having Sunday dinner in the dining room of the hotel, a woman came over to our table.

"I saw you at church this morning and want to welcome you. My husband is president of the college here."

We thanked her politely, inwardly reminded ourselves that there were two other colleges in town, and left her wondering who we were. In the short space of one week, we had already learned that Negro and white people were not supposed to associate. Much later we learned that there were state and local laws prohibiting eating together.

At the college the administration, faculty, and students accepted us fully. I think they thought we were too simple minded to realize the difference between them and us. We were, in a sense, being held on a pedestal; we were treated so well we were spoiled as though we were special guests.

Our search for living quarters was difficult. White people with apartments to rent rejected us. We began to feel the effects of their deeply imbedded race prejudice. We had no way of anticipating the sit-ins that would occur in the spring of that year, and the disruption they would cause to the town

and the nation. Realizing we could not afford to stay at Hotel
Marshall, we moved to a miserable motel cabin. Motels in
those days provided central bathing and latrine facilities and
beds in a series of small primitive cabins.

Mrs. White, a faculty member, had a house for rent she
had inherited from her recently deceased mother. It was
across from a triangle where she and her husband and son
lived, on the corner of South Grove Street and University
Avenue, both muddy streets a couple of blocks from Wiley
College.

The house was primitive with a back porch beyond
redemption. Albert visualized its potential while I could not
imagine how our two small salaries would ever buy furniture
and appliances and make it comfortable. I stood in front of
the house and said, "Don't talk to me about this house. It's
not livable." Albert didn't argue. He waited until we had
suffered through a few more nights in an insect infested cabin.
By that time I was ready to agree with anything he would
recommend. He rented the house and went right to work on
it. The back porch was reduced to a cement slab. He had a
vent placed on the hot water heater. He engaged an electrician
to put switches as an alternative to fumbling in the dark until
a light bulb hit his nose. He put a stove (natural gas) in each
room. He was very busy checking on everything for our
creature comfort.

We shopped for furniture, drapes, curtains, rugs, and
kitchen appliances. Albert, as usual, had no concept of
money, but he gave the impression of being a good credit risk.
It must have been our destiny to meet a furniture store owner
who took pity on us. (Could he have been a "guardian
angel?")

All at once we bought a refrigerator, gas range, dining

table with six chairs, a cherry bed and matching chest, a Posturpedic mattress, a three-piece Simmons couch and three Basset tables to go with it. Prices were greatly reduced because of the volume of our purchase and perhaps because the man recognized our situation.

In the dining room, one wall had been disfigured by a leaky roof. Albert installed a wall-to-wall drape that also covered an air conditioner and beautified the room. We bought a piece of Curtis Mathes furniture housing a Garrard changer and an amplifier, which served handsomely as a buffet. The back bedroom became a study room. Albert built a large study table for me, a smaller one for himself, and a series of bookcases. After he built several bookcases for college offices, he created a special case for my studio in Smith-Nooks Music Hall. It housed instruments and music. A rod was installed so that the drape brought from our Chicago apartment covered the case and the entire back wall of the studio, making a beautiful place for private lessons.

Albert got a splendid dark red rug remnant that fitted our front hall. For the living/dining area he personally installed wall-to-wall carpeting. It was surprising how that little old house turned into a pleasant home. People loved to come to our home. It was simple, but effective. I felt like a newlywed.

I was accustomed to having my hair done weekly. The woman downtown that accepted me as her client asked many questions. I kept my answers brief. Finally it came out that my husband and I worked at Wiley College.

"Your husband is not...?" she asked in a hoarse voice, unable to get the world *Negro* out.

"No, he's Italian, well, he's American, but his parents came from Italy." That didn't seem to help. She was so nervous that my neck got burned. It was obvious I was not welcome. I tried several other places, none of which did good work. Eventually I found a shop in a woman's home where I was not regarded as a dangerous alien.

My first semester's teaching consisted of giving private lessons on wind instruments all day, Monday through Friday, and two hours on Tuesday and Thursday nights. There were fifty music majors; many planning to become band directors. With Mr. Tillis's endorsement, I organized a Brass Choir. After six rehearsals the group proved it was capable of playing serious historical music as well as contemporary works. The Brass Choir distinguished itself with concerts and a coast-to-coast radio program for the United Negro College Fund. A tape for the broadcast was made in an ice cold recording studio in Shreveport along with a vocal ensemble conducted by Henrietta McCallum. We were recording during an ice storm that uprooted large old pine trees.

As chairman of the Department of Elementary Education, Albert had to become acquainted with local schools where he would someday be placing student teachers. He seemed to get along well with his contacts in the schools, but he frequently related his frustration about his departmental meetings. I'm sure he wanted to imbue his colleagues, one man and two women, with a philosophical orientation to elementary school teaching. They expected something more on the level of how to make effective bulletin boards for each season. He would come home and say, "Soon as I'm beginning to make a point, one of the women will say, 'Well, fine. Now I gotta go home and cook.'"

We had been invited to a fish fry dinner at the home of Dr. Leonard Haynes, a professor of religion and humanities and ordained minister. He had given me a little piece of paper with directions about how to get to their home. I was driving slowly when suddenly the local police stopped me.

"Let me see your license." My license and tag were still from Illinois.

"What did I do wrong, officer?"

"Nothing, we stop all out of state cars on this road. You were driving too slow." Then he wanted to know where we were going and why. I showed the slip of paper with directions since I had never been there and didn't really know how to say where it was.

"Follow me, I'll escort you." We arrived at the Haynes' home under police surveillance. We got out of our car and the policeman said, "Now you children be good!" We just said, "Thank you."

Dr. Haynes was impressed with Albert's grasp of philosophy and religion, especially his concept of "the giving of Grace." Later when Dr. Haynes would meet me on campus he would shake hands with me saying, "Today I'm giving Grace."

Albert's special concept of the giving of Grace cannot be easily described, only felt or surmised. He didn't talk much about it. Perhaps it was a way of accepting each person from a world perspective as one he could bless, live in peace and harmony with, promoting universal brotherhood. It was as though his personal **self** was available to render a healing—yet devoid of any self-love or ego I myself believe he had some type of special healing powers. When he disliked someone, as he rarely did, it made him sick.

NOTE: Leonard Haynes III became Assistant Secretary of Education under the Bush administration. When we went to the fish dinner he was about 12. He returned from Washington to work in a Louisiana University. His father had received his Ph.D. at age nineteen.

During the second semester of our first year at Wiley College, the "sit-ins" occurred. The spring of 1960 was full of civil rights events. Our students, following the sit-ins in Greensboro, N. C. and in Houston, Texas, attempted to be served at a lunch counter in a downtown drug store and counters in Woolworth's. After that they marched to the county courthouse to protest the arrest of "lunch counter sit-down demonstrators" as a local newspaper put it. A newspaper photo in *The Shreveport Times* dated March 31, 1960 showed firemen holding a hose on students from Wiley and Bishop colleges.

We were sympathetic to the students, but never participated in any speeches or marches. As the only two people of non-color on the faculty that year, we learned that we were under scrutiny by persons on both sides of the conflict, from the Texas Highway Patrol to the local white banker. We just behaved normally.

There was one dramatic incident during which Albert was able to educate the local law men and reduce their fears. His office was in the old Pemberton House, about two blocks up the road from our home. One evening he was carrying books and papers, starting for home when a group of officers confronted him, told him to get into their car to be taken to jail. In those days to be taken to jail was like having a badge of honor. Albert had no intention of going with the officers because he had no need to go. The muscles he had developed working at the National Safety Council were still strong, so when an officer tried to put him into the car he resisted. He came home and said, "Guess what happened to me? They grabbed me, but I was stronger than they were. I just gently, but firmly, pushed them aside with one arm." Any white person seen with a Negro was considered circumspect as though a potential instigator of a riot. He wrote in his second semester journal an account of what happened to him on Saturday night, March 26, 1960, entitled *The Sheriffs Stop*.

"Hey there, come here." There were three county sheriffs in a police car. "What's your name? What are you doing in this neighborhood? Where do you live? Where were you born?" There was an initial period of adjustment during which I answered their questions. After I admitted I had been talking with students on campus and that they were my friends, "they are my students," serenity developed and they expressed their opinions that:

(1) Negroes (that's not what they called them) have no self-discipline, they get drunk.

(2) They would fail a 7th grade exam, they can't be educated, will always be wild, are not safe, and they will turn on you.

(3) God made them to be segregated, different; (They are not people is the gist of the argument.)

(4) Some big old n___s would take care of the sit-downs themselves if they asked them.

(5) One sheriff said, "If one gets close to me, I would not hesitate to shoot, FBI or not."

(6) White people from the north are stirring them up; they would not be troublesome otherwise.

(7) Money from Marshall and rich whites goes to Negro colleges and now look what thanks they're getting.

(8) Communists are causing the trouble. (I was asked if I had ever been to Russia.)

(9) Schools are up-to-date for Negroes and they should stay in them.

(10) A white man (like me) should not lower himself to their level by teaching them.

(11) Some of these old farmers will be "looking for you", better get out of town, etc.

(12) Would a child of mine be permitted to marry a Negro?

Journal entry: The fear and the inconsistency are secular.

The points I made were that:

(1) God tells me I should be here.

(2) They (the sheriffs) and Marshall people are sincere persons.

(3) If you only knew how nice our Wiley students really are you wouldn't be afraid.

(4) I don't believe in violence myself and had nothing to do with the sit-downs.

(5) Some day white southerners will be glad I'm here, that I'm doing good for all concerned.

(6) I call them Negroes (not "niggers.")

(7) They are not quite as educated as students in white schools, but then they have had teachers who were not as good.

(8) Marriage is a divine thing, and if love happened it would be God's will.

(9) This is a passing form of protest (sit-downs) and whites as Christians should be patient and show mercy.

(10) The officers have an obligation to protect all in the line of duty (including myself).

(11) I will ask God as to what I should do.

(12) Would **you** leave? "Situation not the same."
(13) On parting, I said, "God bless you all," and
also that Hackney (local banker) knows I'm here,
Southern whites are very kind people. I defused
the impending threat of violence.

When Albert told Reverend McCallum, a religion
professor, that the sheriffs had stopped him, he said, "They
knew everything they asked you already. They only wanted
to find out what you'd say. Their idea was to frighten you."

In later months we would be driving in Marshall and I
would see an officer tipping his big hat to us.

"Who is that?"

"Oh, that's one of my county sheriff friends." Whatever
he said to them had been effective. We did receive a few
threatening phone calls. "I'm not threatening you, but if I
were you, I'd get out of town." We felt quite safe in our
home.

Wiley students marched to the Courthouse and sang
hymns. The "city fathers" turned fire hoses on them. They
did not lose their dignity, retaining their composure as they
returned to the campus. They had an unusual degree of faith
in what they were doing. There was little or no disruption to
their studies. They seemed so dedicated and committed to
self-improvement with spiritual overtones during the spring
of 1960. Reading the editorials from newspapers of that era
makes one wonder at the amazing illogical defenses claimed.
There was a point when police officers confused Albert with
a light skinned Bishop College professor, a former
Communist, who just happened to be in Woolworth's during
a sit-down.

I was honored to receive an invitation to give the "Women's Keynote Address" at the 30th annual Lacy Kirk Williams Ministers' Institute on May 3, 1960 at Bishop College. After I had agreed to make the speech, Roscoe Turner, one of my trombone students, happened to meet me in the Music Hall.

"I hear the Brass Choir is going to play at Bishop," he said.

"Where did you hear this, I don't know anything about it. I have been asked to give an address."

"Oh, I just thought it was to be the Brass Choir."

"What's the matter? Don't you think I can make a speech?" "Well, I don't know. I've never heard you make one, but wouldn't it be better if you took the Brass Choir?" I assured him I agreed, but at present I was preparing a speech.

That program started at 7:00 p.m. A series of preliminary episodes included music by the Bishop College Choir and "devotions" by Rev. Banks who preached a full-length sermon, then the introduction of me by a woman who had never met me. By this time I was thoroughly conscious of what was expected of me. I commended the choir and previous speakers, recounted what Roscoe Turner had said. The audience was receiving me well. A great feeling of privileged responsibility swelled over me as I looked out at some seven hundred ministers and wives. My address, as assigned, was "Communicating the Gospel through Religious Education." Later I was commended by members of the Bishop faculty.

The next day I spoke informally to a group of women. That afternoon Albert and I attended a group meeting with some Bishop students. One gave an account of a sit-in by himself and several other young men.

They were seated at the lunch counter in the local bus station. An officer came in brandishing a pistol and yelling, "Get up and leave or I'll shoot." The young men did not move. "Leave or I'll shoot." After several more threats the somewhat overweight middle-aged Texan became desperate. According to the student he behaved "like a two year old." "Oh, PLEASE, won't you please leave 'cause I'm a gonna lose my job." At that the young men slid off the counter seats, said nothing and left. Another story from those days was also told at Bishop. Parents would call up the president and say, "Dr. Curry, don't you let my son go on those sit-ins. I don't want him killed." Later after the sit-ins appeared to have run their course, parents would come to the campus and say, "My son, he's a hero." During that period of time when Wiley students were in jail, the Bell Tower on campus would be rung to signal to the community when they had returned to campus. Once when I thought I should visit the women in jail, I was saved from that unnecessary experience by their release. I was so glad to hear the bell ring.

After our first semester (1959-60), I taught a variety of Music Education classes, conducting, orchestration, brass and percussion, and string classes for the music majors, in addition to giving private lessons. During the second and third years of our four years at Wiley, I held the title of Chair of the Division of Education. That was only because I was the only one with the necessary credentials to meet accreditation standards. My duties were to sign papers when asked, and to hold monthly meetings. We held them in the Music Hall. Albert was the best secretary possible, keeping almost verbatim notes. Everyone knew that Mr. Chandler was in charge of all the Education departments and courses and that I was just the "titular" head of the division.

After our first year we went back to Chicago for the hot summer months. Albert spent time preparing for a one-day, all college seminar. I worked part time at MusiCraft and prepared a plan and resources for a one-day clarinet clinic to serve the bands and directors that came to a Band Festival and Sight Reading clinic that Mr. Tillis conducted annually.

During the second year, Mr. Fred Hall came as instructor of speech and drama. He had just completed his MA at Boston University. In the spring semester, Mr. Hall produced Lorraine Hansberry's *Raisin in the Sun*, a play that both black and white people had either seen or at least heard about from its successes in New York, Chicago, and other places. The play deals with, among a few other things, discrimination in housing and calls for one white man to play a real estate agent; all other characters are black. The play was presented at Wiley during the week of "Founders Observance," March 19-25, 1962.

Mr. Hall asked Albert to play Karl Lindner, the real estate man. Albert refused on the grounds that he was not a capable actor, never had been, and he simply did not want to do it. Mr. Hall asked me to talk him into it. I suggested a part time man from Centenary College. "No, I want Mr. Trobian, you convince him." So I did. He had trouble learning his lines. The play itself allowed for Karl Lindner to be nervous. That worked out naturally. There was something special, sort of tongue-in-cheek, about the way Albert delivered his parting lines: "I hope you folks know what you are doing!"; that the audience found highly amusing. For the remainder of the semester, Albert was a celebrity. The play was taken to Jarvis Christian College in Hawkins, Texas (associated with Texas Christian College in Fort Worth) and was reported to have been a big success there. While the play was in rehearsal, a young woman named Liewanda became friendly with Albert. Getting ready to go to rehearsal one evening, Albert was in the kitchen collecting nuts.

"What are those for?" I asked.

"They're for Liewanda's pet squirrel she keeps in a box in her dorm room."

"Oh my! Be careful! That's illegal you know. Your friendship with the Dean of Women will be jeopardized if she finds out." He took the nuts with him. I knew Dean Hollis was fond of Albert. He had a way with older women, but he should have known not to encourage the keeping of a "rodent" in a dorm room.

Later there was a dance in the gym. I think it was equivalent to a Debutante Ball. Liewanda wanted to go, but it was necessary to have a "father" to dance with and she had none. Albert could not dance and it would have been "inappropriate" for him. At the last minute Albert and I talked Dr. Korossy into going as her "father." He was a Rumanian refugee. It was too late to rent a tux, so we fixed him up in his dark blue suit, a stiff white shirt, and I supplied a bow tie. He was an excellent dancer and Liewanda was thrilled.

Dr. Korossy was not accustomed to American ways but he was learning. When we were going in our car, Korossy liked to open the car door for me. Albert said, "Don't do that. This is America. We treat women as equals." Albert was an early feminist. He regarded so-called gentlemanly behavior as chauvinist—"An attitude of superiority toward members of the opposite sex." It just came naturally to him. Korossy caught on for the moment, but another time when Albert was not present he said, "Your husband not here. I open door for you." He returned from Easter vacation with a young woman from New York he said was his wife.

There was a faculty talent show in the Chapel one evening. Albert accepted that we would participate. He devised an unusual skit for us using Recorder Flutes (blockflutes) that we called "A Man and Wife Conversation." Here was the scenario: All we needed was a straight chair and a small table. Albert sat on the chair with a soprano recorder. I had a matching soprano recorder on the table. At the beginning I stood playing wildly, ferociously, on a tiny sopranino flute, the highest. I went up and down the scale, let the instrument speak and squeal, thereby portraying the wife ranting and raving at length, figuratively speaking. Albert would just play two notes, sounding like "poo poot." Gradually I stopped the sopranino, picked up the soprano and played less wildly. Albert would still play his two notes, but gradually he moved into a tune while I slowly moved into playing the same melody. The skit finished by my momentarily sitting on his lap playing in unison. We never put anything on paper and we rehearsed at home only once. We were the hit of the evening. People commented on our presentation for weeks.

I was appointed Chairman of the Library Committee. Having no idea what was expected, I asked Mrs. Mason, the Librarian, "What does the Library Committee do?" She said that since she had been there, as far as she knew, it had not done anything. That struck me as funny.

After talking with Albert we conceived a "grand plan." We would publish a journal of writing by students and faculty. I conceived of my typing on my new IBM Proportional on Gestetner stencils and Albert running our home machine in our center hall. The college did not furnish any duplicating service, so we had our own at home. I knew it would be a big job, but Albert was all for it. Bulletin Board announcements invited participants and included an invitation to all whose writing would be accepted for publication to attend an autographing tea on May 1st, the publication date set for WILEY REFLECTIONS. The art teacher, Miss Pettis, designed the cover. Three hundred copies were made. Each of the thirty-three authors were entitled to a free copy. The others were to be sold. How the project was financed I don't remember, but Albert and I must have financed much of it. When all the pages had been typed and collated, Albert arranged for the cover and binding to be done at a local print shop. Front material, back pagers, poetry, articles, and a short story all came to seventy-five pages. The collating was done in our dining room. Sometime during April the college was host to a visiting distinguished science professor. While I was teaching, Albert invited the guest to our house to continue the conversation they had started. When I got home that evening, I was surprised to see how much collating had been done. Albert said, "I just told the visitor to pick up pages as we walked around the table talking. He didn't mind." I was amazed that Albert could have gotten a scientist, a person of importance, to get things done. Looking back on that year, I wonder how we could have done so much.

Since the college was related to the Ebeneezer Methodist church, it was the one we attended. During our second year, a new minister, Rev. Bonner, came to our home for a "pastoral call." He made it clear that we were fully expected to join Ebeneezer, so the next Sunday when the invitation was given, Albert poked me and we walked down the aisle and became members.

I was always easily amused at church services, although I did have respect for Episcopalian practices. So much of the ritual I grew up with seemed ridiculous to me, but I never said so. At Ebeneezer Methodist in Marshall, Texas, I was amazed that right in the middle of the Communion Service they would take time out for reports from the "Building Fund Groups" and then return to the latter half of the Communion.

One Sunday morning at Ebeneezer, we were seated near the back of the sanctuary on the right side. We had no way to avoid being conspicuous. This particular morning, the minister, who had a deep southern drawl, had gotten into the sermon and chose to draw out to extreme length, "You must be b-o-o-ne again." I was trying not to laugh. Everyone else seemed devout. Albert, who could easily read my mind, looked at me with a slight smile and twinkling eye, and I could not help but burst into silent laughter. After church a woman I didn't know asked me, "Did you get **happy** in church today?"

I answered, "Well, sort of, I was inspired by the born again message, unaccustomed as I am to southern drawl."

Albert was invited to belong to the Men's Group and I was invited to be a member of Circle Four. I had no idea what was entailed. A long-standing tradition of monthly meetings in member's homes included certain precisely defined rituals. For both Men's and Women's groups, a hot meal, including hot rolls and punch, would be served immediately after the meeting, and one designated member would stand and present a flowery commendation to the host or hostess, and always say, "a delicious repast was enjoyed by all."

By the time it was my turn to invite Circle Four, I had learned what was expected. It was also tradition that the hostess kiss each member on the lips as she entered the home. I wasn't sure if I should do that; it worried me. However, when it was my turn, it was raining and women got their shoes muddy just getting to our front door, so I greeted guests with paper towels and directed them to the bathroom to clean their shoes. While we were in Marshall, this event happened only once for me and once for Albert. Albert did fine with his dinner, with my help, then he told me that there were no women around at the Men's Meetings, so I went to my studio in the Fine Arts Building. The main feature of his dinner was rigatoni with thin beef steaks, served from a large casserole with two candles underneath.

For the women, I prepared rigatoni and a Waldorf salad with grapes that had been seeded and skinned. Albert's study table, covered with a tablecloth, supported the punch bowl. The next day it was all I could do to get out of bed, but the episode was a success.

Several times we entertained student groups. When my conducting class had produced a Sunday evening service at the church, the class came to our house afterward for a celebration. They were very proud and I was very proud of them. When I was preparing the food, Albert said, "Whatever you're planning, just double it. Provide some paper bags and plenty of paper napkins so they can take some back to the dorms." This we did and the students were lavish with their praise. There were no community events to which they could go so an invitation to our house was considered a social event of importance.

We were invited to the International Fellowship, which consisted of the Indian faculty members and one white woman, a wealthy widow on the south side of town. Dr. C. C. Thomas, a dark Indian religion professor, was married to a white woman with a Mennonite background. When the fellowship met at our house we invited Mr. and Mrs. Wilburn, a new Negro couple on the faculty. The white woman who had entertained us once declined to come. She felt she could not come into the "N" neighborhood and dine with Negroes. Anyway, we had quite a crowd. We added two tables to our dining room table and borrowed chairs from the Music Department. Albert and I provided rigatoni and a tossed salad. The Indian women cooked in our kitchen. Mrs. Thomas brought her specialty: curried chicken in a pressure cooker.

The main dish was prepared by one of the Indian wives with Albert and me looking on. She brought her large steel pot, splashed a little oil in the bottom and with her own sharp little scissors cut tiny pieces of very small hot peppers into it. In another pot, potatoes were cooked for mashing. Two packages of frozen cauliflower and two packages of frozen peas were put into the pot. After the addition of the mashed potatoes, spices were added, curry and cumin. That mixture was all mashed together and served from one of our extra large Italian dishes. It was said to be exceptionally good. It was a noisy evening and everyone seemed quite happy.

Some other home entertaining was sometimes done after the four o'clock Vespers that occurred each Sunday afternoon. This we did by spontaneously (we had planned ahead) asking various faculty persons if they would care to go home with us for a visit and a snack. This too was successful.

Still not accustomed to the Texas heat, the second summer we went to Denver. I took a Kelly Girl job as a typist in a bank. One of the bankers was working toward a specialist's diploma in mortgage lending. He was not very nice to work for, but we enjoyed Denver anyway. We especially liked having dinner at a restaurant that employed four vocal students to sing opera excerpts and a waiter that bragged continuously about "such good Denver water." We also attended a few university addresses.

Our third year at Wiley was the final year for Bishop College in Marshall. New buildings were built on a new campus in Dallas. Albert and I had occasionally had lunch at Bishop, sometimes with Miss Inez Jenkins, Dean of Women and Director of Bishop Hall, a dormitory for women. On a Saturday afternoon, while we were enjoying a visit from the Ridgel's, former Wiley faculty who had moved to Kentucky, a knock came on the door. A taxi driver held a piece of paper for me to read, saying he was not to leave until I had complied with Dean Jenkin's request. The note said she had to buy a new coat for Easter because her public expected her to look good and she knew of no one but us to ask for cash to assist in said purchase. *Give $15 to the cab driver.* I did not have $15. It was embarrassing while guests were there. I asked Albert if he had anything in his wallet. He didn't know but found the wallet. I gave $15 to the driver. He wasn't about to leave without it. She had already borrowed from us without repayment. Later we heard, "She owes everybody in town."

Dean Jenkins was the last person, according to her, to leave the bishop campus. Albert had promised her that on the day scheduled for her departure, we would take her to an early morning train. We did. After we got to the train station she remembered she had left her Bible and a couple of magazines on a chair in Bishop Hall. She had put the Hall keys in a mailbox at a house down the street where the grounds custodian lived.

I was **assigned** to drive back to the campus, steal back the keys from the mailbox, enter Bishop Hall, retrieve the Bible and magazines, return the keys to the mailbox and get back to the train station by 4:00 a.m. I was scared stiff, but I did it all in about fifteen minutes. In the meantime, Albert and Dean Jenkins were "holding" the train until I returned. Think what a story if would have made for the papers in those days, "White woman steals keys from house in Negro neighborhood. Trial pending."

Albert planned an event for the middle of the Winter Semester, 1961-62. After working out details, he begged Rev. Bivens, college pastor, and the president to give full support. Bivens was named Director with Albert as Co-Director. "The First President's Seminar for Faculty and Students" was subtitled "The Mid Term Orientation and Guidance Conference." Albert had been relieved of responsibility for the Department of Elementary Education and transferred to courses in Philosophy.

For the seminar there were five main topics, each to be discussed by two sections of students with assigned faculty lecturers, faculty recorders, and two student leaders. The five topics were (1) The Ethics of Scholarship; (2) The Place of Morals on Our Campus; (3) Student Maturity, Health and Discipline; (4) Student and Faculty Relations; (5) Campus Citizenship and Dormitory Living. A General Assembly in the Chapel opened the day and a Social Hour was held in the evening. Albert kept the entire recorder's notes and wrote an extensive evaluation for the president. Although it was a successful day there was no comparable day the next year. By that time, Albert had been assigned to work in the Library and prepare a special report on the Wiley College Library for the president.

Much of my success in the Music Department was due to the excellent work already done, and being done, by Mr. Fred Tillis, a graduate of Wiley, a composer, theory teacher, and Band Director. (Tillis received his Ph.D. from the University of Iowa and later became Associate Provost, Vice President,

and Director of the Arts Center at the University of
Massachusetts at Amherst.)

During our third and fourth years, I directed Concert and
Marching Band while Tillis was working toward his degree.
I organized a small orchestra for two programs. Each year the
Marching Band went to the Cotton Bowl in Dallas for a
traditional football game with Prairie View A and M
University.

After I had done a series of articles on the use of
instruments in church services for *Music Ministry*, a journal
for church choir directors, I was invited by Abingdon Press to
write *The Instrumental Ensemble in the Church* (Abingdon
1963). It sold well and received good reviews.

After four years at Wiley, Albert was invited to become
the Dean at Rust College, a black Methodist school in
northwest Mississippi. I was offered the Rust music
department chair. We never knew who recommended us or
why, but because Albert was no longer happy at Wiley and
anxious to move on, we were open to the invitation. That
Rust College president told us to attend the annual summer
Higher Education Conference at the Methodist conference
center in Nashville, and enroute to stop at Philander Smith
College in Little Rock, Arkansas to meet him and sign our
contracts.

While at the conference, Albert held a short conversation
with some of the Rust faculty. I observed that from a
distance. The next hour I was in a meeting with persons from
other colleges. During an interlude, the young campus
minister from Rust talked to me praising whatever ideas
Albert had expressed. Then he said, "He's like a Messiah for
our age!" I was very touched, feeling a moment of rare
understanding between the two of us. I had become

accustomed to people attributing a certain unusual "holiness" of some sort to Albert. His deep-seated kindness, his soft voice, his way of moving from childlike innocence to explaining the wisdom of ancient sages, something in his Italian background resonated with thoughtful black men and women. Perhaps his years of service as a Conscientious Objector, denigrated by his stepfather, gave him a special perspective in working with young black people.

It was a three-day conference. People from black colleges were housed in a building adjacent to the center. We stayed in a motel. Albert had occasion to talk with one of the black faculty men and had visited his housing to be shown some papers. At one point the next day Albert took Dr. T., a large, tall, black Methodist Higher Education executive, to task because the housing he had seen for black faculty was not clean and not up to standard. He quietly said, "How long have you been here? You don't take care of your own?"

We stayed an extra day to talk to executives, including the head of the Board of Methodist Higher Education. During our conference with the black executive who had a relationship to the black colleges, he got a phone call to which he answered, "Yes, I've got his number." Albert thought that was a negative reference to him. After we left the building Albert was shaking. Out on the sidewalk I took him by the shoulders and calmed him. We walked to our motel where a wire was delivered offering me a job as Band Director at West Virginia State College at Institute, W. Va. My reply wire: "Not available." We drove back to Texas.

When we got home there was a letter to me from the Rust College president. "You should have shared with me that your husband was emotionally unstable." The offer for him to be Dean was revoked. We were still under contract, some other position would be found for Albert. This was unacceptable. I was not about to see him subjected to such indignity. It was not easy, but I wrote a polite letter rescinding our contracts.

Underneath my calm exterior, I was infuriated at the entire Rust College episode. If Albert had been black with a previous administrative position, a loud Public Relations controlling man, and one who was a "yes" man engaging in small talk and showing that he intended for faculty to "toe the mark" instead of being capable of sensitive reactions, could he have been Dean?

Albert's dedication was obvious; no one could have been more sincere or more capable of working with black faculty and students. The behavior of the Methodist hierarchy was unethical, unkind and cruel. Having once signed a contract, he should have had his chance at the Deanship. There was something strange about the entire job offer. Why was everything so vague and unexplained? Why did we have to meet the Rust College president enroute to Nashville? Why did we never go to visit the Rust campus? To have signed contracts that were not to be honored hurt me deeply. For years I wondered why we were not meant to fulfill that momentary opportunity. We wasted no time discussing the situation and I kept my anger inside myself.

Albert took this strange turn of events in stride. He didn't rant and rave, didn't seem disturbed, didn't need to discuss it. We had resigned at Wiley; it was August and we were unemployed.

Dean Njoku tried to get us to return to Wiley. Under the circumstances we did not want to. I sent a letter to Dr. Curry, president of Bishop College, since we had been invited to move to Dallas when Bishop left Marshall. Dr. Curry had no vacancies, but he recommended us to the president of Florida Memorial College in St. Augustine, who had two jobs open. After Dean Chao talked on the phone to Albert, I had the impression we were going to two jobs in Florida. When after a few days there was no confirming evidence, I called Dean Chao to see if I could find out our current status. He said, "I thought your husband said not available this year." I assured him we were both available. He said he would call back in a few minutes and he did with, "Let me be the first to welcome you to Florida Memorial College."

Albert gave away the furniture, rented a trailer, packed it with our heavy things like the Gestetner printing machine, the new file cabinet, the typewriters, some instruments, heavy books and papers and anything else we chose to take. Winter clothing was given away. In three days we were in our 1962 Buick Invicta, trailer attached, ready to depart for Florida. In the meantime, I had developed intestinal flu, something that would happen to me when I was nervous, so I didn't take it seriously.

I was heavy hearted to leave our house and the Wiley music department which had given me so much professional happiness and pride. We had even made arrangements with Mr. Holz who we knew from our Parkersburg days, a salesman for the Martin Company, to activate Trobian Music Company so we could buy instruments at cost for needy students and a much needed baritone sax for the "Collegians," the Wiley College Dance Band.

I was so sad to leave just as Dr. Tillis was returning from graduate study to chair the music department. Everything seemed so awkward, so unnecessary. Yet it was inevitable, as though Albert's destiny came ahead of everything else. This was our destiny at this time. In my childhood experience of moving every year, I had been taught to focus on the new place and not to emphasize memory of the former place, but this was different. I was very unhappy. The Nashville experience and the Rust College contracts had left me in a peculiar state of mind. Was this a nightmare? My emotions were kept under control, as I had been accustomed to doing all my life. Albert seemed to work toward moving as if it was just one more time he could enjoy giving things away. It was natural to him. He was good at it. I was good at loving him, putting him first and foremost regardless. The more troubles we shared the more deep the roots of our love. It would always blossom no matter what would happen to us.

New Teachers Added to Staff. (Pictured) left to right.—Mr. A. Wilburn, Dr. Helen Trobian, Mrs. J. L. Pollard, President T. W. Cole, Mrs. Mary Wilburn, Dr. J. L. Haynes, and Mr. Albert Trobian.

A. Wiley College, August 1959.
B. Albert Trobian teaching a class at Wiley College, Marshall, Texas, 1960.

Chosen

Wiley College Concert Band, Helen Trobian, Conductor.

Wiley College, Marshall, Texas

Brass Ensemble, Wiley College, 1961-1962

Chosen

WILEY COLLEGE

DEPARTMENT OF MUSIC

presents

The
Wiley College Brass Choir

HELEN TROBIAN, Conductor

DANIEL ADAMS BRAINARD CHAPEL

Sunday, April 16, 1961

4:00 P.M.

You and your friends are cordially invited.

Wiley College Brass Choir Program, 1961.

234

Wiley College, Marshall, Texas

PROGRAM

I

Sonata No. 24 - - - - - - - Gottfried Reiche
O Crux Ave - - - - - - - G. P. da Palestrina

II

Contrapunctus I }
Contrapunctus III } - - - - - - J. S. Bach

III

Toccata "Athalanta" - - - - - Aurelio Bonelli

IV

Negev, Tone Poem for Brass - - - - John Hartmeyer
Passacaglia in F Minor - - - - - Frederick C. Tillis*
Frederick C. Tillis, Conductor

V

Theme and Variations - - - - - Verne Reynolds
Introduction and Passacaglia - - - - - James Marks

*Member of Wiley College Faculty

THE WILEY COLLEGE BRASS CHOIR

DR. HELEN TROBIAN,
Director

Trumpet

Charles Archie
Arthur Guidry
Newell Brown
Hugh Johnson
William Drumgoole
Wesley Bell
Robert Carpenter

Horn

Larry McGriff
Arthur White
Jerry Wilhite
Howard Polk
Howard Austin
Richard Gayden

Trombone

Robert Watkins
Roscoe Turner
Algia Jones

Baritone

Alvernon Jones
Adolphus Taylor

Tuba

Willie Thibodeaux
James Jackson

A.-B. Wiley College Brass Choir Program

235

Chosen

NEGRO DEMONSTRATORS (upper photo) leave the Harrison County courthouse in Marshall, Tex., yesterday after being arrested when they gathered downtown to protest the previous arrest of lunch counter sitdown demonstrators. In the lower photo, firemen hold a hose after hosing down about 60 demonstrators and using hoses to push back other Negroes. Some 200 Negroes were arrested and formal charges were filed against 49. Later the Negroes—students from Wiley and Bishop colleges—gathered in the Bishop auditorium and staged a rally. (Times Photo by Lloyd Stilley)

TWO NEGRO STUDENTS are escorted to Marshall's city hall yesterday after they attempted to receive service at a segregated lunch counter in a downtown drug store. A total of 16 were arrested in the Friday sitdown movement, making a total of 73 taken into custody by police since the demonstrations began last Saturday. The 16 today were placed under a $100 bond each. Police are behind the two Negroes as unidentified spectators watch the action. (Times Photo by Lloyd Stilley)

Home at Wiley College.

CHAPTER 17

Florida Memorial College
and "Ending Unemployment"

When we reached Ruston, Louisiana, about forty miles east of Shreveport, we stopped for lunch and checked into a motel instead. I had started to cry and couldn't stop. The trailer had jiggled the car all the way. I was downright sick and I feared the trailer was hurting the car. I had not told Albert about my sickness.

He went out on that hot day in August and redistributed some things in the trailer. He came back into the room completely soaked, as if he had been in the swimming pool. I felt so sorry for him I quit crying. Why cry when we were together and so much in love?

In the morning we drove down the road to the first filling station showing trailers for rent. "Please take this trailer off this car." We were taken to a back office with a Teletype. We supposed our things could be put on a truck. Then a "guardian angel" took over. The station man said, "I have an aunt who received a big display in a wooden box from the Smithsonian Institute. It's big enough for your things." We arranged for the box to be delivered to Florida Memorial College since we had no place to live. I still think that man was some kind of "angel" in a sequence of such helpful people progressing through the various problematic situations of our lives. It turned out the trailer was over loaded and not properly hitched to the car. It may have been providential that we stopped when we did. There could easily have been a real catastrophe.

When we arrived in St. Augustine we had dinner at Dean Chao's house. He took us to see a place, not far away, that provided living quarters. We accepted a one room apartment over a garage.

The college, according to information in print, was on U.S. Route 1. In reality it was five miles west of St. Augustine on the edge of a jungle. Albert taught education courses and supervised elementary student teachers. I taught music education courses and supervised three student teachers in Jacksonville. The college buildings were decrepit: a combination gymnasium/auditorium, main building, women's dorm, library (small), post office (small), and a three room shack where music was taught. (A pet snake lived under the building.) In the winter it was frequently too cold for the eight o'clock music education class to meet. That was taken for granted. By noon it would be quite hot. Once when it rained hard there were tiny frogs all over the walks.

Albert had an office, but I didn't. When I was not teaching, I went to the library until those resources were exhausted. During the spring semester, I got the college to order band instruments from Metropolitan Music in New York at wholesale prices I negotiated. They arrived just in time for one concert to be given before the end of the school year.

Just past the edge of the campus was a stand of tall bamboo. I had previously made Shepherds' Pipes following the English tradition, but I had not experimented with bamboo flutes. Since I didn't have an office and didn't feel free to practice on my instruments, I sat on the campus in my free hours and made bamboo flutes.

Due to road construction, there was a detour from the regular route. Once when I was driving alone the car was shot at during a new wave of civil rights activity. One period of time we were let into restaurants by waiting for the front door to be unlocked. Sometime during the spring term, Mrs. Peabody, wife of the Governor of Massachusetts, came to St. Augustine and led a march. We happened to be downtown at the time and were caught up in a crowd of marchers. That detour was also the route we were on one afternoon in May returning from the campus to our apartment. We were suddenly engulfed in a flash flood. Water rose up over the hood of the car. I kept my foot on the accelerator and thought positively toward getting to a higher ground soon. It took a day in the sun to dry out the car. The red leather interior took less time to dry than some other cars we saw. That was a distinctly frightening experience such as I never want to have again.

The faculty at Florida Memorial, a black Baptist college, was like a United Nations gathering: Chinese, Israeli, Hungarian, Japanese, Korean, African-American, and a few others, along with some like us.

While the civil rights activity was prominent in town, a sociology professor from a northeastern university visited the campus. He was researching "civil rights history." I was with a group of students congregated outside the post office building when he came running up, all excited, "Jane S., one of your students, is in jail." The members of the group remained calm and disinterested. The man expected something to be done about it. The group was quiet. Then one of the fellows obliged with, "So what, she's been there plenty of times."

One night a week I played cello in a small senior citizens group of violins, piano and percussion. It was more a social event than a musical one. We played in homes; spouses were considered vital members of the group as audience and helpers to serve dessert to close the evening. The prime mover for the group was Hugo Wolff, a designer of stained glass windows with a studio near his home. He and his wife played violins.

I played viola one night a week in the St. Augustine Symphonette. The only other viola was Henri Erkelens, retired from the Boston Symphony. He encouraged me to continue playing viola.

Holidays and vacations we drove up and down Florida like regular tourists. In some respects the entire year had a vacation feeling, partly due to the weather, partly because we had no committee work.

Albert and I chaperoned the Senior Prom. On the way home Albert said he was glad there had been no drinking. I didn't tell him I had seen three barrels of bottles picked up. What he meant, without knowing, was there was no drunkenness.

The college was planning to move to Miami and did a few years later. Not only did Albert not wish to live in Miami, we both felt our mission to education was unfulfilled. There were too many substandard features. We declined to accept contracts for the coming year. The president kept asking Albert why we would not stay. His answer: "Because I have decided not to."

For the summer, we attended a String Institute at Eastman

School of Music, University of Rochester, New York, where we enjoyed the instruction and many concerts. In September after no response had been received to any of our application letters, we left Rochester for Washington, D. C. We put the car in storage for the month of October while we spent our time at the Library of Congress. We rented a room in a house not far from the Capitol and got our mail at General Delivery at the post office near Union Station.

After all we had been through together, it seemed strange to be unemployed once more, but one thing was clear to me, I would have to be the breadwinner in the family, although I never told Albert. I think that was also his idea. Not that he was in any respect, lazy. He simply regarded us as a family team, even if I was the one to bring in the paycheck.

We applied unsuccessfully for the Job Corps. Our misfortunes were partially alleviated by receiving in the mail two bonus checks from Florida Memorial that took the edge off our worrying.

The mail brought an invitation from Dean Njoku of Wiley, for us to go to Africa to work in a school he sponsored in Nigeria. We did not want to go, although we were assured of transportation, State Department endorsement, and other accommodations.

Tired of living like temporary tourists, we took the car out of storage and headed south.

The first of November, we rented a cottage behind a house in Daytona and stayed there a month typing numerous letters of application. The cottage, especially the bedroom, was mildewed, but it was the best we could do. We had a steady diet of hamburgers and beans. Our love was strong enough to withstand mildew, unemployment, and anxiety about the future.

As a result of sending out letters, for some reason I came to believe I could have a job as administrative assistant to a scholar; professor of music at the University of North Carolina. Albert thought he would like to study philosophy, perhaps even work toward a degree if I could land a job at UNC.

We left Florida, got a student apartment in Carrboro, and spent our time in Chapel Hill at the university library.

The professor I had hoped to work for died. I took a two-day employment test for clerical work at UNC and passed with no problems. After the woman who interviewed me said, "You are just looking for temporary work?" that was the end of all that effort.

In December I received an invitation to interview at Bennett College in Greensboro, North Carolina. Several inches of snow covered the Bennett College campus the day of the interview. Albert thought it better for me to go alone, there being no invitation for him. President Player was home in bed with a cold that day so the interview was only with the Dean. Apparently Wiley College had been contacted and had given an affirmative response. When I left the interview, I had no idea whether I would be offered a position.

At eight o'clock in the morning between Christmas and New Year we got a phone call in the apartment. Dr. Player did not waste time with details She had not even met me, but she offered me a position as Director of the Humanities Summer School. She had gotten a grant from "Miss Doris Duke of New York City." My job would be to spend a semester designing plans, then execute the summer school and join the regular faculty for the ensuing year. The summer school was a three-year project. She said she would send details and a letter of contract, but she wanted my answer. I said I wanted to discuss it with my husband. She said she would hold the phone. Albert emphatically said, "Take the job," so I did.

After hanging up the phone, I got a bad case of the "jitters." I could not stop shaking. Albert put all our coats and bed covers on me and fed me hot tea.

The job was to start February 1, 1965. We had the month of January to use the UNC library and to find a place to live in Greensboro.

We were fortunate to find the right side of a duplex house available and partially furnished. Once again we were either lucky or were recipients of divine providence. Basic furniture was provided. We lived in that house for a year or more before buying living room furniture. The house was comfortable, although the heating unit in the basement that served ancient steam radiators was made from a do-it-yourself kit, according to Albert.

In 1965, when we moved to Greensboro, we had been married eighteen years during which we had inhabited at least twenty-one miscellaneous types of living quarters. We had both known professional employment interspersed with periods of unemployment. We had worked in at least seven states: New York, West Virginia, Ohio, Illinois, Pennsylvania, Florida and Texas. This new job presented unusual opportunities to use my background and administrative leadership. Was it going to be temporary? I thought we were both ready to settle down and regardless of any reactions I had to any circumstances, I made up my mind to like this job and that we were going to stay located. (Well, at least for three years!) There were so many husbandly roles Albert played so well that my new colleagues accepted us as partners.

Chosen

246

CHAPTER 18

Bennett College, Greensboro, North Carolina

There is an awkwardness about being a new faculty person at the beginning of the second semester. I was not introduced until much later at a faculty meeting where I was asked to stand as Director of the Humanities Summer School.

No matter how awkward my situation might be, I was resolved to prove myself worthy of the opportunity. Employment on a beautiful historic campus, a quadrangle with magnolia trees, a splendid Chapel, helpful people—what more could one want after a fearful semester of homeless unemployment?

Why did this wonderful opportunity have to be in a college for women? My best music education students had been young men. Who would have thought that I would wind up in a woman's college in the south and one that had no intention at anytime of hiring Albert? It was clear to me that some negativism from his past had been relayed. I was hurt by that: it was unfair, but nothing could be done about it. Albert seemed reasonably happy that one member of his team was working. He applied unsuccessfully for various jobs, then used his time to type excerpts from his Wiley College journals and to visit libraries.

Dr. J. Henry Sayles, Director of the Science division, who

had directed a National Science Institute for many years, was asked by President Player to show me the rules, regulations, paper work, and all pertinent information so that I could create a Humanities Summer School to parallel the Science Institute.

Dr. Sayles was very kind, accepted me as an academic equal, did what President Player had asked and more. There were many pieces of paper to be produced—brochures for recruiting, application forms, financial plans, letters of admission and ID cards. Dr. Sayles gave advice about the writing of the Student Handbook, handling budget for meals, student assistants, and dormitory discipline. He recognized that the Humanities Summer School would be different although some things would be similar to the Science Institute. No one could have been more helpful, and he was never overbearing. As a result of Dr. Sayles' professional assistance and understanding of the situation, I was able to conduct planning with expedition and my own creativity.

In addition to a Library hour and Humanities Assembly, students could choose two morning courses from Literature, Philosophy, Social Science and Creative Writing. In the afternoon one activity was elected from Art, Drama, Music, Dance, and Creative Writing. The next year, French and Spanish were also available. Evenings were occupied by concerts or other special events. No student had any time to waste, nor did we! Albert was a gracious host to colleagues and out of town guests and an overnight printer of the daily newssheet for the Humanities Summer School. Usually we would entertain evening guests after a program, by two o'clock prepare the newssheet for the Gestetner Stencil and at six o'clock in the morning I would deliver the "daily news" to each dormitory for the student assistants to deliver to the rooms.

President Player had made arrangements for the faculty to include a Poet-in-Residence, John Tagliabue, from Bates College in Maine. He was a delightful addition. The next year, Edward Lowe, professor of music and a choral director, joined the staff as Associate Director and was responsible for performance of the Eastern Philharmonic Orchestra, conducted by Sheldon Morgenstern on July6, 1968 in front of the Chapel. He was also helpful in obtaining guest artists. Each summer a detailed evaluation and statistical report presented to the college president was given high commendations.

Bennett College, one of two black women's colleges, (Spellman is the other) was considerably different from each of the other colleges where Albert and I had worked. I think he enjoyed my working in a college for women while I adjusted slowly to the "single sex institution." As a pre-college institute the Humanities Summer School admitted both boys and girls. I was grateful for that.

Albert became a househusband after not being pleased to be a philosophy student at Chapel Hill. As a househusband he was superb. No housewife was ever as good. I could always count on him to be as loving and lovable as ever. He appeared on campus when needed—reception lines, Sunday Vespers and an occasional special event. Had it not been for his constant endorsement of my endeavors, our sense of being a team, I could never have achieved such splendid results. From time to time a student would tell me how much she had enjoyed talking to Albert at a reception. I was proud of my marriage and grateful to persons who would comment on our love, although there were never any public displays of affection; the reality of deep love could be sensed.

The Humanities Summer School grant was stretched to a fourth year. After the remarkably successful 1965 session, I was appointed Humanities Core Chair. For seven years (1968-1976) I served as Director of the Humanities Division and continued as Director of the Interdisciplinary Studies degree program.

Twenty-four years of service to Bennett College encompassed the initiation of black studies, women studies, computer labs, academic options, student designed courses, extensive proposal writing for everyone from the custodian to the president, administration of grants, continuous numerous committee responsibilities, new courses—in addition to a full load of teaching and student advising.

Summers were never vacations. In the summer of 1969, Albert and I accompanied (as chaperone representatives) four Bennett students to the University of Graz, Austria along with students and faculty from more than thirty colleges, for seven weeks of study in Europe under Associated Colleges and Universities for International Intercultural Studies. For Albert and me it was like a European vacation with an adopted family. Three of our students were in music so I joined that group and Albert joined a philosophy/psychology group. In addition to places in Austria, we visited Venice, Italy; Zurich, Switzerland; and Munich, Germany.

During 1970-73, several weeks each summer were spent in Boston with faculty from other colleges working on curriculum plans, under auspices of Institute for Service to Education. Albert was home alone during many of my weeks out of town. Sometimes he would visit his sisters, but once I came home from a short trip to find the round coffee table in the living room completely extended with dogwood obtained from the forest behind Woodlea Lake.

"Oh, how beautiful, Bunchy, but why is it so big?"

"Because that's how much I love you!" Albert said as he threw his arms wide open.

In 1976, I represented the college at the Summer Institute for Women in Higher Education Administration held at Bryn Mawr College. Albert drove up with me and took a train home, returning at the close of the program to drive home with me.

As the years went by, I gained more and more respect for Bennett as a college for women. Aspects of college life, outside of classrooms and faculty committees, took on an impressive distinctive importance. Functions on campus from Sunday Vespers to events in the Student Union were conducted with grace and style and a tradition of gentility. Close ties evidenced by the alumnae from year to year carried on inheritance of the college culture. It was an honor to become part of Bennett College history. I treasure my memories of Retreat conferences I led on Mt. Pisgah and Peaks of Otter, of lasting faculty and student friendships, of many long hours in extended committee meetings, classroom moments of high accomplishment, and my opportunities to read papers at professional conferences. Being an active part of a larger unit making a very definite difference in the lives of young women was an enterprise that engaged my time and energy day and night.

I had loved my work with young men at Wiley College. They were fine music students and I enjoyed their devotion to any tasks they were given. In those days instrumental music was my only concern. At Bennett I was amazed at the difference I felt in being regarded as a leader in the education

251

of women. Every type of job I had held before had had a good measure of success, but this tenured professorship and administrative opportunity presented an ongoing challenge. It seemed as though all the miscellaneous jobs I had suffered through had laid a foundation. In a place least expected I was able to make a meaningful contribution. Very few people of non-color have ever known the whole-hearted acceptance which I received at Bennett College. Sometimes I would be told that I was different from other whites. "You're one of us!" was a rare compliment.

When I started getting federal grants, I was told that I was the first person who ever did "anything good" for the faculty. A testimonial dinner was held at a local motel to honor me after receiving the grant for the Interdisciplinary Studies degree program. I was embarrassed, but I played my part and after everyone else had spoken, Albert got up and talked a little too long. He said, "She's pulling on my coat tails, but I'm not quite through." (He wanted to use the opportunity to do a little "educating" of his own.) After I had retired and President Miller had retired, Mrs. Miller told me that many students told her (she was a counselor) that "if it hadn't been for Dr. T" (as I was known on campus) they could never have graduated.

In 1975, the first interdisciplinary graduates presented me with a plaque bearing this inscription: "You have shared our yesterdays and todays, and influenced our tomorrows." I have fond hopes that the influence is a continuous sense of self-esteem and new self-discovery as I experienced in my time at Bennett College.

After 1968 when Barbara Walker had been a student at the summer school, she "adopted" us as another set of parents in addition to her foster parents, Eva and Daniel Perkins in Richmond, Virginia. She was small, quiet, shy, and well behaved and wanted to study music. She quickly learned viola enough to play in a summer school group. She took naturally to all the wind instruments and made rapid progress on the piano. Originally it was her widespread interest in a diversity of instruments that was our connecting link.

Albert told her she could be a member of "The Lori Family" a sort of imaginary group, (his real father's name was Luigi Lori), and we would name her Robin Lori. In August 1972 after her graduation from Bennett College, Barbara, who had married in Richmond, gave birth to Robin and Felicia, identical twins. Barbara said she would call her firstborn Robin Lori and she did. After a short-term marriage, divorce was inevitable and she came back to Greensboro and served for two years as my assistant on the staff of the Interdisciplinary Studies degree program.[1] During this time, Albert became a sort of father figure, or "uncle" for Robin and Felicia.

Albert was instrumental in getting Robin and Felicia into a splendid nursery school: The Gingerbread House. He became one of several baby-sitters and told me after one evening, that as he was diapering Felicia (something he was good at) she looked up and said, "man" and he instantly became self-conscious. When the children would come to see us and I would open the door they would say, "Where's Albert?" Albert wanted to be sure that did not hurt my

---

[1] For the philosophy of the funded degree program and student comments, a detailed account can be found in *Small College Creativity,* Vol. I, No. 2, pp. 66-75, edited by Dr. Lynn Sadler.

feelings, but I was delighted and told him so. He had unusual ability with young children. Robin and Felicia grew up to be splendid adults. Without children of our own, we felt favored by their loving regard. Our years at Bennett were made more enjoyable by the several Thanksgiving and Christmas visits made to the home of Eva and Daniel Perkins who became our friends as a result of Barbara's friendship.

On Saturday, October 5, 1985, at 6:00 p.m. Albert and I were formally dressed and honored to be seated at the "Family Table" for the banquet honoring Mr. Perkins at the John Marshall Hotel in Richmond. The Major of Richmond declared it Daniel Roy Perkins Day in tribute to his dedicated contributions to community life. Barbara gave a speech as his daughter, and Robin and Felicia, introduced as granddaughters, sang. It was a splendid occasion with many speeches including one by Governor Elect Wilder. Eva Perkins has come to see us in Tennessee. We value the friendships Barbara engendered.

We also became close friends with Joyce Calloway, a lay minister in the AME Church, a security guard who worked the exit desk at UNCG library and was also an International Police Chaplain. She had been born with a cleft palate, only getting a prosthesis as an adult. Albert got acquainted with her at the library and invited her to our apartment to continue their extensive conversations on religion. He helped her to improve her reading and writing skills. Joyce arranged her vacation schedules so she could attend summer sessions for lay ministers at Duke Divinity School. At a reception after an award ceremony, she introduced Albert and me as her "Godparents." She told me she had seen Albert in a vision before she met him. We regard her as a member of "The Lori Family." Frequently we went to Sunday dinner together. She has made several trips to see us in Tennessee. Our lives have been enriched by this relationship.

Albert had opportunity to demonstrate his nurturing skills in December of 1986 when I was sent home from Wesley Long Community Hospital with both arms in casts. I had fallen down in a parking lot behind a dormitory building. My left wrist was "shattered" and after being repaired I was put to bed and given a hot meal. I said to the nurse, "I hate to tell you, but I can't get the fork to my mouth. Do you think my right arm should be x-rayed?" The next thing I knew I was back in bed with another cast—broken right elbow. It was the third time that elbow had been broken.

It was the end of the semester and all my exams had been duplicated and made ready for distribution to my classes. My office was neat and orderly as usual. The next four weeks were January break, so I had chosen a good time to be absent from work. With both arms in heavy casts, I was virtually helpless. Dr. Sue said, "I'll let you go home, but you will need someone to take care of you."

I said, "My husband can do that. He's a natural born medic!"

Albert rose to the occasion; he even drove the car. He was better than any nurse. He coped with people who came to see me and brought food. He also cooked. Everything necessary was done without embarrassing me. He was in complete charge and seemed to enjoy himself.

After four weeks we had an appointment to have the right arm cast taken off. I had an old three-piece knitted pantsuit that could be worn, but getting support panty hose (the only kind I had) on me was a comedy routine. Once the right arm cast was off, I could drive, but it was a long time before the left cast came off. Through it all, Albert was magnificent.

President's Reception

Albert at the President's Reception, Bennett College, 1970.

A.   B.C. Students, Helen and Albert, Austria, 1969.
B.-C. Helen and Albert dressed up for Bennett College
      events.

Chosen

CHAPTER 19

From North Carolina to Tennessee

Seventy-one was retirement age at Bennett College so after twenty-four years, I retired on September 1, 1989. That first year I spent most of the time trying to learn to relax. (I had classic burnout.) After that I decided I was not ready to quit working. I felt that my administrative experience was valuable and could still be used some place. I responded to advertisements from several colleges. That yielded nothing; it just stimulated my desire to continue working.

Albert and I attended several national conferences on brass and woodwind instruments. I toyed with the idea of touring the country as a clinician on "The Brass Choir." It was a wonderful fantasy full of precise details, but nothing seemed to take care of the need to continue employment.

We decided we should look for a house for sale in Greensboro, but we found nothing desirable in our price range. We began to feel that retirement in a new location would be best for both of us. We settled the concept of moving and found numerous reasons for leaving Greensboro. Just as when we left Salem, West Virginia, not knowing where to go or why, once again we had no precise criteria on which to focus our hunt for a new location.

Between 1990 and 1993, we made several trips to Illinois

and Pennsylvania to visit relatives that Albert had not seen since childhood. In the summer of 1992, we attended the Keystone Brass Institute in Colorado. The National Youth Orchestra was in residence providing a concert each night of the second week. Albert took just as much interest in the concerts and clinics as I did. Sometimes when two sections each were of special interest to me, Albert would go to one and take notes, which he reviewed for me later. He was totally companionable and capable of analyzing the special presentations made.

Detouring on the way home from Colorado, Albert suggested, "While we're this close let's go pay a visit to Wiley College." In spite of my reservations, I went along with his desire. We talked briefly with a Vice President and I contributed a volume of programs to the Wiley College Library Archives. Downtown Marshall was like a ghost town. The hotel was for sale, the Courthouse was a museum which we visited, getting a kick out of seeing some pictures of people we knew about. Although the college had some new buildings, we were dismayed at the lack of landscaping and the condition of some buildings. The Chapel and other old buildings had been torn down after the college inherited the Pemberton High School, formerly the Negro school. Everything seemed different. We had had a similar experience as we drove through West Virginia on one of our Pennsylvania trips, stopping briefly to see Salem College, now Salem-Teikyo University. What a big difference a few years could make! It seemed to surprise me that nothing had stayed the same. I began to wonder if we were still the same persons who had worked there thirty-two years before.

Back home after we had definitely decided it would be preferable to move, I said to Albert, "Now it's your turn to be in charge! Let's try you being my agent for a volunteer college position and see if it may be our destiny to serve one more church related college."

"Sure, I'll be glad to be your agent. We've always been a team. You compose the letter and I'll sign it."

The next step was to research the most likely colleges to send my agent's letter.

After lengthy research in UNCG library, I picked twenty-two colleges as possible locations, then condensed the list to ten. He wrote a short letter to each. Berea College sent a polite rejection. From the other nine colleges one phone call was received. Ruth Loving, Assistant to the Dean at Milligan College, Tennessee, said Dean Weedman would be willing to talk with us and she set up an appointment.

Like two youngsters with very little information we eagerly prepared for a trip across the mountains. I typed up a listing of our assets and liabilities just in case we should need it. We were ready to look for new housing, a new community, and a new job, without pay.

Staying at the Red Roof Inn in Johnson City, we studied real estate development and went exploring. We drove in the vicinity of the college not finding what we were supposed to be looking for, when we drove by a brick house with a "For Sale by Owner" sign in the front yard.

Albert said, "Oh, stop here!"

"No, no this wouldn't be for us."

"STOP!"

I turned into the long driveway and we knocked on the front door. A woman opened a door that obviously had not been opened recently, and told us she was ill but, "Come back tomorrow and I'll show you the house." She really was sorry she couldn't do it that day. I had no feeling that we had found

261

our house. Albert, however, was already dreaming about remodeling the house and building his own private school on the spacious front lawn. Little did I know the extent of his fantasy at the time.

The next day we met Carolyn Holt, a beautiful young divorcee who was a daughter of the original owner, the Phillips. She had lived alone in the house for the past three years coping with diabetes while she made quilts, and planned to go to Louisiana to be near her daughter's family, especially to assist in raising an infant grandson. We saw the house. It had been remodeled a time or two. From my viewpoint, it had numerous faults. On the other hand, it also had some "plus" features.

There were two back doors, one of which entered into the quilting room, and off that room was a little sewing room. The rest of the house was a combined dining room and living room (with a fireplace), two bedrooms and bathroom. There was a fireplace and a shower in the basement.

Outside the house the front entrance was almost unusable, side porch steps had settled dangerously uneven. It was nice that the house set back fifteen hundred feet from the highway, with a circular driveway at the back along with a two-car garage and an attached tool shed. An extensive back yard included a "valley" (looked like a big ditch to me) and a hill, which we were told, required a "bush hog man" at regular intervals. There was a beautiful old pine tree at the entrance from the highway, another near the garage and another on the hill. Several other trees were obviously deceased. On Milligan Highway five minutes from the college, it was an attractive location in a well-kept area of Carter County known as Pinecrest.

After seeing the house and grounds we sat in Carolyn Holt's kitchen, discussed the purchase price, why she wanted to leave, why other potential buyers had not bought, the nature of the community and the distance to Milligan College. Then Albert, who had not made any "big" decisions for a quarter of a century said, "We'll take it. We don't need to go to the car to discuss it. We'll take it."

I didn't bat an eyelash, got out my checkbook prepared to write the "finder's fee" or whatever was necessary to clinch the deal. In my mind I already realized Albert would plan to do extensive remodeling and I was saying "Oh, no! Not Parkersburg all over again?" I kept still, ignored the feeling, and put my trust wholly into Albert's decision. He seemed so secure; who could mistrust such an angelic person? And we hadn't even had our interview at Milligan College yet. When we did, Albert told the Dean we would be living close on Milligan Highway. He was an impressive "agent." The Dean was pleasant and brief, made contact with the music area chair (they have no departments) who called us at Red Roof Inn. A prince of a fellow, a distinguished organist, he arranged for an interview and accepted me as an adjunct faculty member to give lessons on wind instruments.

We went back to Greensboro and waited four months until we were approved to purchase the house. The delay was attributed to some kind of personnel changes in the Bank of Tennessee. During the four months, we occasionally wondered if we should cancel, but Albert who packed everything well in advance of departure, was secure that we were buying the house. We had discussions about various repairs and changes to be made. I asked Albert, "How did you know we didn't need to go to the car to discuss it? What if I had not agreed?"

"You would never have found anything you really wanted. We couldn't afford to buy land and build. Look how handy that door to the quilting room will be if you want to give lessons at home, even if you don't, it will be a good music room." He knew I didn't want to teach at home, but he wanted to encourage me to play my instruments since playing in the apartment inhibited me.

On January 31, 1993, a beautiful calm sunny day in northeast Tennessee, our *Allied* truck arrived at Box 129, Route 8, on Milligan Highway.* At long last we were finally moved. This was our house and I was listed on a Milligan College brochure as "Adjunct Professor in Music" and also listed in the college directory. The "going back to work" and the retirement location were no longer problems. I knew there would be other problems eventually, and yet whatever they were, it was all worth it to see Albert, "my agent", so happy and successful with his decision.

* now 1390 Milligan Highway

CHAPTER 20

Feathering the Nest for Retirement

The sales person from Dockery's who installed our nine feet wide vertical blinds in the living room, recommended a contractor. We had already decided to turn the little sewing room into a second bathroom and a walk-in closet for instruments. Under Albert's watchful eye many repairs and much remodeling was done. We had dead trees taken away. We planted flowering trees and bushes to add to rose bushes, lilacs, crepe myrtle, forsythia and other nameless plants.

Albert hired a helper to build his grape arbor. He engaged two bricklayers to improve the fireplaces, and to add a low, divided brick wall in front of the house. A college student laid down a patio Albert had designed for the front entrance. He added an artistic glass block and brick enclosure for the back porch. By the time Albert got through with the basement, it was almost completely new.

While the extensive repairing and remodeling was going on, we were also busy buying furniture and appliances. We shopped in Elizabethton, Johnson City, and Kingsport. Once again it was like we were just married. We found ourselves always in agreement about what to buy. Albert was about as "liberated" as any man is likely to be in our culture, but it was difficult to get everything to suit him. Things had to be just the right size and that was sometimes difficult. Several little problems developed. There was a problem about the refrigerator we bought at Loew's. The kitchen door opened onto a door to the basement and there was a very small space to negotiate the fridge through. It was impossible. The solution was to take it through the front door. That worked except that it was a little too tall for the cabinetry it was to fit under. Albert hastily sawed and chiseled until it would fit. The two delivery men from Loew's worked valiantly to get the fridge settled and leveled, but they couldn't get the levelers on the bottom of the fridge to fit. Since they simply would not fit the floor properly, Albert told the men, "Take this back, I don't want it." They looked amazed, but he was so definite they took it away.

We went back to Loew's, shopped some more, found a refrigerator we liked better for a few hundred dollars more, bought it and arranged for delivery through the front door. This time Albert had measured the height carefully and he was sure that this fridge would fit. As I once more stood by as a silent spectator, something was not going to suit Albert. I kept my fingers crossed and hoped we could soon check out of the motel and into this house, even though it was still being remodeled. Albert explained to the two men who delivered the fridge, "I don't want it exactly level. I want it so the doors will close automatically." It meant a fine adjustment of the levelers. The two delivery men were mystified so Albert demonstrated. He said as he illustrated opening the door, getting both hands full, "See, it's like this. When I'm cooking I want to go to the stove and let the doors shut themselves." He did look funny enroute to the stove (wearing a red stocking cap), but he didn't mean to be comical. The two looked at me. I didn't say anything, just acted as if that was

266

perfectly normal. (Albert talked about cooking more than he cooked!) I was afraid they would laugh at him, but they got busy and didn't leave until Albert was satisfied. The doors do close with their own momentum. Albert was determined to have things the way he felt they should be and his perseverance was effective.

He also made the brick masons redo part of the little brick wall he had designed for the front of the house. When one of the pillars did not meet Albert's specifications, he took it apart and explained how he wanted it done. The side porch steps were only done after Albert had worked more than the masons had. He wrote detailed instructions about his design for the back porch glass block and brick, but when the time came Albert just worked with the two men until he got what he wanted.

When flimsy light covers were placed on the two ceiling lights he'd had installed in the living room, Albert said, "That's not what I expected, such junky looking things." We went to a lighting retail outlet and found something he thought appropriate. As usual cost was no item. We had credit cards. Oh yes, we had lots of credit cards.

When the contractor was planning to put both the blower and the light in the new bathroom on one switch, Albert wasn't getting his wishes so we went to Paty's where a nice man showed us blower and light mechanisms. We went home and Albert told the contractor, "There's no problem of separate switches. I saw them at Paty's." The contractor, who was trying to get everything done on minimum expenditures, blushed a little and the switches were installed.

The contractor had sent us to look at bathroom fixtures and to state what we wanted in tile, tubs, and sinks. In the process of shopping, we happened to see a tub at a marked down price because of an injury to the finish.

"Look at this," Albert said, "This is just painted paper. I don't want anything like that and I don't want that 'wrap around' he's planning to put in."

Albert told the contractor that he wanted the tub in the new bathroom to be cast-iron.

"Cast-iron!" Ken (the contractor) emoted. "There's only one of those in the region. It's white and will cost extra. Besides, it'll take three men to lift it." Albert still wanted it and he got it. After he saw the tile we chose for the new bathroom (mine) he had all the old plastic tile and the window taken out of the existing bathroom (his) and new tile and fixtures installed. He was told that the heater in his bathroom worked fine. Albert said, "It's old and rusty. I don't want to take chances. Put a new one in."

When he found out the plumbing was not copper pipes, he had it all changed to copper and a water filter put in the basement, also a dehumidifier for which he fixed a drain so that it would never have to be emptied.

When the fireplace came under study, both the one in the basement and the one in the living room were thoroughly examined by Robert Lyons, a delightful professional chimney sweep from Elizabethton. A piece of marble was ordered for the mantle of the new fireplace in the basement. It took six months to get it, but Albert wanted marble and he got it. He got everything he wanted and never raised his voice.

We had only been in Tennessee a few weeks and had just gotten the new roof on the back half of the house when the historic March 1993 blizzard occurred causing us to use the basement fireplace for cooking while we lived without electricity for several days. Fortunately we had a small transistor radio. As we snuggled up in bed with warm clothing, we learned what the people of northeast Tennessee were really like. People without electricity were advised to take refuge in temporary shelters. Many people were willing to share their **4x4** vehicles to distribute wood, to share their limited supply of kerosene and food. The outpouring of generosity was amazing.

Soon after the blizzard, Albert broke his wrist while clearing the brush from the hill where he planned to have an orchard. I was sure his wrist was broken and desperate to get him quickly to medical attention. I called Mrs. Pritchard, our neighbor on the east and asked where to take him. I didn't even know if it would be Sycamore Shoals or Johnson City. Mr. Pritchard, who was recuperating from a broken foot, came over and rode with us to the ER in Johnson City Medical Center. When we got there the parking lot was crowded so Mr. Pritchard parked the car for me to avoid further delay. When Albert picked this location he certainly picked wonderful neighbors. The Greenes, the Renfros, and the Pritchards are very special "angels" who assisted our relocation in many ways.

In the process of getting the broken wrist taken care of, we were transferred to an orthopedic surgeon at Northside Hospital who discovered a blood test analysis showing Albert's platelet count was dangerously low. Back in Greensboro in 1990, he had successful colon cancer surgery and at that time he was told that he had a negative liver condition. From then on we watched our diet carefully and I was inspired to do more Italian cooking. When my cooking would evidence special effort Albert would say, "What are we celebrating?" Sometimes when we would eat out he would say, "Shall we go for a repast?" He never stopped using that word he had learned in Texas.

Having learned about the blood count, we commenced regular appointments with a liver specialist and a cancer and blood specialist. When his doctors were not attentive to his itching skin problems, I studied the phone book and intuitively chose a dermatologist. While I had no real basis, I felt there was probably a connection with the liver. After making the appointment with Dr. Hudson, I notified Dr. Witt, Albert's Gastroenterologist, and he sent Dr. Hudson a letter introducing us. From then on Albert had "light-box" treatments that eliminated the terrible itching.

We occasionally visited the orthopedic doctors for a leg problem, a back problem, and for a broken finger. None of these health problems prohibited Albert from doing his landscaping, improving the soil, or whatever he wanted to do. He was hospitalized several times during the next three years.

Although visiting Albert so much during his several hospitalizations helped me overcome my fear of hospitals, I never developed a liking for making hospital visits, not knowing appropriate things to say, but in April of our second year in Tennessee, Albert and I visited our elderly neighbor friend (also a county commissioner), Mr. Dave Renfro at Northside Hospital where he was undergoing treatment for pneumonia. Early that morning we had completed some outdoor work, taken showers, and were getting dressed when I remembered

"What about the flowers? We forgot to fix the flowers!"

"You get it started," Albert said. "Bring in some flowers and some greenery.'

Outside the house a special one-of-a-kind variegated tulip

caught my eye. It was easy to find other spring blossoms like forsythia, violets, spirea, and flowers whose names I never knew. I quickly took them into the kitchen where I found a tall jelly glass to serve as a vase. Albert came and said he wanted to get something special from Mr. Renfro's yard. He came back with a sprig of a flowering crabapple tree. Together we hastily prepared a creative work of art. I put several sheets of white tissue paper around the glass, tied it with some green ribbon, and we were amazed at what a professional looking bouquet we had to take to the hospital.

Albert was wearing a blue suit and starched white shirt, which surprised the Renfros as they had only seen him in old drab outdoor work clothes. When we arrived at the hospital we entered the waiting room where the desk clerk was so intrigued with the flowers she requested permission to show them to a colleague in another room who said to also show them to the woman in the gift shop. A woman in the waiting room showed curiosity so Albert went to her and explained about the flowers being from Mr. Renfro's neighborhood. Everyone seemed excited by Albert's obvious expression of delight. He was so pleased with our creation that he was smiling from ear to ear, looking like a happy little child. At the hospital room, Mr. Renfro and his daughter, Mrs. Janet Grant, were appreciative. Albert said, "We did it together." They sensed it was special. Two days later Mr. Renfro passed away and we miss him dearly. We were honored to be invited to lunch in his house with his extended family the day of the funeral.

In September 1996, Albert had been referred to a surgeon for analysis of his liver condition and a hernia. While he was getting dressed after the examination, the surgeon took me aside and told me there was no point in a biopsy that Albert

271

had terminal cancer with tumors in both lungs and "his liver is hard as a rock!" It was not a big surprise to me as Dr. Witt had once asked me if I were prepared for the end of Albert's illness. At the time I had said, "Yes, but not right now."

On September 19 I took Albert hastily to the hospital and the next day he had emergency surgery for an incarcerated hernia. I was told that he might not survive. I understood that, yet he had always survived the other emergencies so I thought he would survive this one. He spent five days in ICU, several days in a regular room, and then was transferred to the "Transitional Floor." I had begun to take for granted that Albert's illness would be overcome. His mind was clear and he understood what was happening. My mind was secure that he was a survivor no matter what the surgeons told me.

I kept going two or three times a day to the hospital, mowing the lawn and working between trips. It took me only fifteen minutes when the traffic was light, but walking from the parking lot to the hospital room was more time and energy consuming.

On Saturday night, October 5 I was rushed to the hospital with "congestive heart failure." I am forever grateful that Barbara Walker, who we regard as a member of our family, was here. I had no idea what was wrong with me, I just knew that the cough I suddenly developed and a strange feeling meant I was not safe to stay home alone. I told Barbara, "Call 911. I'm going to the hospital." I had hastily packed a small suitcase and through some providential intervention I included my little daily book with addresses and phone numbers of relatives. That was Saturday night.

When Albert was in ICU he had said, "I love you so much I just hate it that I'm putting you through all this." Now I hoped that my bout with "congestive heart failure" would not impede his recovery. He made the "Transitional Floor" monitors let him come to see me. He said, "At first they didn't understand, but I was adamant." He came in a wheel chair on Monday morning and came back in the afternoon walking with a cane. Monday morning while both my hands were linked to machines, I heard him tell hospital personnel outside the door, "She's a jewel, she's quick witted, has a sense of humor, and..." They told me he was grinning from ear to ear as he held a vase of flowers for me. We agreed to just talk to each other on the phone for Tuesday because it was so difficult for him to get an escort to bring him to my room, and I was constantly interrupted by numerous medical technicians. We held hands briefly and I noted how bony he had become in the hospital. Wednesday he sent me a bright orange high-rise balloon from the hospital gift shop and we talked briefly on the phone. By that time, my doctor had made arrangements for me to go to the Transitional Floor on Thursday morning where we could be together. We were pleased and Albert said he hoped we could go home together soon.

Wednesday evening a phlebotomist was having difficulty getting my blood sample from me. A young doctor was standing in my doorway and I smiled at him, wondering vaguely if he was some kind of supervisor. There seemed to be so many doctors, nurses, and technicians. I was amazed when one of the male nurses told me they almost "lost me." At that time I thought I was meant to go before Albert and imagined his sisters taking care of him after I passed on.

Finally the technicians cleared out, the young doctor in the white coat came in and without prologue said, "Your husband passed away this evening. He was peaceful." I held his hand a long time. That was Wednesday night. Strangely enough, after forty-nine years had come to a screeching stop, I was very calm. When the nurse asked me "Do you want anything?" I said I would not break down now, but could wait until later. It was more important to me to get the friends and relatives notified. I showed the nurse the persons to call in my little red book. I appreciated the hospital personnel doing the notification to relatives. The idea of a funeral and burial wasn't even on my mind. I was amazed that right away that night, local friends came to see me. Then the next day Albert's relatives came. I love them all dearly and could never have made it without them.

The burial and other necessary arrangements were made at the foot of my hospital bed. Barbara Walker came and saw me through this heartbreaking episode which was finally over. People thought I didn't grieve because I didn't cry nor have hysteria. That would not have been natural to me. The hospital kept me until Friday night and with the burial on Saturday my grief was numb; I was eager to get back to bed with what little energy I had left.

I grieved silently deep within myself, as I still do, but I am grateful for the forty-nine years of happy married life with a most exceptional man who was lover and all things to me. If prior to marriage I had set up in my imagination some criteria for the perfect mate, I could never have conceived of any man as wonderful a mate for me as Albert had been. What had I done to deserve him? Heaven had smiled on me and I wanted to be worthy.

When he came home from his first weeklong hospitalization, Albert told me as we drove in the driveway, "I feel like a millionaire. It is such a thrill to come home to our own home that we have fixed for ourselves, just as I wanted."

Not long before he was taken to the hospital for the last time, we had been watching a TV movie: *"Sleepless in Seattle."* Albert said, "I know **our** marriage was ordained in heaven." I agreed and he said, "And I have never had any hesitation."

"You are my angel."

"And you are **my** angel."

Chosen

EPILOGUE

Not until after I was married did I lose my embarrassment about the sound of my voice. By giving me new self-esteem, marriage somehow alleviated some of the difficulty I had in speaking, but I would still become hoarse and get a sore throat if I spoke at length.

I learned to use the "advantage of a handicap" by specializing in group work. As a result I spent much time in organizing my college classes for small group projects and in providing ways for groups to prepare their own creative efforts. Their learning experiences were enhanced by built-in self-evaluation procedures and my classroom sessions were popular with students.

Once during the eighties I was teaching a class in a large basement room in a Science Building. Feeling the need to project my voice in giving assignments in that room, I experimented with a small PA system. It was awkward and made me self-conscious. After class a student told me, "You should stop worrying about your voice. I'd rather listen to you any day than those high-pitched teachers. Besides you are a seasoned teacher."

I never knew if "seasoned" meant **aged** or **capable** or something like salt and pepper, but I considered it an insightful comment and stopped using the PA system in favor of always distributing duplicated assignments. Having our own duplicating machine was helpful in many ways to my work as a teacher and administrator.

Barbara Walker tells me that my early childhood throat disaster and salvation was a prophetic event that set the tone of my future's movement. She described voice texture as an *auditory sensory impression that causes people to take notice of you as a trustworthy capable individual—a chosen one.* I had never thought of it that way, but because of the experimental surgery and special prayers of Mercy Hospital Sisters, I now think that my life is a special gift meant to be useful and helpful to others. Even today I have a sense of a continuing destiny.

The story of my life is one of profound happiness paralleled by continuous struggles. In every instance of impending disaster some special intelligence or some special "angel" took over just in time. It happened often enough to be beyond coincidental and I am deeply grateful.

The light of my adult life was Albert Lori Trobian. His presence, his influence, is always with me. He was more than a husband, a lover, or a mate. Could he have been an angel spun off by the Universe for me?

Could it be that mutual empowerment now exists with a new friend and mentor, once more an angel provided for my particular needs at present?

The problems encountered in my early life were instructive. Perhaps I inherited personal independence from my mother and I am sure that from my father I inherited his regard for people, his love of books, and creative talents. All the aspects of my life added together are more than the chronological sum of their parts. They represent a personal synergy.